THE KINDNESS OF DRAGONS

An Akitada Novel

I. J. Parker

I • J • P
2018

Published 2018 by I.J.Parker and I·J·P Books
3229 Morningside Drive, Chesapeake VA 23321
http://www.ijparker.com
Cover design by I. J. Parker.
Cover image by unknown Korean painter
Back cover image : Japanese fabric.
Publisher's Note: This is a work of fiction. Names, characters, places, and incidents are a product of the author's imagination.

The Kindness of Dragons, 1st edition, 2018
ISBN 978-1724666789

Praise for I. J. Parker and the Akitada Series

"Elegant and entertaining . . . Parker has created a wonderful protagonist in Akitada. . . . She puts us at ease in a Japan of one thousand years ago." *The Boston Globe*

"You couldn't ask for a more gracious introduction to the exotic world of Imperial Japan than the stately historical novels of I. J. Parker." *The New York Times*

"Akitada is as rich a character as Robert Van Gulik's intriguing detective, Judge Dee." *The Dallas Morning News*

"Readers will be enchanted by Akitada." *Publishers Weekly* Starred Review

"Terrifically imaginative" *The Wall Street Journal*

"A brisk and well-plotted mystery with a cast of regulars who become more fully developed with every episode." *Kirkus*

"More than just a mystery novel, (*THE CONVICT'S SWORD*) is a superb piece of literature set against the backdrop of 11th-cntury Kyoto." *The Japan Times*

"Parker's research is extensive and she makes great use of the complex manners and relationships of feudal Japan." *Globe and Mail*"

"The fast-moving, surprising plot and colorful writing will enthrall even those unfamiliar with the exotic setting." *Publishers Weekly,* Starred Review

". . .the author possesses both intimate knowledge of the time period and a fertile imagination as well. Combine that with an intriguing mystery and a fast-moving plot, and you've got a historical crime novel that anyone can love." *Chicago Sun-Times*

"Parker's series deserves a wide readership." *Historical Novel Society*

"The historical research is impressive, the prose crisp, and Parker's ability to universalize the human condition makes for a satisfying tale." *Booklist*

"Parker masterfully blends action and detection while making the attitudes and customs of the period accessible." *Publishers Weekly* (starred review)

"Readers looking for historical mystery with a twist will find what they're after in Parker's latest Sugawara Akitada mystery . . . An intriguing glimpse into an ancient culture." *Booklist*

Characters

Japanese family names precede proper names

Main characters:

Sugawara Akitada	nobleman, official
Yasuko & Yoshitada	his children
Tora, Saburo, & Genba	his retainers
Nagaoka Kojiro	Akitada's brother-in-law
Yoshiko	his wife, Akitada's sister

Characters associated with the bandit raids:

Shinsho	abbot of the Dragon Temple
Taro	a murdered farmer
Kuniko	his daughter
Sergeant Shibata	the local police officer
Miyo	an outcast woman
Otomo Muroya	a provincial nobleman
Tabito	his son

Characters associated with the Asano murders:

Asano	a well-to-do farmer
Toshiyasu	his son
Maeko	his daughter
Sadamoto	Asano's nephew
Moroe	Asano's servant
Shigeie	Asano's slave

Minor characters: **Unjo** (a dwarf), **Jugoro** (a hunter), **Ikugoro** (an outcast); as well as owners and managers of brothels

1

Monkey in the Rain

Akitada had gradually become aware of their danger. This journey should have been easy and fast. It turned out to be neither, and now he began to fear for their lives.

They were headed for his sister's home in Mino Province. The distance from the capital was not great, and he had decided to aim for even more speed by riding and taking only one pack horse. His position as senior secretary in the Ministry of Justice provided him with ample tokens for service and horses at the inspection stations. It was midsummer, a dry, pleasant summer without any ominous forecasts from the *onyoryo*, the Bureau of Divination. And they would travel only during daylight hours when there was plenty of other traffic on the roads.

He was in the company of his children and of Saburo, his secretary. The children, Yasuko and Yoshi, had seemed quite mature to Akitada at twelve and ten respectively, but close contact with them for the three days of travel had alerted him to the fact that they were still children and very dependent on him. Add to this that he missed Tora, who normally accompanied him on his travels. Saburo, while resourceful and agile, had never been a fighting man. He had been a spy and a monk in his colorful past. Neither experience was useful against robbers.

The early part of the journey on the Tosando, the central mountain road, had passed quickly and pleasantly as they traveled along Lake Biwa. There had been frequent changes of horses due to liberal tips handed to grooms at the post stations. But then they had to leave this comfortable government highway just before Sunomata to turn into the Mino Mountains.

At this point, the weather had changed abruptly.

A thunderstorm moved in with violent squalls, cracking thunder, and frightening lightning strikes. They were caught in the mountains, on a steep, slippery track, and in a thick pine and cryptomeria forest. Saburo and Yoshi rode ahead, and Akitada had his daughter beside him.

They were drenched. Akitada, Saburo, and Yasuko wore straw rain gear—Yasuko with many complaints—but Yoshi had disdained such garb as unmanly and now sat on his horse shivering in his thin, wet clothes.

The storm abated eventually, but the rain did not. Yasuko fell silent. Akitada feared she was crying. And they could barely see the track, let alone watch out for hostile attacks.

Akitada had expected to have reached his sister and brother-in-law's place by now. He had carefully gone over the map and discussed the route with the station master at their last stop. That was where he had picked up the first warning about bandits. If the man was to be believed, the entire Mino Province was in the hands of highwaymen.

Akitada doubted this. His sister had not mentioned it in her letters. But then the storm had come and it had turned dark early, and they were alone on this god-forsaken track. Both he and Saburo rode one-handed as they gripped their swords.

And his daughter *was* crying. She was unused to riding, unlike Yoshi.

"I saw a monkey wearing clothes," Yoshi called out suddenly.

"What?" Akitada gave him an anxious look. Was the boy hallucinating?

But Yoshi turned his pale face back to him, wet hair plastered about it, and said through chattering teeth. "I did! Just for a moment. He jumped from a tree and disappeared."

Saburo asked, "Could it have been a man, Yoshi?"

Yoshi shook his head. "Too small for a man, I think. Maybe I just thought I saw clothes."

Yasuko gave a sob. "How much longer, Father?"

"Sorry, Yasuko. I'd hoped to reach your uncle's house before now, but the rain has slowed us down."

"It's getting dark. I'm afraid."

"I know." Akitada would not admit it, but he was also afraid. He and Saburo both had wondered if Yoshi's sighting meant that robbers had posted a look-out who had gone to announce them. To reassure her and himself, he said, "When I looked at the map, I saw that there's a temple on this road. It's on top of the mountain, and we are almost there. We'll spend the night there."

The next half mile was nerve-racking. He expected an attack at any moment, but then the trees receded a little on either side, it grew lighter, and he saw that they had reached a plateau. On the plateau was a huddle of dark buildings with a small pagoda.

Akitada pounded on the gate. All was silent within. Saburo was scanning the road and the surrounding forest

"Patience, Yasuko," said Akitada to his sobbing daughter, "we'll be inside in a moment and in some dry place. We'll have you both warm in no time."

Yoshi said, "I'm hungry. I was hungry at the bottom of the mountain and now my stomach hurts."

"Food, too, will shortly appear." Akitada pounded again on the gate and shouted, "Open up! Travelers ask for shelter."

Finally the gate creaked open and an elderly monk in a threadbare robe looked up at them. "We have no room for guests," he said. "This is a very poor temple."

Akitada glowered and moved his horse forward. The monk raised his arms to stop him but then stepped aside. When they were all in the courtyard, Akitada snapped, "Close and bar the gate. I don't want any unpleasant surprises. Tell your abbot that I'm Lord Sugawara from the capital with my children and secretary. And hurry up. The children are nearly frozen."

The monk started his protest again, but now Saburo brought his horse closer and raised his sword. "You heard my master. Do you want to die?"

The monk fled.

Akitada dismounted, suppressing a groan at the shooting pains in his back and sides. When he helped Yasuko down, she clung to him and he had some difficulty to get her to stand on her own. Saburo also dismounted and gave Yoshi a hand. The children were pale and looked frightened.

Yasuko glanced around. "I don't like it here, Father," she whimpered. "It looks scary."

Akitada could see little in the darkness and driving rain. The temple buildings looked small and quite old. Time and weather had turned them dark. Yasuko was familiar with the colorful temples near the capital, those graceful buildings with blue roofs, red lacquered trim, and gilded ornamentation on their white walls. Here all was dark and forbidding.

Akitada made out a building near the gate that might be a stable. He gestured. "Take the horses there, Saburo," he said. "Then come back. We're going into that main hall to be out of the rain and wind."

The hall was one of the temple buildings, and while it was dry inside, they had stepped into a darkness much more impenetrable than the trail through the forest. Something moved in the murk, and Yasuko cried out and flung herself into her father's arms.

"It's just a rat," Yoshi sneered. "Girls don't have an ounce of courage, do they?"

"A . . . r-rat?" Yasuko shuddered. "You needn't talk. You saw a monkey wearing clothes."

Akitada held her, feeling her slight body tremble and shiver against him. After a moment, he released himself long enough to take off her heavy, wet straw cape and his own. Then he pulled her close again and wrapped his hunting cloak about her. She snuggled into it and. after a while, the dreadful trembling slowed.

"Where is that cursed monk?" Akitada muttered.

Yoshi seemed to be exploring the hall. "Some cushions over here, Father," he reported. "Poor, thin things, I'm afraid. Bet they don't have any bedding. Do monks sleep in bedding like we do?"

"I don't know. These are very poor, I think. If we can get a brazier or a place near a fire, we can make do with our clothes. Saburo will bring dry things from the saddle bags."

"If I can get warm and get some food, I'll sleep like the dead," Yoshi said.

"Don't say 'dead,'' Yasuko reproached him. "This place may be full of evil bandits that cut the throats of poor travelers."

Yasuko was a great one for reading. Somehow this was not helpful at the moment. Akitada said,

"Those stories were written to frighten children. They aren't true."

"Tora says they're true," Yoshi said. "He's seen them cut their victims' throats."

Tora had once been captured by a gang of bandits. Akitada said, "Yoshi! You're not helping. Stop frightening your sister."

Yoshi snorted.

Then they heard voices outside and the door opened, admitting Saburo and the monk. The monk had brought a lantern and the doors admitted a weak gray light and gusts of wind and rain. Yasuko gasped. She was staring at a carved pillar. A dragon appeared to climb it. Such decorations were common enough in temples, and he said, "It's just a carving."

"We don't take guests," the monk announced, raising his lantern to see them. Akitada was about to start shouting at the man again, when he added, "Follow me. The abbot wants to see you."

They went back out in the rain, Yasuko clinging to her father. The abbot's house was not far. It was more than modest but had been kept in good repair. Inside, they found an room with a few mats and trunks, a brazier and oil lamps, and an old man wearing a brocade stole.

"Abbot Shinsho bids you welcome," said the monk and left.

The old abbot peered up at them as they stood there, shivering and dripping. "Welcome," he quavered. "Sit down." He fixed his eyes on Yasuko. "Women are not permitted."

"My daughter is a child. She's twelve. She stays. I wonder at your lack of charity."

"Hmph." The abbot nodded slightly. "You are called Sugawara? An official from the capital?"

"That is so."

The abbot studied him. "Are you traveling alone? Without an escort?"

"We were in a hurry." Akitada was becoming impatient.

"I see. We do not take in guests, but in charity I will make an exception. We are, however, a very poor community." He waited.

Akitada glowered. "I'll pay for the accommodations. We need a dry place, braziers for warmth, food and drink. Tomorrow morning we'll be gone."

The abbot smiled. "Of course."

They stood and waited. Yasuko clutched her father and gave another sob. Akitada took a threatening step forward. "Well? Give the orders! If you don't, I'll report you and your temple to the authorities in the capital. The Bureau of Buddhism will be interested."

The abbot smiled more widely. Then he reached for a small bell. The sound of the bell brought the monk back. The abbot waved a hand, and the monk nodded and said, "Follow me, please."

Back out into the rain and wind. They walked to an outbuilding near the stable. It was apparently used for storage. Bundles of straw, bags of beans, baskets of assorted root vegetables filled half of it. In one corner, near the straw, a space had been cleared and some woven mats had been laid down. Three plain wooden neck rests marked this as a sleeping place. Near it, another mat held two wooden bowls with nuts, and plums and a stoneware basin containing some sort of gruel. For drink they had been given a jug of water. In the farthest corner stood a wooden bucket that the monk indicated was for bodily functions.

The monk looked at Saburo and said, "Your servant can sleep in the stable."

Akitada seethed, but he said nothing and dismissed the monk.

Saburo said he had planned to keep an eye on the horses anyway and went to get their saddle bags with dry clothes.

When he returned, he looked worried. "I don't trust this place, sir," he said, "I think they've gone through our saddle bags. You have the money safe?"

Akitada nodded, patting his waist where a money belt held a sufficient amount of gold and silver. He looked through their things quickly, but found all safe. "I'll keep watch," he told Saburo, who nodded and left for the stable.

Yasuko disappeared behind a stack of rice bales to change. Akitada and Yoshi changed in the open area. Akitada spread the children's wet clothes across the straw and rice bales and wrapped Yasuko, who still shivered, into one of his robes. They tasted the gruel and found it inedible. Nibbling on the plums and nuts, the children lay down and eventually went to sleep.

Akitada sat up, his sword beside him, and kept guard over them. He did not like this place any more than Saburo had, and his charges were more precious than the horses.

It was a strange night. Though uncomfortable and filled with constant imaginings of being attacked, it was also a night when Akitada watched over his sleeping children and felt deeply happy in his love for them. In the way of passing years, he would soon lose them to their own pursuits. Yoshi would become a man and think himself wiser and better than his father—just as the young Akitada had done—and they would no longer be close. And Yasuko would grow into womanhood and go away to live with a husband and raise her children. Even if he could prevail on the young couple to reside in his house, he had no illusions about the arrangement lasting or, indeed, being always comfortable. But he still had them now and he must make the most of the short time.

From time to time, he went to the door to peer out. The rain stopped after the middle of the night, and the buildings lay silent and dark. Dawn came eventually and nothing had happened. The monks rose early; he could hear them chanting.

At first light, Akitada stepped outside into a cool mist, breathing in the clean mountain air, fragrant with pine, and watched the thin golden line that outlined the eastern mountain range grow wider as the sun rose. Birds twittered and the sky turned pearl gray and golden. It was beautiful. Living in the city, he rarely paused to watch this miracle of the new day.

The children stirred behind him, clamored for food, and settled for the remaining plums and nuts. Saburo appeared suddenly like a ghost out of the mist that rose from the forest floor and reported that the horses were ready.

The abbot's hospitality had been cruelly meager, but Akitada wrapped a gold coin in a piece of note paper and left it in the bowl that had held the plums.

They were mounted and on the point of leaving the temple area when the sound of horses and men's voices reached them. Akitada's hand went to his sword again and Saburo moved in front of the children.

The mist was beginning to lift and from its remnants appeared the dark shapes of six horsemen.

2

A Close Call

They came from the east and stopped when they saw the small group of travelers in front of the temple. The light was still poor, and Akitada moved his horse foward to see better. To his enormous relief, he saw that the man in front wore the red uniform of a policeman.

When the policeman called out to him, Akitadaaproached him and saw he wore the uniform of a sergeant.

"Who are you?" the sergeant barked. He was small, almost slight, and had restless, searching eyes.

"Good morning, Sergeant. I'm Sugawara and these are my children and my secretary."

The policeman did not respond to Akitada's greeting but pursed his lips, studying Akitada's appearance and that of his companions. His eyes rested longest on Saburo.

Akitada wondered if he was hard of hearing and said somewhat more loudly, "Has there been trouble? We're on our way to Hichiso."

The sergeant nodded, pursed his lips, and looked at Saburo again. "Report of bandits in the area," he said. "He's your secretary?"

Akitada glanced at Saburo. They had become used to him, and Saburo had changed a good deal since the days when his scarred and torn face frightened children and adults. He had grown a beard to hide the worst scars, but you could still see some of them and, in a way, the beard added a sinister look. It struck Akitada that the sergeant had probably seen any number of bandits who looked a lot like Saburo.

Saburo, for his part, smiled, revealing crooked yellow teeth that had clearly been rearranged in a fight and didn't help his image. He said, "I used to be a monk."

The sergeant pursed his lips again. "Really? What made you give up the holy life?"

Saburo's jaw dropped.

Akitada was not amused. First the abbot who could not be bothered to give them shelter from the storm, and now a policeman who not only did not bow, but seemed determined to arrest them all as suspected bandits. He restrained himself from making an ugly scene as most noblemen in his position would surely have done, not because of his gentle nature, but because he needed the man's cooperation to protect them the rest of the way. He reached inside his gown for his government papers and handed them to the sergeant, hoping the man could read.

He could. He briefly raised them to his forehead when he saw the seals, then unfolded them and read, letting his eyes occasionally rest on Akitada while pursing his lips. When he was done, he handed them back and made a slight bow. "I'm Shibata. You came up this way from the Tosando?"

"Yes. In the storm. We had intended to reach my brother-in-law's house before night but were forced to seek shelter here."

"May I ask, sir, what brings you on this road without a retinue?"

"The wish to travel quickly. Also, we did not expect trouble. What happened?"

"One of the farm women reported her husband and daughter had not returned from market. We went to look for them. Found him with his throat cut not far from here. The girl's gone."

Chilled to the heart by this account, Akitada gasped. "Great heavens. You suspect a gang?"

"Yes," said the sergeant glumly. He glanced toward the temple compound. "Bet Abbot Shinsho was not delighted to see you."

Akitada's head was still in a whirl. "He was not."

"Well, I have some business with the abbot. I suggest you'd better wait and travel to Hichiso with us. You're lucky it wasn't you the bastards found."

Akitada nodded.

The sergeant turned to one of his men. "Go and bring out the abbot and his monks. Tell him it's by orders of the governor."

This surprised Akitada who would have expected the monks to be treated with more respect. The constable–Akitada had decided that the armed men must be constables, though they lacked uniforms–dismounted and walked to the open gate where a group of monks had gathered to see what was going on.

The second surprise was that his order was obeyed. The monks gathered in the yard and the abbot emerged after only a moderate delay, leaning heavily on a young monk. The sergeant dismounted and went to speak to him. Curious, Akitada drew near.

"Are all the men belonging to the temple and monastery present?"

The abbot inclined his head and quavered, "Yes, Sergeant. Nobody else is here."

"What about the big monk? He's been seen in town."

"Jozo?"

"Where is he?"

"He is blind, Sergeant."

"Blind? Bring him out."

The abbot nodded to the young monk who ran off. Shortly after, a huge figure of a man appeared. He was bald like the rest and wore a brown robe like the rest, but he was twice as tall as the young monk and had broad shoulders and muscular arms and legs. He shuffled along slowly, clutching the young monk's robe, his head raised to the sky in the manner of the totally blind.

When they stopped before the sergeant, the policeman said, "So, Kotaro! Passing yourself off as a monk? Trying out a new trick, are you?"

The big monk turned his head in the sergeant's direction. "Who's there?" he asked in a gentle voice.

"You killed a man. Where's the girl?"

"Blessed Buddha!" The big monk shook his head. "How could that be? I was asleep. Am I dreaming?"

"You killed him, and you and your men abducted his daughter. Where is she?"

"I was asleep. As the blessed Buddha is my witness."

The sergeant suddenly raised his baton and charged the blind man. The abbot and several monks cried out, but the blind man did not move. The sergeant stopped before him, his baton an inch from the monk's nose, and lowered it. "How long has he been here?" he asked the abbot.

"He came this spring from Horyu-ji."

The sergeant pursed his lips, frowned, then told his constables to search the compound.

The search turned up nothing, and eventually the abbot and his monks returned to their temple, and Akitada joined the sergeant and his men for the last leg of his journey.

The descent into the Shiragawa valley was uneventful. They did not encounter any bandits. Akitada was curious about Sergeant Shibata's futile investigation of the mountain temple and its inhabitants, but Shibata volunteered little beyond the fact that a particularly infamous bandit had been seen in the area prior to the attack. This man was known as Kotaro and was said to be a giant.

"What made you think he was hiding in the monastery?"

"They give shelter to such people."

"Really?" Akitada glanced back at his children and shuddered. "I take it, this attack did not come as a complete surprise? Have there been others?"

The sergeant glanced at him. "They don't always kill."

"I see. Will you be able to find the girl?"

There was a long silence.

Akitada said, "I'm afraid we may be keeping you from your duty."

The sergeant gave a snort. "It's too late for her. They have taken her to their lair and passed her around." He leaned away and spat. "She was only fourteen."

"But that's terrible. Can nothing be done? Have you no resources? Men to scour the whole area?"

The sergeant looked at Akitada. "We're not in the capital, sir. We're not even close to the provincial capital. And our governor isn't interested as long as the rice tax is collected."

Akitada was appalled. He thought of Yasuko. Would they have dared to touch the daughter of a court official? He rather thought that such men feared nothing and considered themselves safe from the feeble interference the authorities in Heian-kyo could offer.

They rode in silence. In the foothills, the sergeant pointed. "We found him there. Behind those trees."

Akitada turned in his saddle and motioned to Saburo. "Take the children ahead. We'll follow in a moment."

Saburo nodded and herded Yasuko and Yoshi onward.

Akitada asked the sergeant, "Can you show me?"

Sergeant Shibata nodded and they left the road. Akitada saw that the grass on the side of the stony roadway was trampled. Near the trees, they found a great deal of blood on the grass, leaves, and the low branches of the trees. Where it had soaked into the dirt, flies rose in clouds.

Akitada stopped. "They cut his throat, you said?"

The sergeant nodded. "Then they dragged him into the shrubs over there. And left, taking his ox and the girl with them."

Akitada looked around. There was nothing to see except steep mountain sides that were heavily wooded. Tracks had branched off from the road here and elsewhere. How could they find anyone in this wilderness? He said, "It's a vicious crime. What made them kill him, when they haven't done so with other victims?"

"Taro probably fought when they took the girl."

Akitada nodded. They moved on to look at the body. The man lay there, his neck and chest covered with black flies, his eyes staring at the sky, his mouth open in protest. What must it feel like to know that you cannot protect your child?

Akitada said, "Perhaps she escaped."

The sergeant shook his head. "No. And they don't come back."

Shocked, Akitada asked, "There have been others?"

"Oh, yes. Three in this valley. Two on the other side of the mountain. One of those was found at the bottom of a cliff. Jumped or was thrown."

"Dear heaven!"

They were both silent. Akitada suspected that the girls could not return because there would be no welcome for them. Once having been the property of a gang, they would never marry. In some of the backwoods, their families might not want them back because of shame. It was cruel, but people cared too much about what their neighbors thought and said about them.

After a while, they turned away to catch up with the others. Akitada asked, "What will you do?"

"Bring the body back. Ask questions in town. Somebody may know something. But first I'll see Taro's wife. She and Taro doted on the girl." He looked glum, and fell silent.

"You were looking for someone at the monastery?"

"There was a rumor that a gang leader called Kotaro was seen with the monks from the Dragon Temple."

The Dragon Temple.

It was an apt name, the way the place perched on top of the mountain cliffs.

3

Bridging the Years

Akitada did not pursue the matter. He had no authority here and could hardly tell the man what to do. As it was, he was grateful that he had his protection on the way down the mountains.

By now, he was becoming uneasy again about their visit to his sister Yoshiko and her husband Kojiro. They had not seen each other since Yoshiko had married well below her station and against Akitada's wishes. In the meantime they had only exchanged occasional letters, mostly reporting additions to the family. Yoshiko's marriage had made Akitada miserable. He loved her and had always been closer to her than to her older sister Akiko. His sisters and he shared the same father, but had different mothers. The issue of Yoshiko's marriage had arisen after his father's and stepmother's deaths when Akitada had become the head of the family. He had, dutifully, forbidden a marriage to a commoner who was also in jail for the murder of his brother's wife. Akitada had cleared him of the murder charge, but that in no way qualified him as a husband for a Sugawara daughter. Yoshiko, while she had bowed to her brother's will, had declared that she would enter a nunnery if she could not be Kojiro's wife.

All of this had caused much unpleasantness all around, and while Akitada had relented in the end, he was not at all sure of his welcome.

As they descended into the wide valley of the Shiragawa River, it grew warmer. The valley looked prosperous with its many rice fields and tidy farm houses. A town, Hichiso, gradually hove into view. It, too, looked civilized. They were not, after all, entering a primitive world where people lived on roots and grains.

The sergeant explained the way to Kojiro's place. Akitada noted that he spoke of Kojiro respectfully by his family name, Nagaoka. Anxious by now to end their journey, they passed through Hichiso without pausing to look at the small, but handsome temple, the ornate shrine to Hachiman, the city administration with its police station and jail, or any of the shops and merchants' houses along the main thoroughfare.

At the police station, they parted from their escort.

Kojiro's estate lay outside Hichiso in the foothills and amidst lush rice fields. It seemed large, its main house resembling a manor more than a farmer's abode. Akitada had known that Kojiro was an able man and that he and Yoshiko started their lives together in modest affluence, but he had not expected quite such comforts.

The gates stood open, as customary with a working estate where carts and peasants were constantly passing in and out. The large house was surrounded by a grove of massive trees and bore some resemblance to the noble houses in the capital in that it was inside a compound and had verandas and outbuildings in separate courtyards. But its appearance was rustic. The steep roof was covered with straw and the wood of its walls and verandas was unpainted. Still, it looked prosperous.

They halted in the courtyard and dismounted. A youngster came to take their horses. He smiled and called out, "Welcome!" Servants and workers paused to look and bow. They were also smiling. Then the door of the house flew open, and a woman rushed out, her skirts gathered as she ran down the steps.

"Akitada! Oh, Akitada! There you finally are! And safe. Welcome! Welcome!" she cried and flung herself into his arms.

Deeply moved, Akitada laughed and hugged her to him. Yoshiko had gained weight. But as he looked down into her laughing face, he saw that she was still his loving, gentle little sister, though now grown somewhat more matronly, her hair gathered at the nape of her neck, and her gown of ordinary blue and white cotton.

Yoshiko detached herself and ran to embrace the children, exclaiming about their good looks, how they had grown, their charm and distinction until they both laughed and hugged her back. It struck Akitada that neither Yasuko nor Yoshi had ever experienced such very physical proof of affection, and he felt the old guilt again. His own loneliness had filled him to the point where he had paid no attention to theirs.

Yoshiko returned to him, taking his hand and drawing him toward the house. "Come, all of you! I have been cooking for days. I hope you're very hungry." Her glance fell on Saburo and she paused.

Akitada chuckled and said, "This is Saburo. He joined us the year Seimei died and has been a great help to me."

Yoshiko smiled. "I've so looked forward to meeting you, Saburo. My brother has told me the most amazing things about your life. Welcome. Forgive me for not greeting you properly. It is such a joy to have my brother back that my manners have gone missing."

Saburo bowed and grinned. "Thank you, Lady Yoshiko. I have admired your manners ever since you've come to give us such a warm welcome."

The warmth of her welcome did not quite extend to her husband. Kojiro, a few years older than either Akitada or his sisters, had grown grayer and heavier in body and demeanor. He bowed to Akitada instead of offering him a brotherly embrace and seemed ill at ease. Akitada thought that here would be the expected resentment and regretted it. It was his own fault, but he had hoped those past events might have been forgotten by now.

He tried to make his own greeting warm, though he also abstained from physical contact, fearing rejection. "Kojiro! You're looking well. It's a great pleasure to see you again."

Kojiro's smile seemed forced. "Indeed! It has been a long time. How was your journey?"

"Eventful. We barely missed an attack by local bandits."

This caused an outcry, at which Yoshi took over with great excitement, "You should have been there, Uncle Kojiro. There was the worst storm, and Yasuko was crying, and Father and Saburo had their swords out the whole time, and I saw a monkey wearing clothes jump from a tree."

Kojiro glanced at Akitada, raised his brows, then bent to Yoshi. "You did? A monkey? Truly?"

Yoshi grinned. "Well, I could've been wrong. It was raining pretty hard. But it looked like a monkey. The policeman was asking me about it, too."

Kojiro looked at Akitada with concern. "A policeman? We have had marauding gangs in this area lately. You took no harm?"

"None, beyond the weather."

Yoshiko said, "It sounds dreadful. And we were worried when you didn't arrive yesterday. The weather and that road! Where did you sleep?"

"On top of the mountain. The monks weren't very friendly, but we had shelter."

"The Dragon Temple? Oh, how awful. Did they feed you?"

Yasuko said, "Just some plums and nuts, Aunt Yoshiko. The mush in the bowl was disgusting. We're very hungry."

Yoshiko laughed and hugged her. "Oh, you poor things. Come, come. There is food. And a nice place to sleep and dry clothes if you need them." Yoshiko eyed Yoshi's wrinkled robe with a frown and felt it to see if it was dry. She told her husband, "Kojiro, you take Akitada and Saburo to the big room. I'll see to these children." And she hurried off with them, an arm around each.

Akitada said awkwardly, "I hope we're not too much trouble."

"Not at all." Kojiro sounded stiff again. "Sorry about the unpleasant journey. Please follow me."

Kojiro's home was comfortable but not as large as the Sugawara residence. Akitada would have his own room, but the children shared with their cousins. Still, all their comforts had been seen to. Akitada found a desk, books, candles and oil lamps, a clothes rack, soft bedding, and a couple of braziers. The latter would not be needed. It was quite hot already. The valley seemed to absorb the sun's heat and hold it.

When Akitada had expressed his complete satisfaction, Kojiro asked, "Did the policeman say what he was doing on the mountain?"

Akitada had hoped not to have to go into details with the children present. Now he said, "A farmer was found dead beside the road. The police assume that bandits waylaid him on his return from market, probably to relieve him of his money. But they took his ox also." He paused. "And his daughter."

"Damnation!" Kojiro's face was red with anger. "Not again! And they killed him? I wonder who it was. And that poor girl."

"The sergeant mentioned the name Taro."

"Oh, no. Not Taro. And Kuniko's only fourteen. The same age as our Tameko. Oh, dear gods!" Kojiro shuddered and covered his face with his hands.

"I'm sorry," Akitada said , his response woefully inadequate. "You knew him?"

"He's one of my friends. He works the land next to mine."

"Oh. I didn't know. Can nothing be done? For the child, I mean?"

"They'll look for her. And we'll look for her also, but it will be too late. Those men are animals. I must leave. I'll speak to Taro's wife and organize the search."

"Of course. Do you want me to come?"

"No. Yoshiko would never forgive me. Besides, you don't know the area." Kojiro touched his shoulder. "Welcome, brother, even if this is a bad time." Then he left.

The rest of them gathered over dinner, where Akitada met his nephew and nieces. Arihito was the oldest. He was fifteen, good-looking, deeply tanned and sturdy. The girls were Tameko, fourteen, and Masako, twelve. It was a casual occasion and they sat in a circle, with Yoshiko beside Akitada. Yoshi had placed himself next to Arihito to discuss hunting and fishing. The girls were young, pretty versions of Yoshiko when she was their age and seemed timid around Yasuko, who wasted no time impressing them with her knowledge of the imperial court and her stepmother Yukiko.

Yoshiko passed around bowls of food, but she looked upset, her eyes moist and her smiles forced. Kojiro had told her about the murder. Yasuko's comments about Akitada's second wife distracted her for a moment.

She turned to him, her eyes questioning, and he said in a matter-of-fact tone, "I've divorced Yukiko."

His daughter frowned. "They didn't get along, and now Yukiko lives with her father and mother and she's taken the baby, too."

Akitada's sister said brightly, "Well, this sort of thing happens sometimes. I expect it's more convenient for Lady Yukiko when she must serve at the imperial palace."

"I wish she'd take me with her when she goes to court, but Father forbids it."

Akitada caught another sisterly glance, and said bluntly, "What goes on in the palace is not suitable for young unmarried girls."

"Oh." His sister covered her mouth quickly. He saw that she had guessed what had happened. Tears rose to her eyes–for him this time. "That is very sad," she commented ambiguously.

Yasuko wished to argue, but Akitada said, "Never mind, child. Pass that bowl of delicious fish stew, eat your food, and enjoy your cousins. You'll find a lot to do here."

His sister squeezed his hand and passed him the steamed vegetables.

After the meal, when the children had left to explore the house and grounds, Yoshiko said, "You brought shocking news, Akitada. Taro was a good man, a hard worker, and a man who doted on his family. It will be terrible for them. They have no one to take over. And that poor child! Better they had killed her outright."

Akitada said. "She may have escaped."

"I hope so, too, but those men, they've done it before. They take the young ones. And the girls haven't come back."

Akitada shook his head helplessly. "I thought of Yasuko when I heard."

She looked shocked. "Surely they would not dare attack a nobleman's family."

"Why not? The sergeant thought we'd been lucky. Why doesn't anyone do something about this gang?"

She wrung her hands. "Oh, Akitada, they've tried. There's only Sergeant Shibata and six constables that are able-bodied. Another three do paperwork, and the local pharmacist looks at the dead. They don't have time, and there aren't enough strong, healthy men. Kojiro's called his peasants together to make up a search party. Chances aren't good. The villains know these mountains and they hide. And if they are confronted, they fight like tigers." She paused, then asked, "How is Tora?"

"Well enough, though getting older. I worry about him. He would have come, but I sent him north to look after Yasuko's companion who rejoined her family."

"We're all getting older." She took her brother's hand and pressed it to her cheek. "Thank you for coming and for bringing me the children. I loved Tamako, you know."

He nodded. "I know. And she loved you." They smiled at each other. "Are you happy, little sister?"

"Yes, Akitada. Very happy. Kojiro's a good man. I could not have hoped for a better."

He drew her close. "I have missed you."

"Have things been very bad?"

"With Yukiko? Yes. I blame myself. She was young and lovely and I thought I could get a little of my life back."

"I wish I could've been closer after Tamako's death. What was Akiko up to?"

"Oh, you know Akiko. She saw only a great marriage, a huge dowry, and influence at court. But I'm not that sort of man. I did not want any of it and never will."

"Yes, I know. She means well, though."

"Yes."

They fell silent. Then she said, "Forgive me, but I think I'll go now to see Taro's wife. She shouldn't be alone."

Akitada nodded. No, no one should be alone with such news. How good both Kojiro and Yoshiko were to their neighbors! And how different from his sister Akiko and her husband. Though Toshikage, his other brother-in-law, was basically a kind man, their lives in the capital meant that they rarely wasted a thought on the many peasants who struggled in remote areas to provide the food and wealth they enjoyed.

Being left to himself, he decided to do what Saburo had done and walk into town

4

A Terrified Town

Akitada put on a plain robe and his comfortable boots. He enjoyed the walk after days on horseback. After the night's storm, everything was fresh and clean, though warmer than he had expected. The ditches in the rice fields were full of water, and the rice stood tall and golden, waving in the slight breeze.

Hichiso was like many small towns he had seen. It had a modest temple, many statues and miniature shrines of *Inari*, the fox god sacred to the culture of rice, a line of houses with small shops below, a police station, a bath house, and a number of wine shops. The police station looked abandoned but a small group of people had gathered to await news. Others peered nervously from their houses and shops. His sudden appearance among them did nothing to calm them. They stared and he became aware of being followed by children. Even an old man in rags who was sweeping the street paused to stare.

All of this made him uncomfortable and after a while he sought refuge by stepping into a shop where nobody seemed to take an interest in him. He saw right away that the shop sold fabric for clothing, boldly patterned blue and white lengths of cotton of such intricate patterns that he stopped to admire them. Yoshiko had worn a robe that looked like this. Hers had had scattered white chrysanthemum blossoms on a deep blue ground. Most of the fabrics here were simpler, showing stripes and wave patterns or geometric shapes. He wondered how these were made and walked farther into the building. Female voices led him to a room that was open to a courtyard where lengths of fabric dried on lines strung between trees.

Three women were outside, one elderly, one middle-aged, and one young. The old woman sat on a step sewing cloth. The next, her daughter perhaps, stirred something in a large vat, and the young one was drawing patterns on white hemp fabric spread out on the ground. All had hands that were faintly blue from the dye.

He cleared his throat and all three jumped. He apologized. The young woman put down her brush, bowed and came to him.

"Can we show you some of our *shibori,* honored sir?"

"Yes, thank you. I saw the fabric and recalled that my sister had on a very pretty robe like this. I wondered how you make it."

She bowed again. "Is your honored sister in this town?"

"Yes. She's the wife of Nagaoka Kojiro."

All three cried out of this, smiles on their faces, making small bows.

"Oh, Lady Yoshiko. Yes. She bought the chrysanthemum fabric and then brought us some silk for another gown. We don't normally get silk and are afraid to make a mistake." The young woman was refreshingly honest. The older woman reproached her, then said, "I can show his Honor how we work.

He learned some humble facts about dyeing cloth that day. It struck him as tedious work, requiring much sewing, gathering, tying, dipping, washing and drying. Because he had interrupted their work, he bought a length of fabric with white bell flowers on blue ground and asked them to set it aside for him. He hoped Yoshiko would like it.

When he asked them if they had heard the news, they nodded.

"Poor girl," said the girl's mother. "My daughter no longer takes our clothing to market." She sighed. "I go these days and it's a long hard journey for these old legs and this old back. The fabric gets very heavy."

"I'm not afraid," the girl said bravely. "And I'm stronger than you, Mother."

"No," said the grandmother. "You're not stronger than ten of them. They steal girls like they steal money. To them a girl is good for only one thing."

Blunt language. Akitada liked the old woman. "Your Sergeant Shibata and his men are searching for her. It's too bad about her father."

"Too late for her," the old one said. "And I don't know what Taro was thinking of. He has no need to sell his vegetables on the other side of the mountain."

The futility of the searches seemed to be a common theme, but Akitada said, "They'll bring her back if they find her and punish the villains."

The grandmother shook her head. "Nobody'll want the girl."

"I understand her mother dotes on her."

She said nothing then, just shook her head again.

Her granddaughter said softly, "I know Kuniko. She's a good girl. And very pretty."

The grandmother snapped, "The worse for her."

Akitada expressed his regrets that local people were living in fear and departed.

When he reached the end of town, he ran into Saburo. He was standing on the road, talking to someone among some bushes. When he saw Akitada, he waved, then turned back to his hidden companion.

Akitada found that Saburo's acquaintance was a woman who was bent nearly double under a load of sticks larger than she: a wood gatherer. To judge by her rags, she made a poor living.

When she saw Akitada, she tried to scurry away, but Saburo caught her arm.

"Wait, Miyo. He's my master. He'll want to hear your story."

She shook her head. "No. They mustn't find out."

Akitada made a guess. "She knows something about the gang?"

She cried, "No," and pulled away from Saburo.

Akitada realized that she was younger than he had thought. She was very thin, and her bare legs and arms were nearly black from being outside. Her face was quite ugly, having a broken, flattened nose and a crooked mouth. He reached into his sash and pulled out a silver coin. "This is yours if you can give us some information about the bandits."

She fixed her eyes on the coin and stretched out a trembling hand for it. "Please," she whispered, "and may the Buddha protect you."

Akitada moved the coin out of her reach. "What do you know?"

She gave a small sob. "I lived with them for five years."

Akitada raised his brows. "Five years? Were you abducted by them? People say none of the girls the robbers take come back."

She said defiantly. "I didn't want my son to become one of them."

Akitada and Saburo exchanged glances. Saburo looked grim and nodded.

"They let you leave?"

"No. They caught me the first time I tried to run. I was pregnant then." She gestured to her face.

"They beat me and cut me and said they'd crush the child in my belly if I tried it again."

Akitada did not know what to say. He grimaced. "But you did escape. You went back to your family?"

She shook her head. "No. I came here with my baby. But they've come here, too." She had not taken her eyes off the coin and extended her hand again. "Please. For my boy. He's hungry and I have no food to give him. I can find them for you." She spoke through scarred lips, her words distorted by the missing teeth.

"You said you're afraid of them," Akitada said dubiously. "Afraid that they'll take you back."

She shook her head. "I'm too ugly now. They have younger women. Prettier ones. But if they find me, they'll kill me, and then my boy will die."

"Yet one of them is his father?"

She spat. "They all are, the devils."

"All? How many?"

"There were fifteen or twenty then. Fewer here, they say."

Akitada shuddered. "They took another girl yesterday. Could you show the police where they have taken her?"

"I can find out, but you'd have to be quick. They move all the time."

Akitada reached a decision. "Take the coin. Tell Saburo where you live and he'll find you when we need you."

She took the coin, kissed it, and then fell to her knees before him, kissing his boots. Akitada stepped away quickly, and walked back into town.

Saburo caught up with him at the police station. "There's a settlement outside town. They're outcasts. That's where she lives."

Akitada nodded. By now, several constables had returned and he went to speak to them. They looked hot and tired and said they had just returned for a short rest. The sergeant was sitting inside. He was also red in the face and his uniform was sweat-stained. He looked worn out.

"I see you're back, Sergeant," Akitada said. "Any news?" Shibata tried to scramble to his feet with a groan. Akitada said quickly, "No. Don't get up. I can see you're exhausted." Akitada took a seat on the bare floor. Saburo remained standing, but loosened his robe. The heat was getting everybody down. Akitada saw that Saburo wore his talisman around his neck. That usually meant he feared trouble.

Shibata wiped his face with a sleeve. "Nothing," he said. "We've been up and down the side of that mountain. Nothing. Next we're going to search the next mountain. And so forth."

"Is there any place that would give the bandits refuge?"

The sergeant pursed his lips. "You mean like the Dragon Temple?"

"Ah, you do think those monks may be involved."

Shibata looked away. "I don't know. I was sure this morning, but there was nothing. I expect they have already complained about me and I'll be called back and replaced with someone more respectful of our Lord Buddha's disciples."

"Heaven forbid!"

Shibata shot him a glance and chuckled weakly. "You, sir, should know how things are done."

Akitada returned the smile. "And so I do. Frequently to my regret."

Shibata's eyes went to Saburo. "You were a monk. What do you think?"

Saburo scratched his beard. "They're isolated. And they're poor. They may be giving shelter, no questions asked, for donations to the Buddha."

Akitada said, "That doesn't make sense, Saburo. They practically turned us away."

Shibata straightened up a little and reached for an earthen pitcher. "Some water, sir? It's fresh."

"Yes, thank you. Much better than wine."

"Can't afford that." Shibata passed across the pitcher.

No cups. He probably couldn't afford them either. Akitada raised the pitcher to his lips and drank deeply. The water was cool and delicious. He wiped his mouth and handed the pitcher to Saburo.

"Your water is better than any I've ever tasted," Akitada said.

The sergeant nodded. "It does little to make a man forget his misery, though."

Akitada looked at him with interest. Men rarely talked about their innermost pain. He felt a bond with this man. It was unexpected. They had only just met, and were of different stations in life. His friendship with Tora had developed slowly over the years, but Tora also had that knack of revealing himself readily without embarrassment.

"What is wrong, Sergeant?" Akitada asked. "Can I help?"

Now the other man was surprised. "Help? No, sir. But you're kind. Frankly, I'm not used to kindness from my superiors."

"I'm not your superior, though it's true that I outrank you and could pull strings for or against you. If your troubles are personal, I won't be useful, but if they concern doing your job to bring these animals to justice, I may be able to do something."

The other man gave him a long look. "I'm more used to threats and reprimands from noblemen, those who actually bother with someone like me." He paused. "Forgive my speaking so freely."

Akitada chuckled. "I have a loyal retainer who has been with me since my youth. He can always be counted on to speak too freely. I'm used to it, Sergeant."

For the first time, Shibata smiled. He passed the pitcher back and said, "Well, sir, it's like this: our governor takes no interest in the bandits. He returns every report of their crimes with a reminder that they are my job and that I must be doing it very badly. He threatens that he'll replace me unless I solve the problem."

Akitada nodded. "And that is an invitation to stop reporting."

"Exactly."

"Who is your governor? I haven't informed myself, since this is a personal visit."

"Minamoto Tamenori. You know him?"

"I'm afraid not. I know quite a few Fujiwara nobles. The Minamoto clan tends to be more provincial. But I can speak to him. How far is it to the provincial capital?"

"Nogami is to the north and west. Bad roads and mountain passes." Shibata pursed his lips as he thought. "Three days for a man with a good horse."

"Then it's not possible. I cannot leave my children. Especially under present conditions. I expect the distance accounts for the fact that the governor did not send you troops."

"Not really. These bandits operate elsewhere in the province, though they stay away from Nogami."

"I see." Akitada sighed. "I could write."

"Don't bother, sir. It would do no good and might make things worse."

Akitada looked at him sharply. "These bandits have been here before?"

"Yes, sir. Nobody got killed, but they got a girl and stole horses and cattle. I asked for help. Nothing happened, except a message to handle my problems or lose my job."

Akitada sighed again. Peasants who lost their livelihood or the help they needed frequently abandoned the land. "How then will you manage?"

"We'll do the best we can." The sergeant wiped more sweat from his face and got to his feet. "Time I went out again."

"Wait." Akitada rose also. "There's an outcast woman. She may help us find them."

"A woman?" Shibata frowned.

"She says she was abducted a few years ago and escaped. She earns a living gathering wood."

"Not Miyo?"

Yes," Saburo said. "Miyo. She has a child. Fathered by those monsters."

Shibata nodded. "Miyo's afraid of her shadow and not in her right mind. You can't believe what she says."

Akitada said, "She seemed very poor and eager to earn some money."

"Ah." Shibata shot him a glance. "She lied. And you paid her."

Akitada flushed. "I don't think she lied. She knows the bandits, but she's sure they'll kill her and the child."

"Miyo is a vagabond. She'll do or say anything for money. That's how she got the child. Now if you'll excuse me . . ." Shibata walked out of the door.

Saburo growled, "That man's a fool."

"No, Saburo. He is a good man. And a brave one. And we have no right to trade a chance of getting the farmer's daughter back against two other lives." He sighed. "He may be right about Miyo. I'm going home, but you may want to take a look at that outcast village."

Saburo nodded.

Akitada stopped only to pick up Yoshiko's fabric and then returned to Kojiro's place, feeling helpless and frustrated.

5

The Outcasts

Saburo had already explored Hichiso and walked from the police station to the temple of the war god. There he left the main thoroughfare and followed a narrow side street into a quarter of small houses, twisted alleys and the sort of businesses that catered to working people and the poor. He found a shop that sold used clothing of all sorts. It was run by a one-legged man with a sharp eye for business.

He greeted Saburo with a deep bow, and said instantly, "Twenty coppers for the robe and five for the sash. The boots . . ." he peered more closely, "maybe ten."

Shocked at being offered so little for the outfit he was quite proud of, Saburo was speechless for a moment.

"And I'll throw in another outfit so you won't have to go naked." The old man cackled.

Saburo snapped, "I'm not selling. I'm buying."

The old man's eyes lit up. "Excellent. We have the finest selection. Let me just show you." He flung open a battered old trunk and dragged out a piece of torn and stained brocade. "Feel this. Finest silk. Made in the capital. You won't find stuff like that in the shops on main street."

Saburo glared. "I want some rags. And an old piece of cloth to carry my things in. But make sure they don't stink." Saburo knew that was too much to hope for, given the smell in the shop and the odor emanating from its owner.

It took a while to select a pair of short pants that were badly patched, a shirt with a large tear in it and some strange stains on the sleeves, a pair of ragged straw sandals, and a straw hat. The shop keeper stared as Saburo stripped to his loin cloth, untied his topknot, and then put on his purchases.

"What're ye going to do?" he asked.

"None of your business," said Saburo, tying his own clothes neatly into a checked square of cotton.

"You gonna kill someone?"

"You want to get paid?"

"Sorry, sir. That'll be twenty coppers."

Saburo did not argue, though the price was outrageous and almost as much as the man had offered for Saburo's own clothes.

After picking up a broken bamboo stick, he tied his bundle to it and carried it over his shoulder. Then he strode out in the direction of what he had been told was the outcast village just east of town.

He found the place between the highway and the river, a gathering of sheds and huts in a small grove of trees. A ragged but well-trodden path led to it from the highway, and Saburo took this.

There appeared to be about thirty dwellings of the poorest sort. Some were no more than four bamboo poles holding up a collection of branches and rags. Most of the lives here were spent out in the open. Naked children ran about, their mothers stirred food over open fires, their fathers were largely absent, though there was a number of the aged, infirm, and diseased.

Almost the first person Saburo passed was a leper sitting under a tree. The disease had eaten away one foot and had left his hands mere stumps. He no longer had a nose and whimpered as Saburo passed.

Saburo forced himself to nod a greeting but resisted tossing him a coin. It would not do to alert the inhabitants that he was not poor.

He smelled it before he reached it. The village was small and pitiful. There were such settlements in the capital also. They were in the western half of the city, separated from the dwellings of others by stretches of wilderness and warehouses. They existed here and there everywhere in the nation and housed the outcasts, the untouchables, the defiled, the non-humans.

How they got to become *eta* or *hinin* was not always clear. Certainly those who worked with the dead, like undertakers, butchers, and tanners were untouchable by their profession, because both Shinto and Buddhism abhorred contact with death and prohibited slaughter of animals. But so were also street sweepers, beggars, acrobats, and prostitutes. Some were descended from slaves taken during the wars with the

Northern people. Saburo's wife was one of these. Some used to be ordinary people but committed heinous crimes like incest. And some were rejected for infectious diseases like leprosy.

It was a cruel system, but they managed to earn a living by carrying out necessary services, like tending to the dead and keeping streets clean. Acrobats, players, and prostitutes belonged to the crowd of vagrants who traveled the land offering their services at temple fairs. These had little in common with the more affluent inhabitants of the willow quarter in the capital.

He was hoping to talk to Miyo again. His disguise was meant to overcome her fear of their being seen together. But he also thought it likely that he could pick up some information from the other people here.

He asked one of the women looking after small children if they had seen Miyo and was told that she had not come back yet. The woman pointed to one of the naked children playing in a muddy puddle. "That one's hers," she said. "You'd think he was the emperor's son himself." She laughed raucously.

The boy was covered with dirt from head to toe but looked sturdy. Saburo thought he would soon demand more of his mother than she was equipped to deliver by picking up sticks in the woods. "I'll come back," he told the woman and strolled off.

In the middle of the village, he found some six or seven able-bodied men seated under a huge cryptomeria, shooting dice. All were of middle age or older. He approached and watched for a while. A few curious glances were directed his way, but nobody interrupted the game.

Saburo knew that dice required little skill and rarely earned any rewards unless they were crooked, and then they required considerable skill. He decided these dice were loaded and that the players knew it. It made for an interesting game. The surface of the ground was uneven and if you knew how the dice behaved, you could make them roll in a direction where they would stop on a high score. He could see that three of the men were particularly adept. One of them was a tall fellow with penetrating eyes and a sneer on his face.

Finally one of the gamblers, a graybeard, glanced up at Saburo. "Look, my friends, we've got company. Where's your manners?" They all grinned. "Welcome, friend!" their spokesman said to Saburo. "Care for a game? A copper a throw?"

"Thanks. Don't mind if I do." Saburo eagerly joined them. It seemed a fine opportunity for picking up some gossip. They passed him the dice. He did not bother to inspect them, but rattled them in his hand, and let them roll. The score was respectable. He passed the dice on, and watched as most of the others scored above him.

"Where you from?" the graybeard asked.

"The capital. My name's Genba."

The old man did not volunteer his name. They rolled again, and again Saburo lost.

"What do you do for fun around here?" Saburo asked. "Is this a good place to stay?"

A small fellow with terrible small pox scars said, "What you see, and no. What's it like in the capital?"

"Well, I'm here," Saburo said, making a face.

They didn't mind his lack of an answer. The conversation continued along those lines, and dice kept passing around. Saburo gathered that life was hard, but some made a better living than others. The pock-marked fellow and two others worked for the monks on the mountain. They washed and prepared the dead for funerals. The man with the sneer did not volunteer anything.

"What's it like, that temple?" Saburo asked, rolling again. "They drove me away when I asked for alms."

The three who worked for the temple snorted. "They don't give alms. They take 'em," said one of the undertakers.

"They don't sound friendly," Saburo pursued. "You've been inside. What's it like?"

The pock-marked character shook his head. "Who us? We just work with the dead. They tell us where the bodies are."

Saburo changed the subject. "I suppose you heard about the murder?"

They nodded. The pock-marked man said, "There may be a bit extra in him if the widow feels like it."

"What d'you mean?"

"That Taro has a nice place. Maybe his woman is charitable. Maybe a few extra coins. Or some leftovers from the funeral."

Saburo saw that the pock-marked man measured murder by its effects on himself–not that you could blame these people. They were the poorest of the poor. But it also meant that they were more likely to be on the side of the bandits than of the police. He said, "People in town are afraid of that gang."

The headman gave Saburo a sharp look. "We're safe enough. Got neither money nor beauty." He paused. "Nor land." Someone sniggered.

The undertaker sat beside Saburo. He leaned closer and took hold of Saburo's amulet. "Where'd you get that?"

Saburo had not taken it off when he changed. It identified him as one of the trained spies belonging to Mount Koya. He had kept it after he parted company from the monks to remind himself of his troubled past. He snatched it from the man's hand. "Picked it up at a fair. Supposed to protect me against disease."

Saburo lost again. He had by now lost twenty coppers and won nothing. He frowned. "Something wrong with those dice?" he asked lightly as one of the others scooped up the coppers..

The burly man sitting next to the headman got up, came over and jerked Saburo to his feet. Holding a large fist under his nose, he asked, "What did you just say?"

Saburo gave a weak laugh. "A joke, friend. Just a joke. I'd better stop or I won't eat tonight."

They tried to keep him, but Saburo was adamant. He left the gamblers and went back to the woman who was keeping an eye on Miyo's boy. His luck was in. Miyo was there, sharing out food from a bundle she had carried from town. Other women gathered about with cries of pleasure. The master's silver coin apparently had bought a feast for several families.

Miyo was smiling and laughing until she saw Saburo. Then her face fell and her eyes scanned the surroundings.

He went to her, saying, "Miyo! I'm glad to find you. I wanted to ask you something."

"You!" She stared at his clothes, then took his sleeve to drag him away from the others.

"You shouldn't have come!" she hissed, looking over her shoulder. "It's not safe. Don't talk to me here. Go away now, please."

"But . . ." Saburo protested.

"Now!" She gave him a push. "Go.! Go now!

6

A Noble Neighbor

When Akitada got back to his sister's house, Kojiro was still gone, but Yoshiko had returned and was entertaining a guest. The guest, a broad-shouldered, corpulent man in his sixties, wore a very nice hunting cloak and had his silk trousers stuffed into shiny leather boots. Yoshiko rose gracefully to make introductions.

"Akitada, this is Lord Otomo. He stopped by to pay his respects, but Kojiro is still out with the searchers. My lord, this is my brother Akitada, come for a visit from the capital."

Otomo was a haughty man with sharp appraising eyes. He frowned at the introduction and bit his lip, but nodded to Akitada. "From the capital?" he asked, eying the package of fabric and looking at Akitada's simple robe as if making comparisons with his own rich brown silk coat. "What do you do there, Akitada?"

Akitada raised his brows at the familiarity of the address and glanced at Yoshiko, who blushed. She had neglected to give Akitada his title or his family name and caused Otomo to be rude. With a smile and a bow, Akitada said lightly, "Oh, I work in one of the ministries. Dry work, compared to the excitement that seems to prevail here, sir."

Otomo had already lost interest. "Yes. I imagine." He turned to Yoshiko. "Well, tell your husband not to interfere. I'll pay the money they owe. Not much point in holding on to the land if she has no one to work it. I'll see him later." With another nod to Akitada, he walked out.

"Oh," cried Yoshiko, "I should have told him who you are. I'm sorry Akitada, but he made me so mad."

"It was funny," Akitada said, his good humor restored. "Here. This is for you. I found it in town. They are remarkably skillful at dyeing." He handed her the package.

Yoshiko undid the plain cotton cover and cried out with pleasure. "It's lovely. How very kind of you, Akitada!" She reached out and caressed his cheek, tears in her eyes. "I have missed you so."

That brought tears to his own eyes, but he laughed. "It's only ramie, Yoshiko, not silk."

"Oh, I rarely wear silk these days and do love these *shibori* patterns so. How very delicate this one is." She spread out the fabric to admire it.

Akitada watched her with a smile. Then he asked, "But what has Otomo done to make you angry? Besides not showing you the proper respect owed to a

Sugawara daughter. Or does he not know about that either?"

She blushed. "Well, it's easier to just have people assume nothing."

"Was that Kojiro's idea?" Akitada asked with a frown.

"No, Akitada. It was mine. I'm happy to be Kojiro's wife." She paused. "Happier than I ever was being a Sugawara daughter."

Akitada glowered. "There's nothing wrong with being a Sugawara. Why do you imply your family is something to be ashamed of?"

She flung her hands up in frustration. "No, Akitada," she cried. "That isn't it at all. None of us were happy as children, and Akiko and I spent several years living with our mother when she was already becoming . . . difficult."

"Difficult" was putting it mildly. Akitada's stepmother, the late Lady Sugawara, had had a vicious tongue for the children in the family, though Akitada always assumed her hatred was mostly directed at him. "Oh. Yes, I see. But surely that is no reason to hide your birth from people?"

'Yes, it is. I have chosen to honor my husband. Kojiro is a commoner, and I have become a commoner also. You know that. And you accepted it, or so I thought."

Akitada sighed. "Sorry, little sister. Yes. I was just angry that Otomo treated you that way."

She relaxed. "He treated you that way also. You thought it was funny."

"In the security of knowing that I outrank him so badly that he would have to get on his knees and knock his head on the floor to apologize." He burst out laughing. "I enjoyed that thought. I didn't like him. Who is he?"

"Our neighbor. He controls a huge estate in the next province and has begun buying up land in our valley also. He's built himself a hunting place a little ways up the mountain from us and stays there to hunt when he isn't pursuing business in the capital or elsewhere. He came today because he wants the parcel that Taro was farming. It's a good piece of land and sizable."

"Does Taro have to sell off land?"

"Well, there have been setbacks lately. I suppose Otomo thinks Taro's death is a good excuse to get his hands on the land."

"Can't the widow run the farm?"

"No." Yoshiko turned away. "Oh, Akitada. It was so sad. She is beside herself with grief. Taro was strong and a hard worker. Now there are only women and a small boy. I don't know what Kojiro can do. Otomo was right. They need the income from the harvest to pay back their debts and live."

Akitada felt out of his depth. He could not interfere in Kojiro's business. Besides, he was no farmer. He had left the running of the Sugawara lands to a capable *betto* and Saburo's bookkeeping. "If you need money. . . " he said tentatively.

She turned back to him. "No, Akitada. We don't need money. And it would shame Kojiro, so don't offer."

Akitada nodded. He felt as if he'd walked into a hornets' nest in this mountain valley. Wherever he turned, he found no escape from that stinging sense of utter uselessness in the face of crisis.

He trailed off unhappily to look for the children, but they were still out exploring. Having nothing to do was beginning to depress him. In the end, he decided to take a nap.

Kojiro returned in time for the evening rice. His news was not good. They had found no trace of the bandits or the girl. Informed of Otomo's visit, he grew angry.

"How dare he? The man's body is barely cold, and he rushes over to buy his land. What about his family? Am I to watch them be driven from their home before the harvest, leaving them penniless and homeless to face the winter? We have enough vagabonds already, and men like Otomo are adding daily to their numbers by driving peasants from their land. It's outrageous."

Akitada said, "Do I take it that the widow won't sell?"

Kojiro snapped. "She may have to eventually." He glanced at his wife. "Never mind, my dear. We'll manage something. They will have a good harvest. We can wait it out. And that will give Taro's family enough to survive till spring. I'll hire some workers."

She smiled at him. "Good! I was sure you'd think of a way."

Akitada asked, "Just who is this Otomo? I met him today and didn't care for his manner."

Kojiro sighed. "Provincial family. He and a number of cousins have estates in Owari Province. His own lands are near the border between Owari and Mino, and his family home is in Sunomata. He came to this valley to hunt. In the beginning he bought some unproductive land, mostly forest, but he has now decided that he wants to add rice lands to his holdings. The valley land is rich soil and we have plenty of water from the river. He has offered money to a number of farmers. The money was good and they had their reasons to sell. Now there's little left except my property and some temple lands."

"Really? Temple lands? Belonging to the Dragon Temple?"

"No. These belong to Horyu-ji."

"I'm trying to understand what is going on here, Kojiro. There has been a murder and young girls have been abducted. The town seems to be terrified of a gang of bandits, and your police sergeant— whom I like by the way—adamantly refuses to ask for help from the provincial governor."

Kojiro nodded. "Didn't take you long. Not even a day. Yes, something is going on. Mind you gangs have operated before in this province, but never here. There's simply not enough traffic to make it worth their while. As for Shibata, he doesn't get along with the governor. He told me he went to see him and told him a few things. I was surprised he wasn't dismissed."

Akitada chuckled. "Yes. He's outspoken. Do you think I could help? With the governor, I mean?"

"Do you want to become involved? This was supposed to be a rest for you."

The terrible events of the past spring were still fresh in Akitada's mind, and his body also was not fully healed. But he did not have to think. "Of course, I'll do what I can."

Kojiro nodded and smiled. "Yes. I should have known. Perhaps you could write?"

"Yes. Just give me the particulars about the governor."

The evening rice interrupted their project. The family ate together, something Akitada had missed in his own home during the troubled times of the past months. The children were full of plans for the next day. They were going fishing in the river. Even Yasuko was eager to tag along. Akitada exchanged a glance with Kojiro and said casually, "Excellent idea. I could do with some fishing myself. We'll go together and you can show us city people how to do it."

The faces of his own two fell instantly, but they did not argue.

Soon after the meal had been eaten, Otomo was announced. Yoshiko took the children away and Akitada would have left also, but Kojiro asked him to stay.

Otomo walked in briskly, slowed when he saw Akitada, and said, "I come on business Nagaoka, as your wife probably told you."

Kojiro nodded. "I know, but my brother-in-law has been kind enough to agree to stay. A good legal mind is always helpful, don't you think, my Lord?"

"Legal mind? Oh, I remember. He works in the Ministry of Justice. Hardly useful in this instance. Besides, there should be no problem. I'm merely offering to help you out of a tough spot."

"Please be seated, my Lord. Some wine? Refreshments?"

Otomo sat down. "Nothing, thanks. Now, you know that the Taro farm cannot be run without male labor. Taro had to struggle as it is. And his widow won't be able to hire labor. They are over their heads in debt to you and others."

Kojiro and Akitada had seated themselves also. Akitada was no longer amused by Otomo's offensive manner. The man was a bully, and he was bullying Kojiro. He cleared his throat.

Otomo gave him a surprised look and was about to turn away again when Akitada said quite politely, "I'm afraid my sister has left you with the wrong impression, Otomo. It is true that I work in the Ministry of Justice, but not as a clerk, as you seem to assume. I'm the assistant minister."

Otomo's jaw fell. His eyes bulged slightly. He turned purple. "Is this some kind of joke?"

Kojiro smiled. "Not at all, my Lord. My wife is a Sugawara. You see, I married up, so to speak. And I'd like you to remember her rank next time you come calling."

Akitada wanted to laugh but kept his face serious. "Yes," he said, "I was rather shocked at your rustic manners, Otomo."

Otomo scrambled to his feet. "I . . . I had no idea. You never said. H-how was I to know?" He pulled himself together and bowed deeply to Akitada. "M-my deepest apologies, your Excellency. I . . . we *are* rather rustic here and I'm not at all well informed of matters in the capital."

He was right, of course, and Akitada would have brushed it off with a friendly word, but he didn't like Otomo, and he didn't like what he was trying to pull with Taro's farm. So he merely nodded.

Otomo clearly wished to be gone, but he had come with a purpose and could not just run out. He said diffidently, "Forgive me, Nagaoka. Your lady wife is a most courteous person. I'm in her debt."

As this was a reminder that Yoshiko had been more courteous than either Akitada or Kojiro, Akitada gave Otomo some credit for his comeback. He realized belatedly that they had made the man angry.

Kojiro merely bowed. "What is on your mind, my Lord?"

"The matter of the Taro farm. He owed you money. I believe you paid for his seed rice this year. I came to tell you that I'll buy that debt from you. His farm adjoins some land I acquired recently. I have someone who can take care of the fields."

Kojiro said coldly, "The debt is not for sale."

"But who will work the land? The harvest is imminent. You do not expect one woman to bring it all in? You'll lose your investment."

"We'll manage something."

Otomo bit his lip. He reached into his robe, brought out a folded paper, and handed it to Kojiro." Here is my offer, should you change your mind." Then he bowed deeply to Akitada, turned and left.

Kojiro unfolded the paper, grimaced, and said, "Generous!" passing it to Akitada.

"Generous indeed. But you know, satisfying as it was to teach him manners, I'm afraid we have made an enemy."

7

Monks and Other Villains

Saburo stood on the road for a moment, looking after Miyo and scratching his head. He did not know what to make of the woman. Why was she suddenly getting shy again after telling him where to find her? And after taking his master's money? Maybe she was mad after all, as the sergeant had said. Still, her behavior had looked uncommonly like fear.

He glanced around as he walked out of the outcast village. People who are very poor often become involved with criminals. Those gamblers had been an unpleasant bunch. He had not liked the way that bully had held his big fist under his nose when Saburo had joked about cheating. No, all was not well in the outcast village. With a sigh, Saburo started homeward.

As he passed through town, he saw that Sergeant Shibata had gathered his tired troops and was starting off on another search. Saburo thought that they were wasting their time. He believed what Miyo had said, that the gang was constantly moving. If that was the case, he was sure there would be watchers to alert them long before the tired group of constables had climbed far enough to present a real threat.

For that matter, the number of constables and helpers with the sergeant was fewer than twenty, and they were tired and poorly armed. Only the sergeant had a sword. Saburo had no doubt that the gangsters were well supplied with weapons. If they were in fact confronted, they would fight. His idea of using Miyo to lead them to the current hide-out would have assured success, provided the constables were rested and armed. Alas, it was not to be.

Having no better ideas, Saburo returned to a related matter: the Dragon Temple. He had taken a healthy dislike and distrust to those monks and was especially suspicious of the big blind monk the sergeant had asked to see. From his life as a spy for his monastery, he knew that good training can involve all sorts of tricks and that one of the favorite pretenses of a spy is to appear harmless and helpless. His session with the outcast gamblers had elicited the fact that the three undertakers were not allowed to work inside the temple compound. Added to this, the monks turned away beggars and travelers in distress. This suggested an unsavory secrecy.

He returned to Kojiro's house to saddle his rented horse and tucked a short sword through his sash. Then he rode back the way they had come that morning. The heat improved once he was in the forest. The thick branches overhead kept out the sun, and he rode in a warm twilight. For a long time, he was alone on the road, but then he encountered a woodsman busy with saw and hatchet. He was taking down small trees of a certain size, removing the branches, and stacking them beside the road to be carried away later.

Saburo dismounted to greet the man courteously.

The woodsman returned a nod and decided it was time for a break. Sitting down on a log, he invited Saburo to join him and produced a pitcher of cool water from a bed of bracken. They drank.

"Hot work," Saburo said. "Are you out here every day?"

"Not always here," said the man. "And you? Just traveling through?" He eyed Saburo with interest.

"Giving the horse some exercise. I'm staying in Hichiso. Visiting."

"Ah."

Silence fell. Saburo knew better than to make the man suspicious by asking questions.

The man finally said, "Not a safe road. Yesterday, bandits killed a man not far from here."

"I know. They took his daughter."

The man nodded. "Fourteen."

"So young. Bad."

The man nodded again.

After a long silence, Saburo said, "The police are looking for them."

Another nod. The glum expression on the man's face had not changed.

"I met the sergeant. He seemed like a good man."

"Good enough in most things. Not good enough for this."

"Why not?"

The man offered the pitcher again and said, "They aren't human. They disappear into the air. They change their shape. They fly from mountain to mountain. How can a man deal with that?"

"Ah. That sort." Saburo passed the pitcher back. "What about the monks of the Dragon Temple? Can't they do something? Perambulate? Pray? Read some sutras?"

That got a chuckle. "Sure. If you got the money. They'll do anything for money."

"Really? Anything? The place looked poor."

Another chuckle, but Saburo's companion did not elaborate, and Saburo did not press him.

"Aren't you afraid to be out here?"

"What can they get from me? I have no money. I have no horse or ox. I have no pretty daughter."

Saburo nodded, thanked him for the refreshing pause, and got back on his horse. He had lived among corrupt monks in his youth. Some monasteries and temples were entirely too devoted to getting their hands on money or rice. It was for the glory of Buddha. Such wealth was useful in attracting followers and rising in the Buddhist hierarchy. Perhaps the abbot of the Dragon Temple kept his current place looking modest and insignificant to avoid attracting the notice of the authorities. But Saburo was still puzzled that they had not been robbed on their stay, though it was conceivable that the abbot had been afraid to attack a court noble.

In any case, Saburo intended to take another look at the temple and monastery. The night he had spent there, watching the horses in the stables and keeping an eye on the hall where his master and the children were, had been uncomfortable and uneventful but thought-provoking.

Why, for example, were the stables so well kept when the abbot claimed they took in no visitors? In fact, the stables, though primitive, had looked definitely lived in, and not only by horses. Straw was heaped in one corner, a simple cooking fire had been made in another, and the water barrel held fresh water even though the stables were empty.

He looked ahead where the road curved toward the top of the mountain and caught some movement. A deer? No. Deer are not blue. There it was again, where the trees parted enough to allow a glimpse of the road. A child. A boy wearing a short blue jacket? Less than ten years old, to judge by his size. Where were the adults with him?

But the boy disappeared and Saburo rode on and the site was hidden by trees again. Apparently what had happened yesterday had not frightened people away from this road.

After a while, he passed the spot where the farmer had been killed and paused to have a look. A short distance from the roadway, he found the blood and a few flies, but the body was gone. Saburo looked at the shrubs and back at the road where the attack must have happened. A rabbit appeared briefly, sat up to stare, and hopped off. Above him, the dark shapes of birds of prey rode the air in overlapping circles. If there had been footprints or signs of a struggle, they were gone now after so many feet and horses' hooves had passed over them. He decided that the attackers had moved the body from the roadway to hide it and delay discovery. They had wanted time to leave the area.

He continued his journey up the mountain. The woods closed in again, and it was cooler now. Suddenly, his horse screamed and reared. He lost his seat, and flew backwards. There was a brief, shocking pain, and then darkness.

When Saburo came to, he was lying among ferns, looking up at dense tree branches. He knew instantly that his horse had thrown him, but other details escaped him. Where was he? What time was it? What was the matter with him?

Some of those details could be identified. His head hurt abominably and he had trouble moving. He was in the forest somewhere. It was getting near sunset.

After carefully checking his limbs, he rolled onto his side and hence to his knees. At that point he got sick and vomited. He decided he felt better afterward and cautiously got to his feet to lean against a tree and look around. He was beside a road that led up the mountain.

Memory returned. The Dragon Temple.

He had been on his way there when his horse had reared and thrown him. It would be easy to blame this on some rabbit or monkey spooking the animal, but the proximity to the temple made Saburo suspicious. He recalled seeing the child. A child throwing a rock could have caused his horse to shy. And yes, the animal had cried out in pain. And there in the roadway lay a good-sized rock.

The horse was gone.

A horse that must be paid for.

Several other things were also gone. First and foremost, his sword. That child could do some serious damage with that sword. He felt his clothing. His money was also gone. Greedy little bastard! And so were some useful implements Saburo carried in case he needed to open locks. And so was his amulet. Cut off the silk lace he wore around his neck. The amulet had been hidden under his clothes, but he had been searched. The amulet was a plain wooden disk with Sanskrit characters on one side and a dragon image on the other. It was old and cracked. Most people would think it ugly and valueless. He assumed the boy had used the sword to cut it loose, but it did not seem the sort of thing a child would want.

On the other hand, a small child was hardly alone on a mountain road, especially a dangerous one. So he had not been alone. Had the people who robbed him been his parents? It was all very confusing.

The amulet was important to Saburo, and not just as a talisman to protect him. It identified him as one of a handful of monks who had been trained on Mount

Koya and if the monks in the mountain temple got hold of it, they might well recognize its significance. It was a carving of the *Dainichi mantra,* representing the cosmic Buddha who was worshipped there. And the dragon was the azure dragon, the mark of a secret monastic organization. He had been a spy for them.

He took a few steps and looked up at the sky through the trees. It was still light but he had only an hour before darkness. He had been unconscious for too long and was too far from Hichiso to walk the distance. On the other hand, he was near the top of the mountain and so decided to finish his journey. Perhaps his horse had been caught. Or if it had been stolen, one of the monks might have seen the thieves. At worst, he would spend another night and walk back the next morning.

He trudged on, glad that movement seemed to improve his limp and the assorted pains in his body. His head cleared also, though it still hurt badly.

Saburo was a cautious man. He did not walk up to the gate of the temple and knock. Near the top, he turned aside from the road onto a narrow path that skirted the open area in front of the temple buildings. He wanted to have a good look at the monastery before approaching it openly.

It was nearly dusk now, but Saburo's eyes were good and he was experienced in working in the dark. The path took him along the front of the temple compound and toward its back, where the monks' quarters and service yards must be. The forest was dense here and grew all the way up to the wooden fencing. He moved in the silent way he had learned in his youth, placing his feet carefully, avoiding broken twigs, and keeping as much as possible to the grassy areas.

And he listened.

Then, over the rustling of small animals and an occasional cry from a bird or the chattering of a monkey, he heard faint voices. Saburo checked the sky again. It was nearly dark, and even darker here under the trees. He must hurry.

He looked for a place to climb over the fence when he heard the voices again. Two males were on the other side of the fence. One of the voices sounded familiar, but he could not place it. It was deep and conveyed authority. The other was higher.

A few yards ahead, a dead tree rested against another right next to the fence. Saburo took off his boots. The men on the other side were very close.

The high voice sounded querulous: "He's a good enough horse. Worth some money. We should just tie him up in the woods. The abbot worries too much. Must be getting senile."

Could they be talking about his horse?

The other said, "Don't be a fool. Monks can't be found with government property. This horse is branded."

Yes! His horse!

Their horses had been issued at the last inspection station and were branded. But how had the horse ended up here? Had the bandits robbed him and stopped here for the night? The voices receded, still arguing. Saburo started up the leaning tree, moving quickly, and craned his head to peer over the top of the wall. Alas, the service yard was dark and empty. He guessed he was near the stables. Somewhere a gate slammed shut. Saburo slid back down, put on his boots.

It seemed these two had not been monks. If they were, they ought to be at the evening service. So clearly, others stayed here. Bandits? The family with the child he had seen earlier?

There was nothing ahead except dense woods and shrubbery. The narrow path disappeared. He turned back, convinced he had lost his chance, when he heard noise. Someone shouted. There was the sound of a slap, and then the crashing of something large through the undergrowth. A gate slammed shut, and the crashing receded.

Saburo cursed. They set his horse free and it was gone. He hesitated a moment, torn between wanting to go after the horse and getting a look at the two men. He decided to hurry back to the leaning tree.

Before he reached the spot, he heard them again, talking on the other side of the wall. The one with the querulous voice was still complaining. "That was a good horse. It's all very well for the boss, but the rest of us got to eat, too. And we do all the work."

The one with the deep voice said, "Shut up, you ugly little frog. I'm tired of your bitching. Let's grab some food before going home."

They said no more. Saburo found his tree and climbed it, but the courtyard was empty again. The evening service had ended. He could hear voices in a distance. It would be time for the evening meal. His luck was dismal today.

He started back down the tree, thinking about the problem of finding and catching a loose horse at night in these mountains among rocks and sheer drop-offs, when the boy in the blue shirt suddenly appeared on the far side of the yard. He ran across to another door, and then he was gone again.

Saburo called him a few names under his breath. He wished he could turn him upside down and shake him till his property fell from the thieving little bastard's clothes. And then he'd cut a switch and teach him about stealing.

Then he bent his mind to catching the horse before it had too much time to get thoroughly lost.

8

Family Matters

The next morning, Akitada joined the children for their fishing excursion. His nephew Arihito, who at fifteen disdained the company of his siblings and cousins, had eagerly agreed to be their guide when Akitada joined the group. He wasted no time asking his new-found uncle questions about the capital.

Akitada saw the interest and wondered. Did Kojiro expect his son to become a gentleman-farmer like his father? If so, encouraging young Arihito in dreams of life in the capital would not be welcome.

He asked, "Do you wish to live there or is it just a visit you have in mind?"

The boy blushed with embarrassment. "I hardly know, sir. I know nothing about it. Father rarely speaks of his life there, and Mother doesn't know anything, being a woman."

Akitada laughed. "You do your mother an injustice. It is true that women in our family tend to stay close to home, but your mother was an enterprising girl. Did she tell you how she met your father?"

"She said he was accused of a murder and you saved his life. So I guess she married him."

This got him another laugh. "She had already decided to marry him before he was arrested."

Arihito's eyes grew round. "Truly? Was she allowed to choose her husband?"

"Not really, but she did."

Now Arihito laughed. "I didn't know. She *is* very bossy."

Hearing their laughter, the other children came up to ask what they were talking about.

"Mother made up her mind to marry our father, and there was nothing Uncle Akitada could do about it."

Akitada grimaced. He said nothing, though, because it was true enough. It still rankled a little that he had had so little control over his own family that his favorite sister had chosen such an unsuitable match.

Yasuko said, "I'll find my own husband also. I'll know better than Father who suits me."

Worse and worse. Akitada had no faith whatsoever in Yasuko's choice, and she had already proved to have the same obstinate nature as her aunt.

They had reached the river. The Shiragawa made a bend through the fields here. Its banks were covered with willows and other trees, and the children knew a cove where they kept their boat. It was barely large enough for all of them, and Akitada, who had not rowed a boat since his early youth, felt a little nervous about all of them piling into it. But Arihito knew what he was doing. He used a long pole to push them out into the lazy current, and they slid gently down river.

Fishing rods were handed around, and the morning passed pleasantly with small triumphs as fish landed in a large bucket and Arihito frequently changed the position of the boat. There was laughter and chatter and even Yasuko deigned to handle her first fish, though a cousin had to bait her hook.

Akitada grew quietly happy and forgot about the troubles of the valley for a while.

Indeed, what he saw looked like a blessed land. On either side of the river the valley stretched toward the mountains with fields of ripening rice, and in the foot hills, the paddies climbed upwards, shelf by shelf, till they reached the dark woods that rose toward rocky crags. In this green and golden world, the river provided water to the farmers with innumerable canals and channels. The peasants worked very hard, planting, digging, treading the water wheels that raised the water into higher fields, and now they were about to reap their harvest.

Their houses rose here and there from the fields, small islands among trees, some mere huts thatched with rice straw, some wooden houses with their own granaries. They paid substantial rice taxes to the government, and if they rented their fields, they paid more to the owners of the land, but in a good year they would have enough for their family and for seed rice to raise next year's crop. It had been a good year so far.

He watched idly, as they glided past fields where peasant women in blue trousers and jackets, with their hair tied in patterned cloth, cut and gathered the sheaves and laid them on drying frames. If the weather held, they would next thresh the rice, and store it in a dry place.

The children had caught several fish. Akitada had lost one. He did not care. As they rounded another bend in the river, he thought of returning. The midday rice awaited them, perhaps enriched by their catch. He was about to mention this to the children when he saw a large compound of many substantial buildings close to the river. It was walled with white-washed mud walls and had its own landing stage on the river. He sat up.

"Whose is that?" he asked.

Arihito looked. "That's Asano's place. Asano is Lord Otomo's *betto*." He made a face. "We don't like him. He acts like he's better than we are. Father doesn't like him either. He says he treats his peasants badly."

Akitada was not surprised to hear that the man who worked for Otomo had a bad reputation. Mistreatment of peasants was common enough, and often it was due to the men who had been placed in positions of power by distant owners. Otomo was not as distant as most, but it seemed very likely to Akitada that he squeezed every last grain of rice from the people who worked his fields and did nothing in return. Asano was merely his tool to keep them in line.

He said, "We're taught that peasants are to be ranked above all common people, even the wealthiest merchants. And that is because they feed our nation."

Yasuko protested. "Surely an ignorant, dirty peasant isn't better than a wealthy man, Father."

Akitada frowned at her. He had neglected his children's education. "I hope I never hear you speak of our peasants this way again, daughter. We are nothing without them and their labor."

She gaped at him. Yoshi grinned. "See," he told her, "this just goes to show how spoiled you are. Better watch out or you'll offend the gods with such talk."

The cousins were silent and looked embarrassed. Yasuko glared and pouted. Akitada sighed, his pleasure in the outing spoiled. With a glance at the sun, he said, "I expect it's time to return."

He found Saburo waiting for him. The children proudly carried their catch to the kitchen, and Akitada listened to Saburo's report as he washed his hands at the well in the courtyard. When Saburo had finished, rather apologetically, he nodded.

"There was little else you could have done. Trying to get into the temple compound would have been dangerous. I'm becoming averse to putting my family into danger. I wish we hadn't set out so happily for a short family visit in the assumption that we would be safe." He wiped his hands on the skirt of his robe and frowned. "This is a backwater. I expected bandits on the main highway and made sure we traveled in the daytime and in contact with others. I did not expect them here. It's very strange. They cannot find much to support a whole gang on these mountain roads."

"Maybe they trade in young women."

"Horrible as that is, it seems the only explanation. You'd think men like Otomo and that *betto* of his would do something about it. They have armed men to protect their compounds and fields. I have a good mind to recall them to their duty, but we are guests here. I think we'd better leave well enough alone."

Saburo looked unconvinced. "The bandits did get an ox along with the girl on the last attack. I expect they dined on that. An ox is not much good in the mountains."

"Also very difficult to lead away if you're in a hurry."

"The monastery rejected my horse, but they might accept an ox."

"I doubt it. An ox is best hidden where there are other such animals. The monastery stable was empty, you said. Besides, they don't eat meat."

Saburo sighed. "Well, I'll see what else I can learn. I can't just pretend nothing happened."

Akitada heard the reproach and bit his lip. "Be careful, Saburo! I don't want to upset anyone. And stay away from that outcast woman. The last thing we want is to have her life on our hands."

Akitada went in search of his sister and found her in the kitchen, preparing the fish they had caught.

She said, "What an abundance of fish! The children usually bring only one or two. You shall have my special fish soup."

Akitada's stomach rumbled, but he looked at her wet hands and the old apron tied over her robe and said, "Don't you have a cook?"

"I do, but I enjoy cooking. The cook—her name is Toyo—has gone to help Taro's widow prepare food for the funeral."

Akitada was once again struck by the great difference between Yoshiko and her sister Akiko. The fact that Yoshiko had married a commoner accounted for some of it, but Yoshiko's kindness and care for other people was surely a part of her own personality. Akiko's mind tended to be on promoting her family's position in the world. He felt a little ashamed of this harsh judgment. Akiko had shown him sisterly affection and offered her help in the past.

Now he said, "Can I help?" looking a little helplessly at the gutted fish and the pile of green vegetables waiting to be transformed into something nourishing and tasty.

"You can bring me that iron pot over there and throw another log on the fire under the cooker."

He did as he was told and felt ridiculously accomplished. "Do you want me to cut up those vegetables?"

She smiled at him. "You don't mind?"

"Not at all. I'm hungry."

She laughed and handed him a knife with simple instructions.

As he worked alongside her, he said, "Yasuko said something this morning that upset me." He told her about the incident of her calling the peasants dirty.

Yoshiko threw the fish into the pot, added hot water from another pot, and said, "Well, I recall that we also thought them quite repulsive. They work in the fields and are covered with muck, and their clothes are the poorest imaginable because they just get dirty anyway. And our children are raised to keep themselves clean. It's natural for them to see peasants as beneath them."

"Yes, but it is wrong. If it weren't for peasants laboring, none of us would eat, let alone have fine clean clothes."

Yoshiko said equably. "She's young, Akitada. Younger than you realize. I had a talk with her yesterday. It occurred to me that at her age she might need some information."

Akitada stopped chopping and stared at her. "What information? The children have a tutor. Not only Yoshi, but Yasuko also."

Yoshiko snorted. "Oh, come on, Brother. You're old enough and have had wives."

Akitada flushed. "But she's too young! Surely she's too young."

"No she isn't. But to reassure you, Yukiko has given her a rather thorough-going explanation of what it means to be a woman, so you needn't worry about talking to her."

"Dear Gods! What did she tell her?"

"Nothing to worry about. I think your former wife had a very sensible upbringing and she really likes Yasuko."

Akitada made a face. "Yasuko idolizes her. It worries me still. So all is well?"

"I think you might give your daughter a maid, one a bit older than she is, on future journeys."

Akitada flushed again. "I'm sorry. She didn't say anything."

"She wouldn't. And perhaps you have another year."

Akitada had stopped chopping the vegetables and now stood bemused. "They're growing up. And I'm getting old and thoughtless."

Yoshiko put her hand on his arm. "That's why you finally came, isn't it? Because Yasuko is growing up."

He nodded. "She needs a mother and I have taken Yukiko from her at the worst time."

"And you need a wife."

"I shall not marry again. But I should have kept her companion at least."

Yoshiko smiled a little. "Yes. That was a great pity. Now are you done with those vegetables?"

They had a pleasant lunch. The children were proud of their catch and praised the fish soup highly. Kojiro joined them late.

Akitada asked how the searches were going. He shook his head. "Hopeless. The poor girl. No point in going on."

Akitada was dismayed by such easy acceptance of a child's fate that must be horrifying. But he bit his lip and asked instead, "Who is this Asano who lives in such high style a mile or two down the river?"

"He's all right. He's a *betto* who manages Otomo's lands in this valley. He's good at his job."

His older daughter piped up, "I know his daughter Maeko. She's very nice."

Akitada smiled. "Then there is no more to be said."

Kojiro gave him a searching glance but did not pursue the subject until later when the rest of the family had left and he and Akitada went to sit on the veranda with a cup of wine.

"What is your interest in Asano?" he asked.

"I have no real reason except that he works for Otomo. I don't like what has been happening here and I don't like Otomo."

"Well, I don't like Otomo much either, but I think he's finally given up trying to buy more land. And Asano is a good *betto.* Our troubles have to do with a handful of villains who terrorize people because the governor refuses to take any action. Sergeant Shibata is just not up to it. I was thinking of organizing the peasants to fight back, but it's harvest time. I wouldn't be able to get anyone to leave their fields."

"This Asano has armed men, I hear."

"Some. They're Otomo's. He's not likely to use his own people in a search for a peasant girl."

"I see." Akitada thought that this made both Asano and Otomo very different from Kojiro. He said, "I forgot about the harvest. The truth is, I have a very bad feeling about all of this. I have no authority here, but I can write to your governor and urge action. Do you mind if I meddle to that extent?"

Kojiro raised his brows. "Do you really think something can be done? I'm afraid I've just been praying that they'll move on to richer prey."

"They may, but a man is dead and his daughter kidnapped. Can you just shrug this off?"

Kojiro bit his lip in irritation. "No, of course not. Believe me, if I'd caught one of them I would have killed him. But in this terrain and with no armed men it's impossible. Besides, you cannot imagine how important it is for a farmer to bring in his harvest. At any moment, the weather may ruin the crop, and then he and his family will be ruined. And many people in this valley would starve during the winter months, because the tax collector will take the little they have salvaged. At that point you take care of your farm before hunting criminals. The priorities are different for us."

Akitada knew this and the comment rankled. He restrained himself and said mildly, "I know. I'm trying to help, brother."

Kojiro's face relaxed. "Yes. Sorry. I'm tired and the strain got to me. If you think it may help, by all means write." He added, "But don't expect results. For one thing, we are too far from the provincial capital. It will take weeks."

Akitada said, "We'll see." Kojiro's grudging acknowledgment had done nothing to make for a friendlier atmosphere, and they parted after this.

Akitada found a desk and writing materials and composed his letter to the governor. He stressed the fact that he and his family were paying a visit and found themselves endangered by the lawlessness in the valley and surrounding mountains. He added that the local police officer had been most accommodating, but that Akitada saw a need for armed troops, especially since the criminal activities were threatening the coming harvest.

He hoped that, between the governor's fear for the rice tax and the courtesy he owed a ranking official from the capital, he would remember his duty and send soldiers.

Having signed and folded the letter, he impressed his personal seal.

Then he took up his brush again and started another letter to his sister Akiko and her husband. A third letter was addressed to Genba, who was looking after the Sugawara home.

9

The *Betto* Asano

Almost as soon as Akitada's letters had been sent, a period of peace and quiet descended on their valley. People began to believe that the bandits had left. Akitada did not think the threat to his family was gone, but after two weeks had passed with no other disturbance than that of a fire to a rice barn at the other end of the valley, he, too, wondered if it was all over. The relief came with some embarrassment. What was he to tell Governor Minamoto when he sent the requested troops, only to find that the gang had gone elsewhere, perhaps even left the province altogether?

He set against this his memory of the bloody corpse of Taro and the loss of Taro's daughter. Justice all too often got lost in these backwoods. Everything in Akitada rebelled against this, and he said as much to Kojiro and Yoshiko and was shocked when they countered with sighs and expressions of relief that peace had returned and a normal life could be resumed.

"The gods know, and a special hell will await those thugs when they die," Yoshiko said consolingly. "It's much more important to look after the living.

Thank heaven we have a good harvest, and if the gods are willing, we'll have another before winter."

Kojiro and others had decided to put out new rice plants they had raised in the optimistic hope that the weather would cooperate. Everywhere the fields were flooded again and women walked in lines across the paddies pushing young plants into the mud.

As for Akitada and the children, they frequently rode. Their rented horses, as well as Kojiro's, needed daily exercise. The children thrived. Yoshi had always wanted to live like this, with daily rides, and shooting birds with his bow and arrow. His cousin was a fine marksman, and Yoshi practiced endlessly. Yasuko also took to horsemanship. Akitada watched her, remembering her mother who used to love riding a horse. Every day, his daughter reminded him more of the wife he had lost and this caused him to yearn for the companionship of a woman again.

Toward the middle of the seventh month Hichiso would celebrate the O-bon festival. Akitada had hoped to have left for home by then, but the children were so happy with their cousins and begged to be allowed to stay for the festivities. They made plans to attend the temple fair and talked about the evening market and entertainments in town. They would put out lanterns to guide the spirits of their ancestors to their door, decorate the house altar, and place bowls of food before it. They would fashion small boats from paper, straw, and bamboo pieces that would hold small candles. These they would launch on the river for the ancestral spirits on their return to the netherworld after their visit. There would be special rice cakes and sweets, and a festive family dinner.

Akitada submitted with a smile. It had been a long time since the children had had something to look forward to.

Saburo was the only one who still persisted in his suspicions about the monks. He made several excursions at night to spy on the temple without finding anything to report. His visits to town to talk to people also produced little of interest. The peasant whose rice harvest burned decided to abandon his land and take his family to the city. The barn burning troubled Saburo, but his master seemed uninterested. Saburo visited the outcast village on a day when he knew the woman Miyo was gathering wood and lost more coppers. He did pick up some interesting rumors but decided to keep them to himself until he could substantiate them.

In general, Saburo was frustrated and depressed. He was irritated that Akitada did not push the investigation into Taro's death and seemed to care for little besides amusing himself with the children. One morning, he found himself in town again and in a very glum humor.

It was market day. People mingled among the stalls that sold vegetables, eggs, inexpensive cloth, earthenware pots, and fish. A few vendors sold rice cakes and noodle soup. Compared to markets in the capital, it was more than modest, but it was also cheap.

Saburo was parsimonious lately since he had taken on a family of his own. So he slowed down and looked for bargains. Perhaps he might find some toy that would please his adopted daughter or a small ornament for his wife.

As he strolled and compared, he became aware of an altercation. A man was shouting and then a child screamed.

He saw a small group of people gathered around the incident and went to see what was going on.

Inside the circle of onlookers stood a well-dressed, elderly man leaning on a cane. He was a little corpulent but physically still strong though he had the walking stick. In front of him cowered a ragged boy who was clutching a bleeding dog and crying, "No, please no! Please. He didn't mean it."

"The cur bit me when I kicked him aside. Give him here! I'll make sure he doesn't bite anyone else!" the man growled. The boy did not obey. Raising his stick, the man started forward.

Saburo pushed past the people who were watching. "Let him be!" he shouted at the man. "It looks like you hurt his dog already."

The old man turned. "Who the devil are you? What is it to you?"

"That doesn't matter. I don't like to see children and animals mistreated."

"How dare you? It's none of your business.". The man reached down and seized the boy's arm. The dog whimpered.

Saburo took hold of the man's shoulder and pulled him away from the child. "Leave him alone, I said."

The man's face turned red with anger. "Take your hands off me!" Saburo released him. The old man raised his stick. "Out of my way, scum!"

Saburo stood his ground. He glanced down at the boy and told him, "Take your dog and run!"

The boy ran. The old man cursed and slashed Saburo across the face.

For a moment, the pain was so great that Saburo could neither hear nor see. He reached for his face. When the world swam back into focus, he felt blood on his hand, tasted blood running into his mouth, and saw it dripping down the front of his robe.

The old man gave a bark of laughter. "That'll teach you next time," he said and turned to walk away.

Saburo was seized by fury. "You'll be sorry you did this, old man," he shouted. "People like you shouldn't be allowed to live."

With another laugh, the man was gone.

A woman took off her head scarf and offered it to Saburo. He shook his head and dabbed at the blood on his face with a paper tissue from his sash. It was inadequate, and the woman held out her scarf again.

"No, thanks." Saburo said. "I'll be all right. Don't want to spoil your pretty scarf. Who was that man?"

"Stay away from him," she said. "He's the *betto* Asano. He thinks he's better than the rest of us and gets angry when he's not respected."

"A rich man?"

She nodded. "He lives in the big house by the river. He works for Lord Otomo."

Saburo nodded. "Thanks. I think I'll have a word with him."

Her eyes grew round. "Don't. He'll kill you like he wanted to kill that dog."

He tried a smile and failed. His face felt raw and hurt at every word. "Don't worry," he managed. As he turned to walk away, he saw a memorable face. A tall, bearded man with curiously slanted eyebrows and a mocking smile was leaning against the wall of a shop, his arms folded across his chest. Saburo paused, but the man straightened and walked away quickly.

Akitada found Saburo at the well in Kojiro's stable yard, gingerly washing blood off his face.

"What happened to you?" he asked, noting the large amount of blood on the front of Saburo's robe and the vicious slash across his mouth and nose. Saburo's beard hid most of it, but the washing had opened the wound again and Akitada could see the blood oozing through. Saburo's mouth and nose were swelling and one eye would turn black.

"Asano," said Saburo.

"Asano? You mean Otomo's *betto*? The one Kojiro thinks is such a good manager?"

"I don't know about that. He slashed me across the face with his stick because I stopped him killing a dog he'd already wounded. No doubt, he meant to beat both the child and dog to a pulp."

"But that's outrageous! Come, let's see if my sister can put something on your face to stop the swelling."

Saburo dabbed at his wounds with a sleeve. "It feels tight. Does it look bad?"

"Yes."

"Well, one scar more or less doesn't matter, but that man must be stopped."

Akitada was furiously angry. "I'll see about it. I'm sorry this happened, Saburo. Perhaps we'd better just go home. Clearly we're not wanted here."

Saburo looked at him. "You shouldn't run away."

Akitada flushed. "Look, I made a mistake in coming, and in coming without enough men to protect us."

Saburo snapped, "You think I've let you down. You think compared to Tora and Genba I'm nothing. Well, maybe I *am* worthless," and walked away.

"Saburo! Come back here!"

But Saburo did not obey. Akitada was angry again, this time with Saburo who had not only been critical of him but openly defiant. He went in search of Kojiro to discuss the matter.

His harvest in, Kojiro was in his office, bent over farm records. He greeted Akitada with relief.

"I don't care for book keeping, brother, but it has to be done. Let's sit outside and share some wine. I have been a poor host during your stay here."

Akitada smiled. "Not at all. I'm the last person to complain about a man who takes his profession seriously. I've been far guiltier than you all these years, and my poor children hardly know their father. But if you really have a little time, I have some questions."

They settled themselves on the veranda outside the office It overlooked a side yard between the dwelling and the service area, so there was agreeable smell of fresh straw and wood smoke from cooking fires in the air. In the distance the green hills rose steeply into a blue sky.

"So, what have you been up to?" Kojiro asked after he had filled their cups.

Akitada mentioned the fishing trip and some excursions on horseback, then asked, "About this Asano. You may recall, I asked you about him before. You gave him a good report. Unfortunately something has happened that makes me question that." He summed up what Saburo had reported. Kojiro's face expressed his shock. He shook his head. "Are you sure it was Asano? Asano is elderly and walks with a limp."

"That is probably why he carried a sturdy stick to use on animals and people," Akitada countered.

"Well, he has a temper sometimes, but to strike someone like Saburo? It seems unbelievable. Is Saburo hurt?"

"Yes. He was bleeding and will be scarred."

"Oh. That's terrible. What will he do?"

"Nothing yet, I hope, but he's angry. With me also."

"Why you?"

"Because I've done nothing about the attack on Taro and his daughter."

Kojiro drank down his wine in one gulp and poured himself another. "I wish the gods had prevented this," he said. "I'd give anything to preserve our peaceful life here. Especially now that you have come for a visit. I'm not a violent man, brother. To my mind, violence begets more violence. I want to see my family safe. Surely you can understand that."

"Unpunished crimes lead to more crimes. Doing nothing is worse than stopping the villains."

"But the bandits have moved away. We cannot bring back Taro or his daughter."

"They are killing and raping elsewhere then. But we are getting away from the subject of Asano's attack on Saburo. I'm going to file a complaint with Sergeant Shibata. It may well lead to a cooling of the friendly relationship you seem to have enjoyed with the man. And if he's as irascible as he appears to be, you may find him retaliating. I thought it best to warn you of this."

Akitada had come to this decision only during their conversation. He was irritated by Kojiro's defense of Asano and by his refusal to take action. Ironically, this was the very accusation that Saburo had leveled against his master.

Kojiro frowned. "Don't jump to conclusions. There may be an explanation. Let's go talk to Asano. Saburo must have done something for Asano to hit him."

Akitada said stiffly, "Saburo doesn't lie. I'm going to have a word with Sergeant Shibata."

Shibata was in his office, looking glum. His face brightened when he saw Akitada. "Did you hear yet from the governor?" he asked.

Akitada had not and said so. He was angry about that also and had wasted time thinking of ways to file complaints against Minamoto Tamenori. But he had a more urgent problem now.

"My secretary has been attacked by Otomo's *betto* Asano. He arrived home bleeding from facial wounds. I want Asano arrested."

Shibata pursed his lips. "I rather doubt his people would allow that. I heard Asano hit your man with his walking stick because he tackled him in the street. Self-defense."

"That's a lie. Asano was about to beat a dog to death, and Saburo merely took hold of his arm."

"Well, it might have happened that way, but seriously, you don't expect me to make an arrest, do you?'

"What do you suggest?" Akitada snarled. "Surely lawlessness in this god-forsaken valley hasn't reached the point of people beating other people over the head without some sort of reaction from you."

Shibata sighed. "I'll go see Asano tomorrow and suggest an apology is in order."

Akitada muttered a curse and turned on his heel.

10

Another Murder

Early the next morning, Akitada rode to Asano's farm. He was again impressed by the size of this farmstead that occupied a gated compound and was surrounded by many outbuildings. It was almost twice the size of Kojiro's place. In the courtyard, he dismounted and called out to one of the workers. The man came over and bowed.

"Where's your master? I have business with him."

The man pointed to the main house, a large, square building with a steep, thatched roof.. "He must be inside. I'll go tell him. What is your name, sir?"

Akitada gave his name, and the man ran off.

Walking his horse to the main house after him, Akitada tied the animal to a railing and waited.

The worker reappeared with a house servant.

The house servant, an elderly man, bowed, and said, "I regret that I don't know where the master is, sir. He didn't come home last night. His women are very worried. He's an older man and was attacked by someone yesterday."

Akitada began to feel very uneasy. He had not seen Saburo this morning. "When did you last see him?"

"He returned in time for his evening rice, but he went back out afterward. He said he was going to check the work on the water channels in the high fields."

"Did you send someone to look for him?"

"Of course. This morning when we couldn't find him. We also sent for the police."

Worse and worse.

Akitada nodded, said he hoped Asano would turn up hale and hearty, and rode back home. There he found Saburo, still disgruntled, and asked, "Did you go to see Asano last night?"

"No, sir. But I will today."

Akitada heaved a sigh of relief. "Don't! Asano is missing, and they have called the police."

Saburo frowned. "The police? He can't have been missing long."

"He told his family about his encounter with you, and then went out again. They were afraid of another attack."

Saburo flared up. "Attack? I didn't attack him. He attacked me. So it's my fault if he's gone? The bastard hits me in front of all those people, and when they misplace him for a few hours, they think I've done something to him?"

"Calm down. He will probably show up, but under no circumstances are you to go and confront him."

There was a brief silence. Finally Saburo said, "I see. We're to do nothing again. I think you've changed, sir. You're not the man I came to serve–the man who fought the pirates in Naniwa, the man who stood up to powerful nobles in Kyushu, the man who persisted in his mission in a terrible storm. What happened to him?"

Akitada stared at him, speechless. Then he turned on his heel and walked away.

Saburo's words hurt Akitada deeply. Strangely he was not angry; instead he was saddened. He would have to dismiss Saburo for such insubordination. But Saburo now had a family who relied on his support. No. He could not do it. He had taken him on and Saburo had served faithfully. Until now! He could not send him away into a world that had little faith in former monastic spies and their outcast family. He would have to live with Saburo's disapproval, with the knowledge that he had lost his respect.

His misery was increased since he had, in fact, avoided confronting the outrages that had occurred in this valley.

In the end, Akitada decided to return to Asano's place. He could at least keep himself informed of the search, and when Asano was located, as surely he must be, he could insist on charging the man with assault.

He found that the police had arrived in the meantime. Shibata's men had gone to search the area where Asano had gone the night before, and the sergeant was interviewing house servants and workers in the courtyard. Akitada dismounted and tied up his horse.

The sergeant did not show much joy at seeing Akitada again. "I need to speak to that man of yours," he said after a mere nod.

"Saburo will be very glad to lay charges against Asano." Akitada countered. "Where is the man?"

"We're looking."

"I understand he left last evening to inspect some work on one of the fields."

"So they say." Shibata pointed to a place up on the hillside above the compound. "We looked. He isn't there."

Behind Asano's farm, the rice paddies gradually climbed as far as it had been feasible to carve paddies out of the mountain. "Could he have had an accident? Was he on horseback?"

"The horse came back."

"An accident then."

Shibata grimaced. "Not necessarily."

Akitada snapped, "Saburo had nothing to do with it, whatever it was."

Shibata did not answer. A young man in fine clothes was coming to join them. He was in his late teens or early twenties, slender and clearly not used to working outdoors. After glancing at Akitada, he asked, "What's going on, Shibata?"

Shibata said, "This is Asano's son, sir," and to the young man, "Lord Sugawara came to ask for news."

The young man blinked at the title, then said, "Is it his servant who threatened my father?"

Akitada said mildly, "My secretary suffered an injury from your father's cane yesterday, but he had nothing to do with his disappearance."

"So you say," the young man said rudely. He turned back to Shibata. "Anything yet?"

"No. My men are searching the woods now." He gestured toward the forest above the fields.

"He went all the way up there?" Akitada asked.

Shibata pursed his lips. "We aren't sure."

"He would surely have dismounted before going higher. That doesn't look like the sort of terrain a horse can manage. And I understand he had trouble walking."

Shibata pursed his lips again and looked thoughtful.

Asano's son said, "He may never have got that far if someone was after him."

This was true, of course, so Akitada said nothing.

As they stood scanning the mountainside, they saw a figure emerge from the woods and hurry down the slope, waving his arms.

"Ah," said Shibata and made for his horse. Akitada did the same.

They had found Asano.

He lay among the trees, half hidden by broken bracken, covered in blood, his fine clothes ruined, his corpulent body sprawled as he had fallen. He was very dead, apparently bludgeoned to death with his walking stick. The stick, a heavy, knotted one, lay beside the body, covered with blood and brain matter. Akitada's heart sank when he took in the manner of this death.

Shibata was off his horse and beside the body in a moment. He bent over it, then stood up holding something that dangled from his hand. Turning to Akitada, he called out, "Would you mind taking a look at this, my lord?"

Akitada dismounted and walked over. The item Shibata held out to him was a wooden amulet on a broken string. He recognized it. It was Saburo's.

Ironically, it was at this moment that Akitada knew Saburo had had nothing to do with this murder.

"It's an amulet," he said.

"Well, do you recognize it?"

"Sergeant, such things are sold at every temple fair in this country."

Shibata looked disappointed. "Then you don't recognize it?"

Akitada hesitated. "Saburo had one similar to this one."

Shibata nodded with a pleased smile. He shoved the amulet inside his robe and turned back to the corpse.

The dead man's face was unrecognizable. The beating had been brutal, had been meant to kill

It spoke of a furious anger.

But there was the amulet.

And that spoke of cold and rational planning.

Shibata pursed his lips. "Where is your man??"

"At home. It may come as a surprise to you, Sergeant, that he was attacked on the road to the mountain temple two weeks ago. The robber or robbers stripped him of all his valuables, including that amulet."

Shibata's lip twitched derisively. "Convenient. Neither you nor he reported it."

"You were busy at the time, and the items lost were not of sufficient value to trouble you. He thought he saw a child. The child may have thrown a rock that caused his horse to throw him, but I believe it's more likely the bandits were behind it."

"You claim the bandits did this?" Shibata gestured to the body.

"I claim nothing. Saburo's amulet could have fallen into anybody's hands."

"And the manner of this man's death?"

"It might have seemed convenient to the killer to blame it on Saburo. The encounter between Asano and Saburo was well known in the valley."

"This happened late last evening. Just before dark, I think. Just after Asano came up here to check on the work. Where was your secretary at the time?"

Akitada said, "I don't know. I can find out perhaps."

Shibata turned away in disgust. He directed his men to put the body on a stretcher and take it down the hill to the house. Akitada waited, but the sergeant ignored his presence and eventually set off after the stretcher.

It was frustrating not to have any authority, nor any friends one could call on. Many other men in his position would have pulled rank, but Akitada was not like that. He had seen too much abuse of power. Also, amidst his frustration with Shibata, he felt a certain amount of admiration for the sergeant who refused to be intimidated by Akitada's rank.

He trailed after the police with their gory burden.

11

The Grieving Family

When the stretcher bearers arrived before Asano's house, they set down their burden. Asano's son was waiting. He cried out and threw himself on his father, weeping loudly. The farm workers and house servants approached more slowly. Among the house servants was a tall young woman in the clothes of an upper servant. She came to stand beside Asano's son.

The latter became aware of her and raised his head to search for Shibata. "Have you caught him?" he demanded hoarsely.

Shibata shook his head.

"Then what are you waiting for? Are you so incompetent that you cannot arrest a single man? Bad enough you let a gang murder and rape our people. But we know the vile person who has slain my father. Go arrest him! You know where he is."

Shibata shot Akitada a glance. "In due time, Toshiyasu. He will not escape. Formalities require that I establish a few facts first."

Asano's son was on his feet. He pointed at Akitada. "There's the man who brought my father's killer here. What is he doing here? Is he gloating at our grief?"

The tall young woman cried out, "Toshi! Remember your manners. Let the sergeant do his work."

Akitada gave her a nod of approval. He said, "I'm very sorry for your loss. I'm Sugawara Akitada. Nagaoka Kojiro is my brother-in-law. I take it the dead man is your father?" He looked from one to the other.

It was the young woman who answered. "Yes, sir. I'm Maeko, and this is my brother Toshiyasu." She turned to her brother. "Perhaps we should take Father inside. Then the sergeant can ask his questions."

Shibata thanked her, and her brother reluctantly agreed. Somewhat to Akitada's surprise, Maeko included him in the invitation as she gestured toward the stairs leading up to the house.

They placed the stretcher reverently in the center of the main room, then stood about looking at each other. The silence was perhaps a sign of respect for the dead man's final entrance into his home.

Shibata was the one to break it. "Who knows what happened yesterday after Asano returned from his fight with the man Saburo?"

The son and daughter both raised hands. The son said, "Father was outraged. His color was bad. I feared for his life and made him sit down and rest. He told us how he had been attacked on a public street in front of people. He's an old man, and feeble. And nobody helped him. They just stood about to watch that villain push him about. It was a long time before he calmed down. After his evening rice, he decided to get on his horse to check on some work his peasants had been told to do in the upper fields. He was a most conscientious *betto*. Lord Otomo will tell you what a good man he was. Oh, Father!" Toshiyasu's voice broke and he fell silent. He went to kneel beside his father's body, sobbing quietly.

Akitada said nothing, though this account differed materially from Saburo's and from the injuries the "feeble" old man had done him.

Shibata looked at Asano's daughter. "Is this what happened. Maeko?"

She frowned. "He *was* upset and angry. It seems a dog had bitten him. That caused the incident in town. And he did go out later, even though I thought the matter of the upper fields could have waited till the morning."

Akitada cut in before Shibata could dismiss her. "You say there was no urgency to inspect the fields. Was your father in the habit of going back out after the evening meal?"

The son broke in angrily, "What good is all that? We know who did it. Why aren't you arresting him? I don't care if he works for some big nobleman from the capital. He killed my father." He shot Akitada a venomous glance.

His sister said more calmly, "Let us cooperate, brother. The guilty will be found, I know." To Akitada she said, "One of Lord Otomo's men brought a note asking if some work had been completed. Father went to make sure it was before answering."

"I see. Very commendable. Did the messenger wait?"

"No. I think that worried Father. As if Lord Otomo had heard it hadn't been done and was sending a reprimand. He went as soon as he got the note."

Shibata was getting impatient. He broke in with, "When did you notice your father missing?"

Maeko looked down. "I cannot say, Sergeant. I went to bed. I did not know until a maid woke me in the morning, saying my brother couldn't find him."

Shibata nodded and looked at Asano's son.

Toshiyasu brushed tears from his face and said thickly, "I wasn't here. I got home late and went to bed. When I went to speak to him in the morning, his room was empty and his bedding hadn't been slept in. I immediately questioned the servants. None had seen him after he left the night before. That's when I sent for you." He paused and added, "Now do your job, Shibata."

Akitada thought it interesting that Asano's daughter was dry-eyed throughout, while his son seemed the only person to grieve Asano's death. He asked, "Where is the rest of the family? Aren't there other children? Wives?"

Toshiyasu glared at him. It was his sister who answered. "We are the only surviving children, sir. Our mother died a few years ago. My father has not taken another wife, though there is a concubine."

Akitada nodded. "I'm sorry. I wondered why you were alone to cope with his death."

"What do you care?" her brother snapped. "It's our business. Except for shielding my father's killer, you have no business here."

Akitada nodded. "Fair enough. Sergeant, I shall be outside." Without waiting for comment from either man, Akitada strode out quickly.

At the entrance, he found the same elderly house servant he had talked to the previous day. The man was dry-eyed, but looked upset. Knowing that servants, especially ones who had been with a family for years, felt the loss of a master as deeply as his closest family, Akitada expressed his condolences.

"Thank you, my Lord," the old man said. And after a moment, "I don't know what will become of us now."

Surprised, Akitada said, "Surely Asano's son will take over as *betto*. Or are you afraid that Lord Otomo will abandon the family?"

The servant sighed. "Not Lord Otomo. At least, he will not abandon the family. My master's people have been senior retainers for the Otomo family for many generations."

"What is the problem then?"

The old man just shook his head.

Realizing that loyalty forbade the man to speak ill of the family, Akitada said, "I hope all will be well."

The old man sighed again. "My young lady. I grieve for her."

"I liked her. She seemed a capable and sensible young woman. Surely she will look after her father's people."

"She will try."

Akitada knew he could not press the man further. Obviously, Toshiyasu had not inspired respect or trust in the servants. But Akitada was more interested in another matter. He said, "I understand your master's visit to the high paddies at such a late hour was unexpected. I think he received a message?"

The old man nodded. "There are always messages. He was a *betto.* The Otomo estate is very large. That's a big job. But I think the master just wanted to get away from the house to calm his mind. Too many quarrels. Too many bad things happening yesterday. And he was not a peaceful man." He shook his head sadly. "I'm afraid Master Asano was not like the bamboo. You have to bend with the storms you encounter in life. He did not know how to bend."

That confirmed the temper that caused Asano to strike Saburo. He asked, "Did anything else happen to upset your master?"

The servant hesitated. "Ah," he said after a moment, "they say 'Let each child go its own way even if it leads to a cliff.' Fathers find that hard to do." He bowed respectfully and hurried into the house.

Akitada stood a while longer, looking after him thoughtfully.

He was about to descend the stairs to the courtyard, when the door opened behind him and Sergeant Shibata joined him.

"Still here?" he asked, almost rudely.

Akitada said mildly. "Yes. And you? What are your plans?"

"It's a murder investigation. I ask questions."

"Good. May I come along?"

The sergeant's face closed. "Better not. Go home. I shall be there shortly. Make sure your secretary is available." Without another word or salute, he ran lightly down the stairs and went to speak to a group of constables waiting below.

It was not a good sign. Very worried, Akitada got on his horse and rode back to Kojiro's farm. As he approached the compound, he saw that the courtyard seemed to be full of horses and people. Catching his breath fearing for his children, he spurred on his horse.

12

A Gain and a Loss

Akitada arrived, scattering people and horses, his hand on his sword. There were four heavily armed strangers in the yard and five horses. When nothing happened except that the armed strangers stared at him, he demanded, "Who are you?"

They looked at each other, then one saluted. "Hired warriors from the capital, sir."

Realization dawned belatedly. Akitada jumped down and shouted, "Genba?"

From the veranda above came the familiar gruff voice. "Yes, sir?" Genba appeared at the head of the stairs, beaming. "We made it, sir. Are we in time?"

Akitada dropped the bridle and ran up the steps to embrace Genba. "Thank the gods you are here, old friend." He released him and looked at him anxiously. "The trip wasn't too hard on you?"

Genba was a big man in many ways. He was both tall and heavy. He had been a wrestler when he was younger, and his huge appetite along with his wife's cooking had added more weight over the years. When his hair had turned gray and his life had become less strenuous, he had accepted the fact that he neither had the strength nor the swiftness of his youth any longer. Akitada had turned the management of his properties over to him, and used Tora and Saburo for the footwork. Now, Genba had been called on to fight for and with his master again. He had come eagerly.

"Of course not," he said, grinning more widely. "It felt like old times, sir. I feel good. I brought letters."

Akitada embraced him again, causing Genba to blush with embarrassment. Akitada received the bundle of letters with mixed feelings. Was there more trouble from Yukiko? He had left, reassured that the divorce settlements were satisfactory to all involved, but Yukiko could well have thought up something else to inflict pain on him. He looked through the papers quickly. Only estate matters, and—to his special delight—a letter from Tora and Sadako. Tora was not much of a writer, so most of this letter must be by Sadako. His heart lifted.

They were joined by Kojiro and Yoshiko, also smiling.

Genba said, "It's good to see your little sister again, sir. She's all grown up, and as pretty a young lady as one could wish for."

They all laughed at this. Yoshiko said, "Not so young anymore, Genba, but I thank you. You're most welcome and so are your men. Kojiro will show them where to sleep and eat. You will stay with us."

Kojiro left to welcome the hired warriors, and Akitada saw that Saburo had also come out and recalled the new troubles. He said, "I'm sorry, Yoshiko, Kojiro. I didn't mean to burden you with more people, but I was concerned about the journey home. Setting out the way I did with the children with only two of us to protect them was foolish."

Yoshiko protested, "But surely you're not leaving already? You said you would stay through the O-*bon* festival."

"A rash promise I made the children, but there's another problem now. Shall we go in?"

As they settled in the main room, Genba said, "Saburo mentioned the robbers and that mad old man who beat him. He looks awful."

Akitada nodded. "Yes, but that mad old man is about to be even more trouble."

Yoshiko had sent a maid for wine. Now she asked, "What's wrong, Akitada? Is it something to do with poor Saburo?"

"They found Asano. Dead. Beaten to death with his own walking stick."

Yoshiko cried out, and Saburo drew in his breath with a hiss.

Akitada looked at him. "And there is worse, Saburo. Near the body was your amulet."

"What?" Saburo's eyes widened. "Now that's strange. I told you, that child on the mountain road stole it." He suddenly looked almost pleased. "Well! That proves it. I was right all along. The bandits are still here. They're hiding in the Dragon Temple. Now we shall get at the truth."

Akitada frowned. "I doubt the bandits are behind this murder. It was too well planned. Asano's servant said Asano's setting out so late for the place where he was killed was unlike him. I think he got a message and walked into a trap."

"I see no reason why bandits shouldn't plan a murder," Saburo said stubbornly in a tone of voice that made Genba give him a surprised look.

Akitada said, "That's beside the point at the moment, Saburo. Sergeant Shibata will arrive shortly to arrest you. That, too, was in the plan."

This was greeted with shocked silence. Then Yoshiko protested, "Oh, no. Shibata wouldn't. He's not a bad man."

Akitada nodded. "I agree, but he will have no choice. And I'm afraid I have made matters worse by sending to the governor for help against the bandits. He's ignored that request and will probably put the blame on Shibata."

Saburo glowered. "Well, it wasn't me who killed Asano, though the bastard deserved to die."

"Watch your tongue," Akitada snapped. "There are servants about."

Another silence fell. Then Genba sighed. "I guess you wish now you had Tora with you rather than me." He hung his head.

That was true enough. Akitada was ashamed to admit it. Genba had, over the years, been pushed aside, left to look after home and family, while Tora and Saburo had assisted Akitada.

He said, "When I wrote you, I was afraid for my children. I wanted you here because I trust you to defend them with your life. You are my right hand, Genba."

Genba muttered, "Thank you, sir," and brushed at his eyes.

Saburo stirred. "I'll leave. I won't be here when Shibata and his men come. Sorry, I've let you down. It looks like I was no help to you and the children, and now I'll be arrested for a murder."

Akitada had had enough of soothing feelings. He said, "You cannot run away. That will make things worse. Shibata will assume that I've had a hand in it. What happened wasn't your fault. Instead of bemoaning events or running away, let's try to discuss our options."

Saburo subsided, but he looked rebellious. Genba patted his shoulder. "Don't worry, brother. We'll get you out. And then we'll all go home together."

Yoshiko suddenly had tears in her eyes. "You've finally come to visit us, and this happens," she said to Akitada. "Now you'll never come again. Oh, Akitada!"

It was a depressing gathering all right. Akitada said briskly, "Nonsense," but it was true that he was beginning to take Hichiso and the Shirakawa valley into serious dislike.

Sergeant Shibata arrived late that evening with four constables in tow. They were armed and carried chains to secure their prisoner.

Akitada met them in the courtyard. "Sergeant," he called out. "Please come inside."

Shibata hesitated. "We've come for your secretary Saburo."

"I know, but let's do this peaceably," Akitada insisted, with a glance at the armed constables with their chains. "Nobody here will raise a hand against you."

Shibata dismounted, tossing his bridle to a constable and went into the house with Akitada. In the main room, Kojiro, Genba, and Saburo awaited them. Kojiro offered wine and was turned down curtly.

Shibata eyed Genba with a frown. "Who's this?"

"I sent for Genba and a few men to accompany us on our return journey. Genba is a senior retainer and *betto* for my family."

"His name is Genba? A very common name, is it?" Shibata looked at Saburo. "Is that what Asano did to his face?" he asked Akitada.

"Yes." Akitada pointed to a cushion. "Please sit down. Let's talk about this."

Shibata did not move. "There's nothing to talk about. Asano's dead, and this . . . Saburo is suspected of having killed him. We have a witness."

"I didn't kill him," Saburo said loudly. "I was here ever since Asano attacked me yesterday."

Yoshiko said quickly, "Yes, Sergeant. That's true. He was here."

Shibata's eyes flicked over her and went to Akitada. "I don't know about that," he stated. "All I know is that he threatened Asano's life in town where upward of twenty people heard him. A few hours later Asano's found beaten to death with his own walking stick, the same stick he struck Saburo with, and an item belonging to Saburo is found near the corpse. Can you explain these things?"

Yoshiko snapped, "I don't lie, Sergeant."

Saburo said, "The amulet was stolen from me a few weeks ago. By the bandits. Or someone working with them. You can't arrest me."

Akitada said. "Saburo, I know you're innocent, but the sergeant has no choice in the matter. It's best you go with him until we can clear this up."

Saburo's eyes flashed. "I might have known," he said bitterly. "Well, what're you waiting for? Let's go."

The sergeant went to the door and called for his constables. Akitada said quickly, "No chains, Sergeant."

"I insist on chains, " snarled Saburo. "Let's make sure the people here get what they expect to see. Let Shibata march me back to jail like the hero he is."

Akitada winced. "Saburo, be patient. We'll do our best to help you."

It was the wrong thing to say. Shibata flushed with anger and snapped an order. The constables came, and Saburo was chained and taken away.

13

The Letter

The silence in the room lasted until the door flew open and Kojiro stormed in. "What happened?" he demanded. "Why are they taking Saburo?"

Akitada explained. Kojiro cursed.

Yoshiko touched her husband's arm. "We know he's innocent. Akitada will find out what happened. Shibata is acting strangely. I cannot imagine what makes him so unreasonable."

Her brother sighed. "Shibata is angry with me. I have a suspicion that my letter to your governor has got him in trouble.

"Oh." Yoshiko was startled by this. "Shibata is a good man. Why did you complain about him? He tried his best, Akitada."

Apparently Akitada was doomed to have his motives suspected, no matter what he did. "I did not complain about Shibata. In fact, I praised him. He doesn't have the support he needs to deal with that gang. It's the governor's responsibility to make sure he does. That's why I wrote. Alas, the governor didn't even acknowledge my request for help. Instead he probably blamed Shibata for what has been happening here. Now Shibata is furious. And Saburo has been blaming me for not working harder to locate the kidnapped girl. He thinks I intend to abandon him also."

"But you won't abandon him. And neither will we, right, Kojiro?"

Kojiro said a little doubtfully, "I'll do my best. What can we do?"

Akitada said, "I'm a little surprised that Shibata did not accept Yoshiko's word that Saburo was here at the time. That seems rather high-handed of him. At the very least, he could have asked some questions."

Yoshiko looked distinctly uncomfortable. "Well, I think we'd better let that go."

"Why? The more I think about it, the angrier I get. Saburo cannot be in two places at the same time. Shibata as much as called you a liar."

His sister blushed. "Well, it was a small lie."

"What?"

"Saburo was here to start with, but when it got dark, he said he'd have another look at the temple and left."

This confession was appalling. "You lied to Shibata? When you knew this is a murder case?"

"I tried to help. I knew Saburo would never do such a thing."

Akitada thundered, "How could you know that? You've only met him a few weeks ago."

She flinched at his tone. "Don't you trust him? You brought him to us. That was good enough for me."

Akitada was speechless. Did he trust Saburo?

The truth was that he had distrusted him from the beginning of their relationship. Saburo's confession that he had worked as a spy for warring monasteries meant he was a trickster. And the horrible punishment his enemies had inflicted on him when they caught him was most likely what he himself had been taught to visit on others. Perhaps he had even done so. And yet he had taken Saburo on—out of pity and gratitude. Saburo had proved his courage in the desperate fight against the pirates and perhaps saved their lives. Besides, he had skills that had proved useful in Akitada's work.

But did he trust him the way he trusted Tora and Genba? The answer was "no." And the current situation seemed to prove him right. Saburo acted on his own and against Akitada's orders.

He looked at his sister and brother-in-law and wondered if they blamed him for bringing a dangerous individual into their family. He said, "Of course, I trust him. I've known Saburo now for ten years. But you have not. More importantly, if Shibata finds out that you lied, Saburo is lost."

"Oh!" Tears filled Yoshiko's eyes. "I'm sorry."

Akitada suspected that Shibata had known, but he said nothing.

Kojiro went to put his hand on his wife's shoulder. "Don't fret, my love," he said. "We will find who killed Asano, and they'll let Saburo go."

Akitada nodded. "Yes. Thank you, Kojiro. I shall need your help. I hope this won't make trouble for you with Otomo."

"Otomo? Why would he make trouble for me? I have nothing to do with him."

"Yes, but he seems to have something to do with you. He wants some of your land."

Kojiro laughed. "He probably wants all of it. Let him. He won't get it."

"If Asano was merely Otomo's *betto,* I assume his house and the surrounding land really belong to Otomo. Yet he is considered a rich man."

"Oh, that. The house his family lives in and a good portion of the land is Asano's. He manages some parcels of Otomo's here in the valley and also looks after Sunomata fields where Otomo's main property is and Haguri where he has other properties. But Asano is quite rich in his own right. His family have served the Otomos for generations and built their own fortune through hard work."

There it was again: that note of admiration for Asano. In Akitada's experience, men became rich in land by stealing it from poor peasants. He said, "I asked because I wondered if Otomo might have had something to do with the murder. Asano's servant said there had been messengers that day. Something sent Asano to those high paddies, far enough from his main house and from other fields to escape observation."

Kojiro shook his head with a laugh. "Why would Otomo want his own *betto* killed?"

"I don't know. It remains to be seen."

Genba, who had been very quiet throughout, now asked, "Why did Saburo suspect the temple on the mountain? I never could quite understand, except that he thinks the monks must be hiding the bandits and there's a child there. Saburo said the child robbed him. It didn't make sense. Since when are children robbers?"

"Saburo is a little obsessed with the temple. When we stopped, we saw no evidence that they accommodated visitors. They almost denied us shelter. But something did happen to Saburo on that road. He may have imagined a child throwing a rock at his horse, but the animal did throw him. He hit his head and was briefly unconscious. That's when someone took his sword and amulet."

Genba shook his head. "You know, Saburo isn't a very good horseman."

"I know."

"As for being robbed, could he have lost those things when he was thrown?"

"Perhaps. But that doesn't change the fact that someone is implicating Saburo in this murder."

They fell silent again.

Genba stirred after a while. "So what shall we do, sir?"

Akitada saw the eager look on his face and smiled. "Perhaps we should pay Asano's household a visit tomorrow? For now it's time you got some rest."

That evening, in his own room, Akitada looked through the letters Genba had brought. He saved Tora's and Sadako's for last.

Tora's note was brief and nearly illegible. He reported that the journey had been uneventful, that Lady Sadako sat a horse well, and that he would return after a brief rest.

Sadako's letter was much longer and gave him great pleasure. She shared several small adventures on the journey, praised Tora so extravagantly that Akitada felt a pang of jealousy, and then described her family situation. Her elder brother had succeeded to the property. It had been he who had made a great effort to bring his siblings home. Two sisters had meanwhile found husbands and had families, but Sadako and the youngest, a boy, had returned. Her brother, now head of the Tanaka family, had two wives and four small children. She looked forward to helping raise them. The house and property were in good shape, though some damage had been done by those who had taken them over.

At the very end, she wrote of her gratitude to Akitada for "saving" her. In his own opinion, he had done nothing of the sort. She had helped him over a difficult and painful time. And almost imperceptibly she had become a part of his family and, as he knew too late, a part of him. He should not have let her go, but how could he have stopped her from rejoining her own family?

At the end came a sentence that made him warm with pleasure. She wrote, "My dear sir, I shall think of you and your children for the rest of my life. You, especially, are in my heart."

"You especially are in my heart." It was an extraordinary phrase from a woman to a man she was not married to or in love with. And "my dear sir," was surely also very kind.

He suddenly felt quite breathless. Throwing open the shutters, he looked out at the night sky, star-strewn around a pale moon, and tried to remember her. He only recaptured fragments: how she had looked standing under the plum tree in his garden, rosy with the chilly air and her joy in the blossoms; how she had caught him in Lady Aoi's arms and had run away with a sob; the way she had looked the day they had left.

He had been a fool.

But these memories were futile. It was far too late. Putting them firmly from his mind, he went to bed.

14

Sadamoto

As they rode to the Asano compound together the next morning, Genba looked around and commented, "This is good, rich farmland. No wonder Asano's rich. It will belong to the son now?"

Akitada nodded. "He seemed grief-stricken at the father's death. His sister was quite calm."

"Are you saying that he loved his father more than his inheritance? And the daughter did not care much about either?"

Akitada smiled. "People may pretend feelings they don't have."

"Ah!" Genba chuckled. "But surely killing a parent is too horrible to imagine."

"Nevertheless such things happen."

"Do you suspect the brother and sister?"

"Not yet, Genba. I don't know enough. We are going to learn more, I hope."

When they arrived, they found a stranger with Asano's children. He was a small man, near middle age, who introduced himself as Asano Sadamoto, cousin to Asano's children and their nearest relative. He lived in the next town and it appeared that Maeko had sent for him. He was far more courteous than Toshiyasu, who still seemed in a towering rage and wanted to know what business Akitada had on their land. His cousin and his sister both reproached him, and he stormed off angrily.

Sadamoto murmured, "Our apologies, sir. The youngster is distraught. Please be seated. We're honored by your visit. How may we serve you?"

Akitada replied, "Thank you, you are very kind. I'm Sugawara, as you have perhaps been told. This is Genba, my *betto.* The man Sergeant Shibata arrested also works for me. He is innocent. I'm, of course, very eager to get to the bottom of this."

"Yes, indeed. Please know that we don't blame you, sir. I understand that my uncle mistreated your servant?"

"Yes. He used his walking cane on his face."

"Ah. Terrible." Sadamoto wrung his hands and shook his head. "He had a temper, my uncle."

"Whatever they say, Saburo did not kill him. So it seems someone else must have done so. I am here because the quickest way to get my man out of jail is to find the real killer."

This astonished Sadamoto. He looked at Akitada doubtfully. "Are you connected with the police?"

Akitada suppressed a smile. "In a manner of speaking. I have served in the justice ministry."

Genba added proudly, "My master has investigated crimes for many years now. He's well known in the capital."

"Ah. Yes. I see." Sadamoto bowed respectfully, then wrung his hands again. "Are the local authorities aware of that?"

"Yes." Akitada was actually not quite sure how much Shibata knew. He certainly knew of Akitada's background. It had been explained to him in the matter of the bandits. But if Sadamoto thought Akitada was authorized to ask questions about his uncle's murder, there was no need to correct him.

Seeing Sadamoto hesitating, Akitada said, "I take it that you and your cousins are eager to find out who killed your uncle. As long as Saburo is jailed as the murderer, the real killer is free to strike again." He did not know if it was likely, but there was always a possibility that this case was more complex than just the killing of Asano. The careful and rapid planning to put the blame on Saburo suggested as much.

Sadamoto now looked nervous. "What do you want to know, sir? I cannot speak for Toshiyasu, but Maeko and I will answer your questions."

"I assume you came here to look after your young cousins. Who inherits your brother's property?"

"Toshiyasu, of course. I'm here to see all is done properly. My uncle asked me to witness his will. There's provision for Maeko when she marries, but that will be in Toshiyasu's hands."

"Your nephew is very young. I'm told that Asano's property is large. Do you trust him to manage?"

Sadamoto looked uneasy. "He's nineteen. Well, Maeko is sensible. She'll keep an eye on him."

"She is older then?"

"She's twenty-three."

Akitada raised his brows. "I'm surprised her father has not found a husband for her by now."

"Well, she's a very useful housekeeper. And she preferred it this way."

Genba said cheerfully, "A good daughter looks after her parents."

Akitada could see that Maeko had had a safe and comfortable life with her father and might not have wished to exchange it for the uncertainties of marriage, but she had just encountered the uncertainty of life as a single woman. He said, "Being an intelligent young female, she must have considered the possibility of her father's death. He was getting old and infirm. Does she get along well with her brother?"

"Certainly. They lost their mother five years ago. Maeko has taken her place by looking after her brother and the household."

"I think perhaps you have some doubts as to Toshiyasu's good sense?"

Sadamoto shifted in his seat and said with the same doubtful expression, "Well, he'll settle down soon enough. I'll stay until things are arranged."

"Do you expect he will also inherit the position of Otomo's *betto*?"

"His lordship has expressed his support in the past."

Akitada did not press the matter. Instead he asked, "Has he had a good education?"

"He wished to attend the university in the capital, but my uncle wanted him to learn estate management. It caused some disagreements, I think. Toshiyasu wanted to go to the capital very badly. Now it may have been for the best."

That did not answer the question. Or perhaps it did. And it would be for the best only if Toshiyasu had really applied himself. Akitada's impression of the youngster had been that his interests lay elsewhere. Neither farming nor studying at the university seemed on his mind. Of course, life in the capital offered many attractions for a young man. He wondered what amusements Toshiyasu might have found in Hichiso.

Akitada thanked Sadamoto for his patience and asked permission for Genba to speak to Asano's servants and peasants.

This was granted readily. Sadamoto asked anxiously, "Is there really a chance that my uncle was killed by someone else?"

"Yes. I'm certain of it."

Sadamoto shook his head. "What a thing! Uncle had such a temper!"

Akitada raised his brows. "Do you know of anyone who might have had an argument with him and done this?"

"No, no! Not at all. I was just thinking out loud," cried Sadamoto, horrified. "I don't live here and don't know anyone. Except my uncle and his children, of course."

Yes, but they were crucial. Akitada had often thought that the victim held the secret of his murder, not merely because he knew who had taken his life, but also because something about him or his activities had provoked the deed. And the children were closest to Asano. Love between parent and child was not always a given. Children had killed their parents, and parents had also murdered their offspring. But there was nothing more he could get from Sadamoto at this point. He asked again to speak to Maeko.

Sadamoto left with Genba and returned with Maeko. He offered to stay.

"I'd prefer to speak to your cousin alone," said Akitada.

"B-but she's a woman," protested Sadamoto.

"And I am a family man. I shall observe the proprieties."

"Please, Cousin," said Maeko firmly. "You mustn't insult Lord Sugawara."

Sadamoto flushed and bowed several times. "Not at all. It wasn't my intention. My apologies. I shall go then, shall I? You can always call out when you want me." He flushed again, realizing that he was making things worse, and hurried out of the room.

Maeko raised a hand to cover her mouth and giggled.

"Your cousin cares about you and your brother," Akitada said with a smile.

"Yes. He came to take care of us. It's very kind, but we are too old for that sort of thing."

"Are you?" He still smiled and saw her lip twitch.

"Well, *I* am, anyway."

"Surely not. You seem like a young woman on the threshold of her life."

"Thank you, but I have long since given up thoughts of marriage. Father told me I was needed here and he couldn't do without me."

Akitada noticed that her smile was gone. "Ah. Yes, I can see where a fond father would dote on his daughter, but now you may surely hope for a family of your own."

Her chin came up. "I shall stay on in my brother's house." She sounded quite firm about this, but Akitada saw there was no joy in it, just a hint of pride.

"He's a lucky man, then, but surely he will take a wife some day?"

"Yes, but the business of management will go on."

Akitada finally understood. "You have been helping your father with his work as *betto* for Lord Otomo?"

She nodded. "I have been taught to read and write and I'm very good with numbers." She held up her hands and wriggled her fingers. "You should see me use an abacus." She chuckled.

So Asano had been given a daughter with the gifts he had expected from his son. And he had promptly turned her into his assistant, preempting any hopes she might have had for a life of her own. She seemed well adjusted and not resentful, but Akitada doubted that she was unaware of her position as a servant in her father's, and now, her brother's house. And what about that brother?

"Have you discussed the future with Toshiyasu?"

"Yes. He thinks it's a good arrangement."

"He doesn't wish to handle the management himself?"

She gave a short laugh. "No. At least not yet. He has other interests."

"And these are?"

She stiffened. "He's still young. Young men need some freedom before they settle down."

Since she was not much older than her brother, that seemed astonishingly wise. Akitada smiled and said, "I suppose that's very true. What are those interests? Women? Drink? Gambling?"

She flushed. "Toshiyasu will soon remember his duties. Meanwhile, I'll look after business."

So he had guessed correctly. But which was it? Women, wine, or dice?

He could not press her further or she would realize that he was searching for motives for murder. So he thanked her and asked her to send in the elderly servant.

He found that she had become suspicious. "Moroe has been with us all his life. He's very upset. He practically grew up with my father. I don't want him bothered."

To allay her fears, Akitada said, "Moroe mentioned that your father received messages on the day of his death. It occurred to me that one of those might explain why he went out so late that evening."

She frowned as she thought about this, then nodded. "Very well," She bowed, and left.

The old servant came in quietly, bowed deeply, and waited.

Akitada said gently, "Good morning, Moroe. I'm sorry to trouble you again. Your young mistress didn't wish you to be upset. I understand that your loyalty to the Asano family forbids you to say bad things about any of them, but I think you want this murder cleared up. I think there is some uncertainty that weighs on your mind. Knowing the truth is always preferable to not knowing."

Moroe looked back at him. He did not speak immediately. Then tears filled his eyes. "It is difficult to know what to do. I would have died for my master and I love his children like my own."

Akitada nodded. "I knew this when I first talked to you. You worried about what was to become of your young mistress, and you quoted a wise saying about letting children find their own way. I rather thought that referred to Toshiyasu."

The old man's shoulders slumped. "I shouldn't have said that. Please forget it."

"It *is* young Toshiyasu you were thinking about, isn't it?"

Moroe wiped away some tears. He did not answer.

"His sister tells me that she has been helping their father with the work of the estate and the management of the Otomo property. Apparently her brother had little interest for this."

"She is very intelligent. Her father taught her well," Moroe said.

"He did not teach her brother?"

"He did, but . . . ."

"But Toshiyasu was not intelligent?"

Moroe twisted his hands inside his full sleeves. "He was a good boy. A charming child. There was so much for a parent to love."

"But his father had no patience?"

Moroe sighed.

"And he had a bad temper?"

"He never hurt his son," Moroe cried. "Never. He loved his children equally." He paused, then muttered, "Perhaps too much."

Akitada let the silence hang between them.

After a long moment, Moroe said, "He tried too hard with Toshiyasu. The boy fought him."

"Fought him?"

"I mean, he would do things his father warned him about."

"At his age, I assume that means women, drink, or gambling?"

Moroe nodded. "But it was just his way of proving he was a man. That he could do what men do."

Akitada nodded. "Yes. I see how a young man might want to prove to a strict father that he was too old to be lectured. They have a certain stubborn pride." He recalled his own youth and just such a lecturing father. He had run away from home and found another father in a gentler man. This had saved him from falling prey to the excesses that Toshiyasu might have engaged in. "Did his father know?"

"He suspected. He asked me questions and he asked people in town. I didn't tell him, but someone might have."

"Ah! Perhaps that was the reason for one of the upsetting events the day your master went to inspect the high paddies."

"Maybe. He may have learned something in town that made him shout at Toshiyasu."

"There isn't much happening in Hichiso. What is your guess? Women or gambling? I assume drinking would not have upset his father very much."

Moroe allowed himself a small smile. "No, sir. In Hichiso it would have been a woman. But Toshiyasu frequently travelled between here and Lord Otomo's estates. In Sunomata there are many places with both women and gambling."

"Yes, I can see how his father would be very angry indeed if his son lost a great deal of money on women of pleasure or by gambling."

"That was my thought, sir."

Akitada thanked Moroe. He had his motive. Toshiyasu was clearly resentful of his father and inherited his father's property. And they had quarreled shortly before Asano's death.

Or motives, for Maeko might also have resented her father's treatment of her enough to murder him. She was not very grief-stricken by his death, and she was tall for a woman and looked strong enough to commit the murder. The siblings could even have acted in accord.

But there might well be others. A man with Asano's temper surely made many enemies.

15

Saburo Rebels

Akitada and Genba rode into Hichiso together. Akitada had shared what he had learned about Asano's family with Genba, and Genba had reported what the servants had said. He had done so apologetically.

"I was a stranger, sir. They didn't want to talk. But I got a feeling they are all nervous about what's to happen next. I did discover that Lord Otomo has some of his own men there. I wondered about that. Why would he hire people to work Asano's fields?"

"Apparently Asano supervises some of Otomo's land also. Otomo's been buying up small farms. Besides, he probably likes having someone there to watch over Asano and his family."

"You mean he doesn't trust his *betto*?" Genba sounded surprised.

Akitada smiled. "It's different for us. We're old friends and comrades in arms. Asano comes from a family of retainers who inherit the job. As we have seen with his son, they have an occasional bad nut in the batch."

Genba grinned with pleasure. "That's very true, sir!" he said. "Thank you for your confidence."

"Did you learn anything else?"

"I think they were afraid of Asano. He must have been a hard task master. They said they didn't know why he went up to the mountain paddies but they worried that he'd find something wrong with their work. I asked if they would be punished in some way, but they wouldn't answer."

"You did very well. They probably were punished but were afraid to speak against Asano for fear that his son would find out. And knowing Toshiyasu, they have grounds to be afraid. What about Otomo? Anything about him?"

Genba shook his head. "Just that a messenger came before Asano's death."

"Ah. I thought so. That means Otomo may also be involved."

"But why would he kill his own *betto?*"

"More likely, have him killed. Men like Otomo do not dirty their hands. As to why, I don't know, but I don't like the man."

Genba chuckled. "Then he'd better watch out, sir."

They arrived at the police station and asked to see Saburo.

Shibata glowered, but he allowed the visit. Akitada did not attempt to discuss the case with him. He regretted that his letter to the governor had made trouble for Shibata, but he was also resentful of

Shibata's behavior. In any case, there was little hope that Shibata would answer questions or listen to suggestions.

As might be expected, the jail facilities in Hichiso were meager. The jail was merely a small outbuilding behind the police station, not much more than a lean-to that held only two cells. Saburo sat on straw and rose awkwardly to his feet, chains clanking.

Akitada turned to Shibata and asked, "Was there really any need for the chains, Sergeant?"

"What do you mean?" Shibata stared back coldly.

"Saburo came with you willingly. Why is he still chained?"

"Let's just say that it keeps people satisfied that justice is being done. Asano was well liked, and your man is a stranger here. Furthermore, he's a stranger who uses different names. People in Mino province don't care much for strangers. So this is for his own protection."

"Different names? What do you mean?"

"The witness who heard him threaten to kill Asano knew him by the name Genba."

Akitada's brows shot up. "Did you use Genba's name, Saburo?"

Saburo gave Genba an apologetic glance. "It seemed a good idea at the time. I was talking to some gamblers in the outcast village. That witness is a scoundrel."

"I see." Akitada wondered what Saburo had been up to. Saburo stared back, his face sullen. It was clear that he had not been forgiven for whatever offense Saburo imagined. "How are you faring here?"

"I'm still alive."

"Saburo, we are trying to do what we can. My hands are tied because I have no authority here."

Shibata pursed his lips.

Saburo looked away without commenting.

"Are they feeding you?"

A grunt from Shibata. "He gets fed."

Saburo said, "Your sister brought food." He paused, then added, "It was kind of her."

Yoshiko again! Her kindness always went to those sitting in jail for murder. That had been how she had met her husband.

Akitada told Saburo, "Genba and I have been to Asano's place and talked to a cousin and Asano's daughter, as well as to his old servant. Genba has questioned the workers. It's clear that a number of people may have had a motive to kill Asano."

Shibata growled, "You had no right, sir! As you said, you have no authority."

Unable to contain his anger, Akitada turned on Shibata. "Sergeant, if you'd do your job, I wouldn't have to do your work for you. And Saburo wouldn't be sitting in jail. You think of nothing but your own job and how to preserve it. I had a better opinion of you when we first met."

Shibata clenched his fists. "Are you done? This visit is over and you're not welcome in the future." He glared, then added, "Sir!"

Well, he had managed to make things worse again. Akitada told Saburo. "I'm sorry. Please be patient."

To his surprise, Saburo's mood had changed. He bowed and muttered, "Thank you, sir."

Outside, Genba said, "I think Saburo really liked it that you told that sergeant off, sir. From what he told me when I first came, he thought you'd changed. That you didn't really care any longer."

Akitada snapped, "Saburo's a fool then. Let's hope we can extricate him and ourselves from this mess. After that he may wish to seek service elsewhere."

Genba stopped, aghast. "You'll let him go? What about his family?"

"I'll think of something. Saburo has defied me. I cannot trust him any longer."

Genba said nothing, but Akitada felt he had disappointed him, too.

So be it.

Akitada returned to the house in a glum mood. He checked on his children, found they were well and having a great time with their cousins. He felt marginally better, but now worried again about the attack on the farmer Taro and his young daughter. In the end, he decided to ride to his farm and have a talk with his widow. Genba stayed behind to exercise his warriors by patrolling the mountain road where the attack had occurred.

The fields around the small farmhouse were being harvested. Akitada assumed the men and women were kind neighbors. He found Taro's widow in a shed next to the house. She was winnowing, beating the ears of rice against a propped up board to cause the grains to fall on the cotton cloth spread on the wooden floor. The shed was open on one side to let in light, and very clean.

She was a typical sturdy peasant woman dressed in rough blue cotton with her hair covered with a white cloth. She was still young enough to make another marriage and wore the stoic expression of so many working women. It was clear she had always worked this hard, though Akitada thought it must be even harder now that she no longer had her husband or daughter to help.

The work to produce the rice harvest that fed the nation was sacred, and Akitada watched a while without interrupting her. She knew, though, that he was there, and when she finished the last sheaf, she rose and made him a bow.

He nodded back and said, "I'm Sugawara Akitada. Kojiro's wife Yoshiko is my little sister. I heard about your loss and decided to see how you're getting along. I noticed you have some helpers."

She bowed again, more deeply this time. "You're welcome, sir. Lady Yoshiko and Master Kojiro have been very good to us." She bowed her head and dabbed at her eyes with her sleeve. "May the Buddha bless them. They are such good, kind people."

"They care about you also. Both are full of praise for you and your husband. I am very sorry for what happened. We had hoped that perhaps your daughter might be found."

She shook her head and looked away. "Poor Kuniko. She was a good and loving daughter."

This sounded as if she were dead. Akitada decided not to pursue the issue. It made him angry that these simple people would not accept a child once they thought her ruined. He asked, "Can you think of any reason why your husband was attacked? I was told he had little of value."

She looked at him and said forlornly, "He had Kuniko. Kuniko is very pretty. I should have gone instead."

"So you think they just wanted your daughter, nothing else?"

"What else did we have?"

"You have this farm."

He watched her face. She started to shake her head but stopped. "Lord Otomo wants to buy it and offered us money to go away, but Taro wouldn't sell. But that was before. And the bandits didn't know."

"Your husband refused Otomo?"

"Yes. I wish he'd accepted. After he died, Lord Otomo came back. Only this time, he offered very little, knowing that I was alone and couldn't work the land myself. I agreed to leave with the little ones, but Master Kojiro came and his people are helping me. I'll at least have the harvest. Then I'll go live with my sister."

Akitada nodded. He had suspected as much. The murder of her husband had made her willing to accept a much lower price. It did not prove anything beyond the fact that Otomo was a greedy man who saw a way to exploit the widow.

On the other hand . . .

Akitada took a gold coin from his sash and gave it to her. "You will have unexpected expenses and I expect Taro's funeral has depleted your savings. Please come to me if you need help. And don't sell the farm just yet. Such decisions are best made when your life becomes calmer."

She took the coin hesitantly, saying, "You don't have to do this, sir."

Akitada smiled. "I know. Use it well."

She bowed.

And Akitada left.

16

The Knife

In his brother-in-law's house, preparations for the O-bon festival had begun. The children were very much involved, and Akitada's sister was happily cooking. Akitada, feeling useless, wandered off to his room to write some letters. The first was to his other sister Akiko to report on his visit. He added a shorter note to her husband Toshikage who was keeping an eye on Akitada's household which was, by now, in the hands of women and boys. Tora, he knew, was on his way home, but the distance between Mutsu and the capital was great and Tora might well include a stop here or there to revisit places from his past. Akitada himself was anxious to return home, but as long as Saburo was jailed, he could not leave. He cursed fate spoiling a visit that should have been a joy.

The thought of Mutsu brought Sadako to his mind, though, truth to tell, she seemed rarely out of it these days. Strange, while she had lived in his house and he had seen her almost every day, he had never felt such a longing for her as he did now. This troubling condition started when she left. He had felt an almost physical pain as he had watched her riding off through the gate of his house.

He sat for a while thinking of her and regretting what was lost, then he took a new sheet of paper and started a letter.

"I thank you for your letter, Sadako. I, too, often think of you. I wish I had told you how glad I was to have known you. It is good that you have your family again, but their gain is my loss. I shall watch the plum tree at the New Year and hope that it will flower again. Alas, few things in life return once they have passed. You have left, and the joy went out of my life."

He read through it several times, ashamed at the maudlin tone, and nearly tore it up, then decided it was as honest as he could be. Another debate ensued on how to sign it. Just "Sugawara" was too formal and distant, but he hesitated to use his given name. They were not related and she had never used the name, not even when she tended to him after the attack. But she had seen him naked. Worse, she had seen him making love to another woman. A man and a woman who were not related could not get much closer. So in the end, he signed it "Akitada."

These memories stirred up powerful feelings again, and Akitada quickly sealed his letters and set off to put them into the hand of the man who took such things to the nearest post station before he would turn coward.

Walking back, he wished he had not sent the letter. It was embarrassingly needy. What must she think of him?

Especially when it was all so pointless. They would never meet again.

An empty eternity lay ahead.

Akitada walked sightlessly into the excitement, startled as police constables erupted from the station to gather behind Shibata, who swung himself in the saddle and set off, while they ran behind him.

They passed him, and Akitada finally woke from his depression. Something had happened. As he watched, they took the road that led to Asano's farm.

He could not very well run after them, so he walked home as quickly as possible and got on a horse.

At Asano's farm, the farm workers and servants stood about with shocked faces. Constables were among them, asking questions. Akitada dismounted and asked one of them what had happened.

He was told that someone had attacked Sadamoto. It was not clear if he was alive or dead. The constable, recognizing Akitada, was afraid to say more.

"There's lots of blood!" one of the workers offered, suggesting that things were bad.

Akitada ran up the steps to the main house. A constable inside the door barred his way.

"Let me speak to Sergeant Shibata. My name is Sugawara"

The constable looked unimpressed. "I know."

Akitada bit his lip. Shibata's attitude had infected his men. He worried about Saburo. Keeping his temper, he said firmly, "I think you should inform the sergeant."

The man hesitated, then said, "Stay here," and hurried off.

Akitada stayed obediently and Shibata returned with the constable.

"What can I do for you, sir?" he asked coldly.

"How is Sadamoto?"

"Dead."

"Oh. What a pity. He was a good man, I think."

"Anything else?"

Shibata was rude, but Akitada remained calmly persistent. "Surely the murder of Asano's nephew so shortly after his own suggests that Saburo is innocent. He was in your jail when this happened. You must release him immediately."

"It proves nothing."

Akitada counted to ten, then said quietly,. "Sergeant, believe me I will not allow one of my people to be unjustly imprisoned and prosecuted for something he has not done. With due respect to your position here, I shall make certain that you will never work again for the police if you treat innocent people in this fashion."

Shibata paled. "This may not have anything to do with Asano's death."

"May I see the body?"

Shibata nodded and led the way. The constable remained behind, looking thoughtful.

They passed along the hallway and through the empty main room . Asano's body had been taken away for burial. Behind the main room was a smaller room under the eaves. It was Asano's office and contained a large fortified money chest, assorted ledgers, an abacus, a small desk, and writing things. It also contained the body of Sadamoto.

The dead man lay on his side, his legs at an angle as if he had been trying to run when he collapsed. A small knife lay near his right hand. It was stained with blood.

Akitada was puzzled for a moment. Sadamoto was dead, his clothing bloody, but he had had a knife. A knife is a somewhat unusual item in an office. But then he saw that Sadamoto had been working on bundled documents and had probably needed the knife to cut string. It seemed he had defended himself against an attacker. Or perhaps more than one. Unfortunately, he had been less successful than they.

He asked Shibata, "Do you have a coroner?"

"We use a pharmacist, but he's good."

Akitada approached the body and bent to peer more closely. There were bloody gashes in his clothes. More gashes in the full sleeves, and the left hand had a cut across it. It must have been a ferocious attack.

He straightened. "May I move him?"

Shibata nodded. "Help yourself." He watched, pursing his lips.

Akitada took Sadamoto's shoulder and rolled him on his back. At least two gashes were in his chest and from their position Akitada guessed that either would have been fatal. But there were others: One to his shoulder and upper arm, and several to both forearms. It looked as though he had been surprised, had turned, and had recognized his danger. He had either had the small knife in his hand at the time or had managed to snatch it up.

Akitada turned back to Shibata. "I think the killer was either stronger or there were several. They had come with murder on their mind, and Sadamoto was unprepared and did not have much time to fight back. I also think the killers had larger knives."

Shibata frowned. "Why did Sadamoto have a knife?"

Akitada gestured to the bundled documents. "To cut string."

Shibata compressed his lips and said nothing.

"One assailant was probably wounded in the fight. It should help to find him."

"So you say."

Akitada sighed. "I assume you have asked about visitors? And who was in the house when this happened?"

That produced an angry look. "I know my job, but I just got here."

Akitada gave up. This was not his problem, much as he regretted Sadamoto's death. He had liked the man who had rushed here to help his uncle's orphaned children cope with the estate. He said coldly, "I'll leave you to find the murderers. The two murders must be linked. You'll release Saburo immediately. I'm eager to return to the capital."

"I can't do that. I'm not finished with the investigation."

"But my patience is." Akitada turned away and left.

Saburo returned shortly before the evening rice. He was received with joy by everyone except Akitada. When he came to make his bow and say, "Thank you, sir," Akitada told him, "Don't thank me. Sadamoto was killed while you were in jail. Apparently even Shibata could see that you couldn't have done this crime and should be released."

Saburo flinched and his mouth tightened. "What are your plans, sir?"

"We are returning to the capital as soon as *O-bon* is over. I would leave now, but I have given my word to the children."

Saburo nodded. "May I use the time to find out what happened?"

"Do as you wish, but know that I cannot help you again if you get into trouble."

Saburo said stiffly, "I'm aware of that, sir," and left.

It was altogether a bitter encounter, and Akitada was in a very bad mood for the rest of the day.

17

O-Bon

The first day of the festival had begun with family observances at the house altar where bowls of food awaited the visit of the departed family members. Kojiro's son asked how departed relatives would find their way if they had died in the capital. This raised giggles from Akitada's children who pointed out that ghosts knew where to go.

"Especially if they're hungry enough," Yoshi explained, eyeing the bowl of filled dumplings. "Have you ever seen a hungry ghost?"

His cousins shook their heads.

"We have a picture book. It has hungry ghosts in them. They look horrible, with skinny arms and legs and big ugly heads, and swollen bellies."

His cousin asked, "Why are their bellies swollen if they're hungry?"

"Because they're so hungry, they eat shit," Yoshi cried triumphantly, bursting into laughter.

"Yoshi!" Akitada warned.

The cousins squealed and gagged. Yoshiko hid a smile behind her hand.

Kojiro said, "We have marked the way with lights, and many years ago when we left the capital, we informed our honored ancestors. They'll find the way."

Akitada thought of his son Yori, who had been only six years old when the smallpox epidemic took him. And he also remembered the rainy night of the *O-bon* that same year when he found the lost child. That half-starved young boy wore only a thin ragged shirt and could not speak. He had not been a ghost, though he had made a ghostly appearance from the depth of a forest, and Akitada, lost in grief, had taken him for the ghost of his son, who had died the previous spring. The old grief was still with him, though it no longer made him yearn to hold another small boy in his arms. The lost child had done this to him, and he had nearly lost his mind when he had had to give him up.

Every *O-bon* observance brought memories back. He had also lost Yori's mother several years later, and that had again unsettled his mind. Losing what you love most deeply inflicts a wound on the human mind. It was much like a serious sword wound to the body that may put a man at death's door.

Perhaps it was best not to love too much. Akitada looked at his children as they watched and listened to the prayers Kojiro and Yoshiko performed at the house altar with the ancestor tablets. His sister included her mother and father in her devotions. They had the same father, but Yoshiko's mother had been the second wife. Akitada grieved for neither. He thought about this, and wondered if it was better to love too much or too little. Thoughts of his father and his stepmother brought nothing but ugly memories of a painful childhood and youth. Memories of Tamako and Yori, on the other hand, were mostly joyous. He was glad that Tamako had given him two more children before she had left him. His heart went out to his pretty daughter and sturdy son. They would grow up and become more distant, but he would always love them.

The small ceremony was followed by their morning rice gruel, enriched on this occasion with special herbs Yoshiko had gathered before dawn. Then they walked into town where there was a fair and where the monks were to perform an elaborate service for the dead later that day.

People had come from farms all around and there was a great bustle of people. Stands lined the street in front of the Temple of the War God, offering food, sweets, amulets, and assorted toys for children and adults. The wine shops were open, and already, this early in the day, some men were drunk, shouting and chanting and dancing the dance of *O-bon odori*.

The children hurried from stand to stand, clutching the coppers their parents had provided and comparing values. Akitada and Genba watched anxiously. They had their swords. The bandits and Akitada's contemplation of death that morning had made him edgy. He saw Shibata briefly. The sergeant was standing outside the police station, watching the crowd. His constables were here and there in the crowd to keep an eye out for trouble. It was a wise precaution but meant there would be no progress in the investigation of Sadamoto's death. Probably nothing would happen until after the next day when the ghosts returned to the other world.

The morning passed without disaster. The children bought sweets, kites, beads, and dolls, and the family returned home for their midday meal and a short rest before setting out again for the ceremony and the evening's festivities.

The monks eventually descended from their mountain and arrived in procession, carrying the old abbot in his chair on their shoulders and chanting. The service was outside the small cemetery a short way up the mountain. An altar had been built there and people arrived with gifts for the monks. They brought what they could afford, food, fruit, lengths of fabric for monks' robes, and money. The monks prayed, chanted, read from a sutra, and then passed through the cemetery in procession before returning to their mountain. Temple servants gathered the gifts and followed them.

Akitada had watched them carefully. All were clean-shaven, their scalps faintly blue. All seemed reasonably familiar with the rituals. The big blind monk was missing, but given his handicap, that was to be expected

So much for the monks being bandits. Still, the temple could have served as a hideout for the gang. Akitada had not seen Saburo since the early morning and suspected that he might be using the absence of the monks to search the temple and monastery. He felt a reluctant admiration for Saburo's single-mindedness and hoped he would find something, or at least not get caught by the returning monks. He did not want to have to deal with another arrest.

Night was falling rapidly, and people were lighting the small oil lamps at the graves. More oil lamps flickered along the road into town. A golden haze hung above the roofs of Hichiso, and when they entered town they were met with the magical sight of glowing colors. Paper lanterns in many hues hung above stores and stands.

The children shouted with delight and greeted the sound of music with more applause. *Bon odori* had begun. Already people danced around a decorated platform on which musicians played their instruments, the rhythms carried by big drums. More and more dancers joined in, forming lines that moved in a circle about the platform.

The rhythms and the movements became faster and more frantic, and the children began to hop about, asking to join. Akitada did not like the dancing. He never had. He felt such abandon led to trouble. People seemed to be out of control, moving in some sort of frenzy. He recalled vividly the *odori* years ago when he had held a happy child in his arms and laughed with him at the antics of dancers, loving the feeling of small arms around his neck again–– until the moment when a pair of cruel people tore him from his arms, claiming to be his parents. The *odori* dance would forever spell disaster and loss to him.

But Kojiro and Yoshiko laughed and let their children go, and Yoshi and Yasuko dashed after them. Akitada had started to say "no," but it was too late. So he bit his lip and stood with the others watching. He was the only one who watched the circling dancers anxiously, waiting for the moment when the children would reappear from behind the platform to pass by and disappear again. As the crowd got larger, a second line formed to move in the opposite direction. The sounds of music, laughter, shouts of encouragements mingled in a distracting manner. Worse, the second line obscured the first, and the shifting and moving colors of the dancers' clothes, the colored paper lanterns, and the flickering torchlight made the scene unreal, confusing, and frightening.

At least it frightened Akitada whose memories warned him that children were about to disappear. The next time the original line completed its circle, he no longer saw Yoshi and Yasuko and started forward in a panic. Someone, Yoshiko perhaps, caught at his sleeve, and Genba called out, but he was past caring and pushed through the dancers.

He was looking for his children, but the dancers thought he had joined them. Hands seized him and he found himself pulled forward, joining the line. He resisted at first, but then decided it was the fastest way to get to the other side of the platform. But there was no sign of the children there either. Both of his own and their cousins had disappeared.

With some difficulty he managed to free himself from the frenzy and retreated into the watching crowd. By now he could not find Genba, Yoshiko, and Kojiro either. He moved among the milling people and then walked toward the stands, scanning faces, trying to remember what any of them had worn, feeling increasingly that he had somehow been transported into another world at another time. He saw two constables dragging away a drunk. Their being on the job was not reassuring.

And then he saw a figure he recognized in a gap between people. It was that outcast woman Saburo had found. She was talking to someone hidden between the stands. When she walked away, she pulled someone along behind her. The crowd closed up again, but Akitada had caught a glimpse of a girl in a green gown with long hair tied with a white ribbon. It was Yasuko. Surely it was Yasuko. She had worn a green gown, he recalled. But where were the others? There was no sign of them.

What was she doing with the outcast woman? A sudden fear seized him.

He started to run after them, desperately fighting the throng of people, many of them drunk, some dancing to the music. He passed the stand where he had caught sight of the women, but there was no longer anyone near it. He ran on, shouting, "Yasuko," dodging strangers, stumbling over a child, past the lighted platform again and toward the other side of town.

When the crowds thinned and he saw an empty street before him, he stopped. He had lost them. Should he go on, or return to search the crowds again? He ran on.

And then he saw them in the distance, walking quickly ahead. He shouted his daughter's name again, and she stopped and turned. The woman tried to pull her along, impatient, speaking urgently, but Yasuko tore herself free and ran toward her father. The woman dove into an alley between two houses and was gone.

Yasuko cried, "Father, come quick. I've found her. Come!"

They met and Akitada flung his arms around her. "What were you doing?" he gasped, holding her close. "Oh, Yasuko, you have frightened me half to death. How could you do this?"

She struggled to free herself.

He recalled himself and dropped his arms. "And where are the others?"

She looked a little scared now. "I don't know. They went back. That woman, Father, she knows where Kuniko is. She was taking me there. She said she was ill."

"Who is Kuniko?" he asked, confused.

"The girl the bandits took away from her parents. How could you forget?"

Well, Saburo had also blamed him for ignoring the murder of the peasant and the abduction of his daughter. And suddenly he knew the danger his daughter had been in. He said, "Yasuko, that woman was working for the bandits. What you did was beyond foolish. That's it! From now on, you will not leave the house until we go home!

She paled. "I was trying to help," she whispered.

"We'll speak tomorrow." He took her arm and started back toward the festival site. "Come on. I hope the others are safe."

They were. Genba, who had been looking for Akitada, took them to the police station, where Kojiro had gone with his family to report Yasuko's disappearance. The other children were with them.

Shibata listened to Akitada's tale, looked doubtful, and said, "Miyo's never been in trouble before, but the outcast village is no place for your daughter. I'll look into it in the morning.

And so they returned home. Akitada was silent. So was Yasuko, barely answering the questions of her cousins and brother. The others soon gave up and chattered about the excitement of the day.

18

The Dragon's Lair

Saburo was a desperate man. As he sat in his room, he contemplated his offense and its outcome. He had read Akitada's expression, had understood his words, knew that he was about to be dismissed. There would be little difference between him and those men in the village of sheds and tents who took to the road at a moment's notice, who eked out a livelihood doing the filthiest, most menial jobs. He had lived like that until Akitada had taken him on when no one else trusted him. And this time, Saburo would take his family down with him. His wife and her daughter had been born slaves and could not be saved from his fate. His mother might manage to survive for a while as a servant. But she was getting old and with her temper few households would tolerate her when she lost her usefulness.

The only reason he had not been dismissed instantly was due to the fact that he was still able-bodied and therefore necessary for the return journey. And that would start in two days. He had two days to change his fate, and the only thing he could think of doing was to remove the threat to his master and his family.

It was an impossible task.

For one man.

Who was no longer young.

And in such a short time.

But he had been given two days, and he would try. There was nothing else to do, and it was what he had wanted to do from the start.

When it was time, Saburo put on the rags he had worn to the outcast village. He hoped they would hide his intentions from the sharp eyes of the monks. If he encountered one, he would become a limping beggar asking for alms.

As angry as his master was, he might not forgive him even if he succeeded. But Saburo knew he had been wrong. Jealousy will do that to a man. He was not Tora and would never become like him. He was not even Genba, slow, elderly, overweight Genba. He was a former spy who had begged for a job.

And so he walked away from the farm and took the long road to the top of the mountain, a road that began to climb and tire him. But the physical effort eased his despair. He had time. He had most of the day to get there.

The road was empty. Everyone was in Hichiso for the festival. Above in the blue sky circled birds of prey. The temple brooded on the mountain's top, dark roofs and a pagoda rising from a solid mass of forest trees like some waiting creature. The roofs resembled the wings of large birds crouching there, scanning the plain below. It was the Dragon Temple, and he was going into the dragon's lair.

Shaking off the silly fancies, Saburo rested a while, watching a pair of monkeys dashing through the trees. The sun was past its zenith. With a sigh, he got up again and continued his climb.

When he approached the top of the mountain, he left the road to take to the dense underbrush. All remained quiet and empty on the road and in the clearing before the temple. This was the first time he got a good look at the entrance. It had been night when they arrived and a storm had driven them inside. On his second visit, it was almost dark, and he had seen little as he had crept along the fence toward the side of the compound. Now he saw that only the front of the temple complex with the gate and a few buildings was on level ground. The rest of the buildings were dispersed on the mountain side and partially hidden by the impenetrable forest of cedars and pines. He realized that his earlier attempt to investigate the place had been doomed to failure. Worse, he could have tumbled into a gorge in the dark. Fortunately, the horse had found the road back and had stopped to graze.

Saburo glanced up at the sky again. It was almost time. He sat down to wait.

After a long while, he heard a bell ring. Then the gate opened, and a procession of monks emerged. They carried the abbot in a sedan chair on their way down the mountain for the ceremony at the cemetery. As soon as the line of monks had passed through, two young monks closed the gate. The procession took the road down the mountain toward Hichiso.

The mountain lay again in silence.

Saburo waited. He hoped the temple and monastery would be nearly empty, as empty as he would ever find it. But searching it would still be difficult, especially in the daytime. They had left at least two behind. And the blind monk. And the bandits might be in residence, too. This, among other secrets, he had come to discover.

He had about two hours of daylight left before dark. Enough time to explore the layout of the compound. Later, darkness would be his friend, but at that point the monks would return from the valley.

He watched and listened a few moments longer, and when all remained quiet, he ducked across the open area toward the gate.

There was a tiny gatekeeper's lodge that had been unoccupied on their previous visit. To be safe, Saburo approached it by creeping along the wooden wall and then rising up slowly to peer through the latticed opening. Empty!

The gate was barred but, as frequently was the case, one side had a smaller door cut into it. To Saburo's delight, it had a simple latch that could be released with a special key from the outside. He reached for his small bunch of bent metal hooks of different lengths, then remembered it was gone. Back to the woods to search for a small stick. Selecting a likely one, he returned and set to work. After a few moments of concentrated effort, the lock released, the door opened with a small creak, and he slipped inside.

The courtyard lay as empty and silent in the slanting sun as the outside. He pushed the door shut and locked it again.

Most temples were laid out by ancient rules, and the location and purpose of all the buildings were precisely the same wherever you were. But this was a mountain temple. There was not enough flat land to follow such rules. There were crags and valleys, precipices and gorges. Each building had to find its own small piece of level ground. Each was at a different elevation. The entrance court, modest as it was, was the most spacious. It contained only a small bell tower and reliquary. The main hall was at a higher level with steps carved from rock leading to it.

Saburo had noted little on their first visit; he had been distracted by the storm during the night and by the arrival of the police the next morning. He had not had any chance to explore. Now he looked carefully and tried to guess where everything was. Within the limitations of the terrain, the monks would have attempted to follow the pattern to some extent. He knew that his master and the children had spent a short time in the main hall or *kondo* before being moved to a storehouse.. He himself had been sent to the stables just inside the front enclosure. He began to realize that most likely only the front section of the temple was enclosed by the tall wooden fence he had peered over on his last visit. The temple and monastery buildings extended farther into the wilderness of cedars and pines. They could not be protected by walls and fences, and probably did not need them because the mountain itself was their protection.

Moving quickly along the perimeter fence, he checked first the stable. It was empty and looked no different from the last time he had seen it. Next came a storehouse. This was of interest, but it was locked, and Saburo's "key" did not open it. He turned from the service area to the *kondo.*

It was usually the largest of the halls and used for services, though here it was very modest. Saburo, reassured by the silence in the compound, made a quick dash to it, ran up the stone steps, and paused on the wooden veranda. Veranda and railings were unpainted, the wood stained dark by time and weather. He looked down into the courtyard with its bell tower, gate, and the woods and mountains beyond. The place was deserted. Where did they get worshippers? Clearly, this particular temple had been built for the monks, and perhaps the occasional traveler who passed over the mountain. The current inhabitants were no longer welcoming to strangers, though they maintained a relationship with the people in the valley.

Saburo turned. When he glanced up at the ceiling of the veranda, he was startled to see the image of a huge dragon writhing among clouds. The painting was done in black ink and must at one time have been striking. Even now, after the boards had darkened, it was impressive. Saburo was not superstitious like Tora, but he felt that the dragon's head looked down at him hungrily, with flames coming from its mouth and nostrils. Beyond the head, a scaly body twisted away in violent convolutions, and the dragon's claws seemed to reach for him. He shuddered.

The Dragon Temple.

Dragons were respected inhabitants of the universe. They controlled winds, weather, the seas, and the mountains. Saburo eyed this particular one askance. It did not look friendly.

The doors were not locked, and with another glance at the dragon, Saburo slipped inside the hall. When he closed the door, he was in total darkness. For a moment he paused to listen. He heard nothing, and so he opened one panel of the double doors again a little to orientate himself. He recalled that there had been oil lamps stored near the entrance. Yes. He saw them and went to get one. Setting it on the floor, he nearly closed the door and struck a flint. The flame caught, and he shut the door completely. It was probably not necessary, since the front part of the temple had been deserted, but he planned to be cautious until he knew where everyone was.

The hall was empty and forbidding as shadows danced with every movement he made. The columns had been carved into writhing dragon shapes that seemed to come alive as the light caught them. Saburo nearly jumped when he saw the first glaring head pop out of the darkness, tongue lolling between fierce teeth. The ceiling lay in utter darkness. Ahead was the altar with the seated Buddha figure. He got the feeling that nobody used this hall. Where did the monks worship?

No matter. If they were in league with a gang of robbers, they were hardly devout in their spiritual duties.

Saburo left the *kondo* by a back door behind the altar.

The terrain rose beyond the hall. A path wound into the forest, climbing by steps cut into the rocks. Here, too, everything was silent and deserted. The main path soon split in two. The monks' quarters must lie in one direction. The other path led toward another large roof that rose not far from the pagoda. The roofs were made of cypress bark. The whole complex seemed part of the forest and mountain. The temples Saburo knew had blue tile roofs, red columns, and heavy gilding inside and out. He decided that nobody had spent money on this temple. Most probably it had been built by local labor. It also meant that little or nothing had been spent on it in the meantime. The temples Saburo had served or spied in were big, ornate, heavily supported by the emperor and the nobles, and attended by large crowds. His training as a spy had been due to the hostilities that had sprung up between several of these large and powerful institutions. Now he stood and shook his head at the Dragon Temple. It was a mystery how it existed, a mystery that might well be explained by the fact that these monks had resorted to robbery to survive.

Well, he had to find proof. He moved forward, choosing the path that led to the lecture hall and pagoda. He thought it safer to check out the temple buildings first. The monks who stayed behind most likely returned to their quarters to amuse themselves in the absence of the abbot and the others.

He was right. Neither the small pagoda nor the *kodo,* or lecture hall, showed any signs of human activity. The pagoda was in poor repair, and when he peered into the lecture hall, he saw it had not been used recently, as evidenced by the layer of dust on the floor. Here, too, he saw images of dragons writhing among various statues of saints.

From this area, a small, steep path led uphill to an outlook. Saburo climbed it and reached a place where it was possible to see across a precipice into the valley and toward several mountain ranges. More importantly, parts of the approach roads were visible from here. Such a spot would be extremely useful to that gang of bandits.

Perhaps they had stayed here before the attack on the farmer and his daughter. There were signs of foot traffic in the dirt.

Saburo considered the possibility that they were still here. Suddenly the silence of the temple seemed ominous. He had to remind himself that he had seen or heard nothing beyond a few animal cries, and it was unlikely that anyone other than a couple of monks were here.

He turned back to find the living quarters of the monks. Here matters would become more difficult.

He moved more cautiously when he reached the place where the path had split and took the other fork. Almost instantly he was badly startled by a monkey chattering in a nearby tree.

As is turned out, the path was fairly short and he soon saw buildings again. This time they were low and modest. There were three of them, first a small one with a cypress roof and a small veranda, and beyond that two larger ones roofed with simple boards held down by large rocks. He had found the abbot's house and the monks' quarters and refectory beyond. The kitchen must be part of the refectory. He stood quite still, peering through branches and listening. Unless the two monks he had seen were making free of the abbot's quarters, they must be in one of the buildings beyond.

He decided to risk it, and walked quickly along the edge of the forest, staying behind the abbot's house and moving toward the first of the buildings. As he got closer, he heard human voices. Someone laughed. Saburo stopped, debating what to do next. It would be difficult to see into the refectory without being noticed, but he could investigate the monks' quarters, which were probably empty.

He changed direction, and as he did so, he saw it: a bit of bright color caught in a shrub. He crept closer and reached for it. It was paper and sticks of bamboo, a torn fan.

A woman's fan.

And a woman's fan did not belong in a monastery.

He smoothed it out. The colors had run in the rain, and it was broken, almost as if it had been torn apart, but he could still make out a picture of cherry blossoms: Pink blossoms on a blue ground: like looking up through a flowering tree into a deep blue sky.

Saburo sighed. He hated to see pretty things broken and spoiled. He was about to drop the fan when a thought struck him. The fate of the fan resembled that of the farmer's daughter who had been taken by the robbers. It might belong to her. The thought was not so far-fetched. This fan had been broken not long before the rain, and that was when her father had been murdered and she had been taken. He tucked the broken remnants inside his shirt and started on his search with renewed hope.

He had just crept up to the silent monks' quarters, keeping to the woods, and watching the refectory where he had heard the voices, when a heavy weight fell on his shoulders and knocked him forward. He fell hard, hitting the dirt with his wounded face.

Careless!

The weight on his back was not great, not that of a grown man. A monkey? He gathered his muscles to throw it off when the animal seized his hair, pulled up his head, and spoke.

"Gotcha!" the voice hissed into his ear. Then he felt the point of a knife at his neck.

He was both bigger and stronger than the person who clung to his back, Saburo gathered his muscles to heave him off, but he was too late. The knife was quicker and sank deep into his back.

19

A Killer is Caught

Early the morning after the *O-bon* scare, Yasuko presented herself before her father. She looked pale and properly subdued. His anger melted.

"You shouldn't have gone with that woman," he said.

She nodded and looked at the floor.

"I know you wished to help, but you must understand that people often lie."

She looked up. "She lied? But she knew Saburo. She said he was good to her and she wanted to help him. Saburo told her he was looking for Kuniko."

"Saburo is an adult. He knows how to handle himself. I doubt he would believe every word he was told by this woman." On second thought, perhaps Saburo had indeed believed her and therefore disobeyed.

Yasuko's chin came up. "I'm almost an adult. Aunt Yoshiko said so."

This was an awkward subject. Akitada said firmly, "As it is, this woman planned to take you to the bandits. You would have been as lost as Kuniko."

He saw understanding dawn in her eyes. She flushed.

"You mean those dirty men would have . . . ?" She broke off in embarrassment.

He said bleakly, "Yes."

"Oh." She seemed to crumple.

He cleared his throat, as embarrassed as his daughter.

"I'm sorry, Father. I didn't think."

"Well, be very careful. This is a dangerous place. Stay close to home and if you go out stay close to adults. I hope your cousins will also be careful."

He next checked on Saburo and was told he had not spent the night at the house and had not returned yet. Akitada did not know what to make of this. It was possible that Saburo had been angry enough to leave without a word and return to the capital. He hoped not, but the man's behavior had been very surprising lately.

It was the last day of *O-bon*, the day when the souls of the dead returned to where they had come from. Everywhere in the country, people were gathering at rivers, lakes, and the sea shore to bid farewell to their dead family members. They would be seen off with more festivities.

Akitada had decided his children could participate only in the launching of the little boats they had so industriously built. The little boats held small oil lamps that would be lit, and thus they could watch the departure of their visitors from the other world on the river. He and Genba would stay close to the children. To make doubly sure all would be safe, Akitada decided to call again on Sergeant Shibata.

He found Shibata in his office giving instructions to three of his constables. These concerned arresting drunks, pickpockets, and other thieves, and keeping their eyes open for trouble of other kinds. There was a satisfied air about the sergeant, and the constables had grins on their faces.

When the constables had departed for their duty, Shibata saw Akitada. His face fell and he frowned heavily. "What can I do for you today, sir?" he asked, not bothering to conceal his irritation with a meddling and demanding nobleman.

If Akitada had paused to consider the man's point of view, he might have excused his lack of respect because of the extraordinary pressures he had been under, but Akitada was angry.

He snapped, "What have you done about the woman who tried to abduct my daughter?"

Shibata pursed his lips. "I sent my constables to arrest her. They found her gone."

"Gone where?"

"Who knows? These outcasts are not permanent residents. They pick up and leave whenever it suits them. They're vagrants."

"So you let her go to do her mischief elsewhere?"

"Since you found your daughter, there wasn't really anything to hold her for. Even an outcast cannot be whipped for talking to a child."

"She had hold of her and was pulling her after her. She told her she was taking her to the abducted girl who was sick. My daughter was foolish enough to believe her, but that doesn't change the fact that this woman had bad designs on her. Saburo told me that this Miyo used to live with the bandits and has a child by one of them. How much more do you need to arrest her as their accomplice?"

Shibata's face closed. "I'm sorry you find my work so unsatisfactory, sir, but I have other duties. It is *O-bon* after all, and we have had a murder."

"Three murders," snapped Akitada. "And what progress have you made there?"

Now the complacent look was back. "We have arrested Sadamoto's killer. He has confessed. No doubt he'll soon also confess to killing his master."

Akitada was struck dumb for a moment. Could it have been this easy? Shibata's lip twitched.

"You mean it was one of Asano's servants who killed both? How did you find out?"

Shibata grinned. "He was celebrating. My constables brought him in with the other drunks. That's when we found he was bleeding from a knife wound."

"But that only proves he was in a fight."

Shibata stopped smiling. "Sorry to disappoint you, sir. It seemed too much of a coincidence. He also took Sadamoto's money. That's how he got so drunk. As soon as he sobers up, I'll get his confession."

Well, they had their ways of getting confessions, but Akitada had thought better of Shibata. He frowned. "Did he say why he killed his master?"

Shibata was not inclined to discuss the case. He rose and said, "Please excuse me while I try to do my duty to the best of my negligible abilities." He walked past Akitada and out of the station.

Akitada grimaced. Clearly he was not going to get either information or help from Shibata. Somewhat surprisingly, the man appeared to be better educated than one expected of a lowly police sergeant in a backwater like Hichiso.

But he had enough mysteries on hand without wondering about Shibata. Why had Asano's servant killed his master and then his master's nephew?

Strictly speaking, this was none of his business. Now that Saburo was free, his business was getting his children home safely. At the moment, they were under the watchful eyes of his sister and Genba. He had a few hours before tonight's departure of the souls. There was nothing to prevent him from asking a few questions.

He walked to Asano's place. As far as he could tell, everybody was at work as always. This grieved him. The death of Sadamoto was so recent, and he had liked the man who had rushed to the aid of his young cousins. Of Asano's family, he had been the only one who had not seemed to hide the truth from Akitada. He would have been a good influence on Asano's children.

He was greeted by the old servant who took him to Asano's daughter. She was in her father's room, bent over paperwork, clearly trying to keep things together. When she saw him, she rose and bowed. She was pale and her eyes red-rimmed.

Akitada said, "Forgive me. I hoped to speak to your brother. Is he not here?"

"Toshiyasu has gone to Lord Otomo. Can I be of assistance?"

"Perhaps. I see you are at work again. Will you be able to manage without your cousin?"

"I must. This," she waved a hand at the account books, "is work I'm very familiar with, but there are many things my father did. He thought me useful for ordinary duties, but I know nothing about legal matters or about arrangements he had with people." She paused. "Won't you please sit down? I apologize for receiving you in this place."

"Not at all." Akitada sat. "Let us both sit. I know something of the law. Perhaps I can be helpful."

She hesitated. "Thank you. Perhaps later. Things are so unsettled still."

"Yes, of course. Sergeant Shibata tells me they have arrested the man who killed your cousin."

Her eyes filled with tears. "Yes. I cannot imagine what possessed him. He must be mad."

"I wondered if he wished to help you or your brother."

She stared at him. "If he thought that, he is truly mad. Sadamoto came because he cares about us.

He is . . . was the kindest and gentlest of men." A tear spilled over and she wiped it away.

"I'm sorry. I did not mean to upset you. Forgive me."

She swallowed. "It's not your fault. It's just that I'm so worried about Toshiyasu." A few more tears fell.

"Can you tell me about it?"

She looked down, clenching her hands in her lap. "He's very young," she said softly and sniffled.

Akitada remembered what the servant Moroe had said. Toshiyasu had apparently been in trouble. He said, "Yes. Nineteen is a dangerous age. Young men feel torn by so many wishes and desires and yet so unsure of themselves. They are likely to overreact in order to prove how grown-up they are."

She looked up gratefully and nodded. "Oh, you understand. That is exactly the way Toshiyasu is. I have been praying that he would find his feet and settle down, but then our father was killed and after him Sadamoto. I'm afraid this has unsettled him completely."

Akitada sensed that he was on the track of something. He felt a little guilty to be taking advantage of this nice young woman, but it was very possible that her beloved brother was not just a confused youngster but had in fact been involved in murder. At the very least, he had some knowledge of something very ugly indeed.

He said, "You're afraid that he has made a dangerous decision? He went to visit Otomo. I thought this was on business or because he hoped to become Otomo's *betto* in his father's place."

She hung her head again. "I think he went to see Tabito. They formed a friendship and have been spending much time together. I don't think it's time well spent. Our father did not think so either."

"Who is Tabito?"

"He's Lord Otomo's eldest son. And his heir." She paused, clenching her hands for a moment. "He is five years older than Toshiyasu. Toshiyasu idolizes him."

"Ah." Akitada smiled a little at her serious face. "That also is something young men are prone to. Do I take it that Tabito has some admirable skills?"

She made a face. "Well, he's quite good at hunting, I hear. No, Tabito attended the university in the capital and that makes him wonderful in Toshiyasu's eyes."

"Ah! And that is why your brother was so anxious to go there?"

She nodded. "I wish Father had permitted it. Toshiyasu would have received an education, and those professors would have seen to it that he didn't run off to gamble, drink, and sleep with loose women." She blushed a little and looked down again. "I'm not supposed to know such things, but Father had a very loud voice when he was angry. You see, he got upset about money." She gave Akitada a sidelong glance and added, "But I think perhaps that also is something young men do."

Akitada chuckled. "It is indeed. And I think, Maeko, that you are quite mature enough to know such things."

She sighed. "Yes. I'm getting old."

"What do you mean?"

"I'm already twenty-three years old. Most girls are married before they are twenty. Nobody cares what I think."

It was clear she meant no men would care to marry her. "Nonsense," said Akitada, his thoughts going back to Sadako who was probably some fifteen years older than this girl and still a most desirable woman. And Aoi was older than Sadako and no woman had matched her sexual passion. Yet here was this attractive girl, grieving over her lost youth. "I daresay you will have many offers soon."

She smiled a little sadly. "You mean now that my father can no longer forbid my marriage?"

Appalled, he said, "Did he do that?"

She bit her lip. "I shouldn't have said that. No doubt Father had his reasons."

"I'm sorry. Was it someone you loved?"

"Someone I respected." She said this with great firmness and in a tone that forbade further questions.

Akitada nodded. "This man who is accused of killing your cousin: do you have any idea why he would do such a thing?"

She gave him a sad look. "Yes. Shigeie. I still cannot believe it. He must have thought Sadamoto meant to hurt Toshiyasu. You see, they quarreled."

"Who quarreled?"

"Sadamoto and Toshiyasu. Sadamoto had been going through the accounts and didn't like that Toshiyasu had spent so much money. Toshiyasu told him it wasn't any of his business and that entertaining Lord Otomo's heir was expensive. He was right, but our cousin wished to correct my brother. My brother is now Father's heir. Cousin Sadamoto should not have spoken to him this way."

Akitada was not sure what to make of this, but he recalled that there had also been a quarrel between Asano and his son, and Asano was dead. He said, "I see. Do you believe Shigeie guilty?"

She regarded him with a frown. "He must be. He was very upset that my cousin disrespected Toshiyasu."

"And do you believe that this Shigeie also killed your father?"

"I'm afraid he probably did. You see, that was also about Toshiyasu. My father threatened to disinherit my brother and pass his property to Sadamoto. Shigeie heard him. Father would not have done this, of course, but Shigeie may have believed him."

And of course, that would have given Toshiyasu the best possible motive to murder his father. But the story was becoming more interesting. Sadamoto stood to inherit if Asano changed his will. Akitada said, "Forgive me, but I find it difficult to think that a simple servant would go to such extremes to protect his young master."

"Oh, they grew up together. Shigeie is a year older than Toshiyasu and they were always together. When they were old enough, Father gave Shigeie to Toshiyasu as his own servant. Shigeie came to us as a slave."

"I see. I'm afraid Shigeie's loyalty will mean his death. A slave who raises his hand to a master will not receive any pity from a judge."

She nodded and hung her head again. "I wish," she said in a soft voice, "that Toshiyasu would settle down. Money isn't everything."

It was not everything, but it had led many to murder, though Shigeie's actions might have been due to loyalty. Unless . . . . Yes, thought Akitada, this is becoming very interesting.

Akitada thanked her, reminded her to call on him if she had questions about settling the estate, and departed.

20

The Kindness of Dragons

Saburo knew he had reacted too late! And with that came the knowledge that he had no time to waste. He rolled, pushing the creature on his back partially off, then threw himself on top of him. It was a risky maneuver if the knife had still been in his back, but it was not. The force of his reaction had caught his attacker by surprise and his knife hand underneath his body. Saburo seized him by his neck and squeezed.

But he had a child in his grip and released the pressure. Immediately his attacker fought back with astonishing force, gurgling and kicking, and Saburo realized that he was an adult male, though hardly full-grown. He had a dwarf in his grasp. Increasing the pressure again, he looked for the knife, but it was too dark already.

He had felt no pain, but now he became aware of warm blood running down his back. His clothes felt soaked already and a strange dull paralysis spread across his shoulders and into his right arm. He was badly wounded and there was no time to consider what to do with the dwarf who started bucking and kicking again. Saburo quickly finished the job by breaking his neck.

He felt light-headed and nauseated when he got to his feet. Looking around carefully, he found the knife and put it in his boot. Mercifully, the dwarf had been by himself. He bent to take the small man's arm and pulled him into the dense shrubbery, then he staggered away, gasping as the pain began, back toward the front of the temple. He was not quite sure how he got to the entrance. The blood loss had weakened him and made him dizzy.

He paused. Escape seemed impossible. It had been hard enough climbing this mountain when he had been well and rested. He could not manage to go back the way he had come while losing more blood all the way.

It was very nearly dark even in the open area in front of the *kondo*. He dragged himself up to the veranda and collapsed there. The wound was still bleeding. He could feel it. Gritting his teeth against the pain, he used the dwarf's knife to cut the legs off his pants and the sleeves off his jacket. The sleeves he fashioned into a thick pad. The pants legs he cut into strips. Then came the hard part. He had to place the pad under his jacket on his wound and tie it down firmly by looping the makeshift bandages across one shoulder and around his back, bringing them to the front and knotting them tightly. This was made more difficult by the fact that his right arm was little help. He had to stop twice to rest. The first time the pad slipped and fresh blood ran down his back. During his labors, the crumpled fan fell from his jacket. To keep it safe, he wrapped the bandage over it. The second time the pad stayed in place, but Saburo passed out as he tried to get up.

When he came round again, he was lying on his back, looking up at the image of the dragon. It seemed to him that the dragon no longer looked ferocious. His expression was almost kindly. Protective! They regarded each other like friends. Saburo closed his eyes again. His back hardly hurt and he could not feel fresh bleeding. He sighed gratefully and looked up at the dragon again. This time, he noticed a slight frown on the beast's face.

"What?"

The dragon seemed to shake his head.

"What's wrong?"

The frown deepened and the lips drew back over those ferocious teeth.

"You want me gone?"

Was that a nod?

"I can't."

Then he heard it. Sounds. From beyond the gate. People calling out. Coming closer. At first he rejoiced. Help was at hand. Then he remembered: the monks were back. And here he was, lying in full sight on the top step of veranda of their main hall.

Saburo got his knees. The pain came back, stabbing fiercely. And the dizziness. He knew he must not pass out again. As he looked for a place to hide, he saw the door. Heaven forbid they decided to end their observance of *O-bon* by a service in this hall.

He shuffled to the door on his knees, opened it, and crawled inside, pushing the door closed behind him.

Darkness enveloped him. He took it for a blessing, lay down, and waited. A bell rang. Apparently those outside were impatient, for it sounded twice more before there was a response. Outside sounds were muffled inside the hall, but he heard only ordinary sounding exchanges, and then even those died away.

He was safe.

And he hoped the dwarf had not been found.

He needed a few hours to rest. The blood loss had made him weak and very tired, and his survival was still in doubt. He might die here, or he might be found before he could get away. And the way down the mountain was long and hard and might kill him after all. In any case, it could not be undertaken in the dark. Saburo sighed and closed his eyes.

He fell asleep instantly, but it was a strange and troubled sleep. It seemed to him that he had fallen into a dragon's nest, resting there among the dragon's unhatched eggs. Fear assailed him that the dragon would kill him, or when the eggs hatched, the hatchlings would gang up on him. He tried to climb out of the nest and fell, plunging through immense space to be dashed below on the sharp rocks of the mountains.

He woke, covered with perspiration and gasping. Scooting upright, he hissed with the sudden pain. There had been some bleeding. He could feel it, sticky on his back, but it did not seem too bad.

The moon must have risen. It shone into the hall through openings high up under the rafters, silvery rays that lit up a column here, a writhing dragon there, and a sparkling bit of gold on the Buddha's head on the altar.

Saburo had no idea what time it was, but he knew he must not stay. He needed to be on his way down the mountain before it got light. He still did not know if he would have the strength to reach the valley, but he must try or death would be certain.

Only he was so tired.

He thought about dragons. They lived in the clouds or in the sea. The dragon king had his palace in the sea. There was a story about a man who had visited the dragon king and married his daughter. He forgot how that ended.

Why build a dragon temple on a mountain? Rain. That must be it. Dragons controlled rain. Rain was needed for crops. So a temple on a mountain top overlooking farmland with rice paddies made sense.

He closed his eyes and dozed.

Rain and monkeys on their journey.

Dragon temples and monkeys.

His eyes popped open again. Yes. That monkey Yoshi had seen in the rain storm had been the dwarf he had just killed. The dwarf had been a lookout for the robbers or the monks. And he had been the child who threw the rock and took his sword and amulet. It was proof that he had been right, but he wished he could have searched the monks' quarters better.

To keep himself from dozing off again, he crawled to the door and peered out. It was still night, but the moon had moved. The air was cool and fresh. Perhaps he had better sit outside again so he would not miss the dawn.

He leaned against the wall and looked up at the dragon again. "Thank you," he murmured, feeling foolish. But you never knew, and so Saburo eventually shifted to his knees, bowed his head, and prayed. The prayer gave him new strength, and when he checked the sky again, he saw a first lightening above the tops of the pines. It was time.

He got to his feet and shuffled down the steps by holding on to the railing all the way down. There he paused. All was still silent, but monks woke early. He started off across the courtyard, pleased to find that the stiffness left his legs, though he was still ridiculously weak.

The small door in the gate opened easily from the inside, Saburo was free and started down the road to the valley.

His strength did not last. He stumbled, then fell. It took forever to get back on his feet, and when he did, he was so dizzy that the road seemed to buckle and twist before him like a giant serpent. He fell twice more, and twice more he got to his feet. The incline made his legs move of their own will, but he had no control over them.

He was also very cold. At first he thought it was the mountain air. Then he blamed it on his bare arms and legs. The cold was a numbing kind and made him more tired than he had ever felt. Only will power carried him forward.

In the end, it was too much. Saburo fell, rolled a few feet, and lay still.

21

Akitada Changes his Mind

Akitada was thoughtful as he returned to the house. It struck him that what Maeko had told him might contain explanations not only for the two murders, but also for the activities of the bandits. Suddenly he was not so eager to turn his back on all of it and return to the capital.

When he got back, he asked for Saburo. Saburo had not yet returned. He decided that this was not like Saburo. He had been wrong to think that Saburo would leave without a word. No, it was more likely that Saburo had gone again to the Dragon Temple to prove his point, and something had happened to him there. It was a frightening thought. Saburo had been right, and Akitada had been wrong not to listen to him.

He sent for Genba and then paced as his brother-in-law and his sister watched him nervously.

"He'll be back," his sister said. She had said so before..

"He may have gone back to the capital. You were rather rough with him," Kojiro offered.

Akitada paused pacing. "I thought so at first, but Saburo would not have done that. No, he was upset and wanted to prove himself. I told him he had two days."

They did not know what to say.

"Well," Akitada said, having made up his mind, "I must find him. Thank heaven, Genba is here with the men. Will you look after my children?"

Yoshiko cried, "Of course. How can you ask?"

Her husband gave Akitada a look. "You think there's trouble, don't you?"

"Yes. And I'm very worried about Saburo."

"Saburo struck me as an experienced and careful man," Kojiro said.

"He is. Normally. But I think he expected me to dismiss him for disobedience. It may have made him desperate. If something happened to him, it will be my fault."

Kojiro frowned. "That makes no sense. Whatever he's done was surely by his own volition."

Akitada's sister said softly, "Akitada has always been quick to take the blame for disasters."

Akitada said, "Nonsense."

Before he could argue the point further, Genba came in. He was dressed for the saddle and looked anxious."

Akitada said, "Good! You're ready to go. What about your men?"

"Ready also, but sir, we were on our way to look for Saburo. He hasn't returned and something must be wrong."

"Yes, Genba. Thank you. You were quicker than I was. I'll be ready in a moment and join you. We're going up to that temple."

The sun was already high as they rode up the mountain road. They were all heavily armed. When the road had become rougher and the incline steeper, their attention was on handling their horses, and they almost missed him.

Genba called out, "Sir? There's blood on the road." He reined in and dismounted. Akitada came to join him. He saw only a small patch and said, "It's probably from some rabbit, killed by a fox or falcon."

But then one of the men cried out, "There's a body in that bush."

And so they found Saburo. Not dead, but only barely alive.

The transport down the mountain was difficult. Akitada had briefly checked Saburo's makeshift bandage and decided to leave it in place until they were home. Genba and his men constructed a stretcher. Two of the men carried him, taking turns with the others. And so they arrived slowly but safely at Kojiro's place.

Kojiro and Yoshiko, having been alerted to their coming, waited in the courtyard.

"Is he alive?" Kojiro shouted.

"Yes."

"Oh, thank the gods!" Yoshiko came running. "He's hurt? What happened?"

"Someone stabbed him in the back."

"Oh, no! Is it bad?" She put a hand on Saburo's forehead. "He feels cold. As cold as death."

Akitada swung down from his saddle and came over, peering anxiously at Saburo, feeling his face, and heaving a sigh of relief. "He's breathing. He must have lost a lot of blood. His clothes are soaked in it."

Yoshiko waved her hands. "Into the house. Hurry. We must send for Kanchu."

Akitada frowned. "Kanchu?"

"Yes. The Dragon Temple's medical monk. He's quite good."

"No!"

She looked at him.

"Someone at the temple did this to him. They cannot be trusted."

"Oh." She looked shocked.

"You and I and Genba must manage."

"They placed Saburo on the raised section of the main room and removed his blood-soaked shirt and the bandage. The crumpled paper fan fell out.

"What's that?" Genba picked it up and showed it to Akitada.

"A fan. A cheap one. The kind they sell at local markets."

"But why put it in the bandage?"

"He thought it was important and didn't want to lose it. Help me turn him on his side."

Saburo's upper back, near the right shoulder was crusted with dried blood. Yoshiko washed it gently, and Akitada and Genba inspected the wound.

"A knife," said Genba. "Struck from above, I think. Only a giant could have delivered such a blow while Saburo was standing. Didn't you say there's a giant at the monastery?"

"Yes. They claimed he was blind, but he could have pretended. But Saburo may not have been standing."

"True," said Genba, scratching his head, "Though a blind man could do this if Saburo stood before him not suspecting anything."

Akitada thought about it. "Yes, I suppose so."

Yukiko interrupted, "You can discuss this later. He must be bandaged and made comfortable."

"Yes, of course." Akitada moved aside to give his sister and her maid room to work.

Saburo did wake up briefly during these ministrations. He stared at them blankly, ignored their questions, and passed out again.

"What do you want to do?" Genba asked later, as they stood again on the veranda. The hired men still waited below with their horses.

"Dismiss them. They can eat their midday rice and rest. I'd like to know what happened. Perhaps Saburo will wake again." He sighed. "He's lost a lot of blood."

Genba looked grave. "He may not wake."

Akitada moved abruptly. "Don't remind me of my guilt. I'm fully aware of it."

"I wasn't. I didn't mean . . ." Genba broke off in confusion.

"Let me see that broken fan."

Genba took the remnant from his sleeve. "It wasn't your fault, sir. Saburo must've slipped up somehow."

"He went alone into extreme danger because I was angry with him. I don't want to talk about it." Akitada straightened out the bits of crumpled paper and the broken spines. The picture had been rough and the colors had mostly run, but he did not think the fan was old or that it had been discarded because it was broken. "I wonder where he found this."

"I've wondered, too. He hid it so carefully. A little piece of trash like that. It will never be new again or of any use."

"Yes. Curious. I think he must have found it in the temple grounds."

"Never heard of monks or bandits using a fan like that. It looks like something a child would buy at a fair."

Akitada brightened. "You've hit it!" He slapped Genba's shoulder. "You've found the answer. Genba, that was excellent."

Genba looked confused. His jaw sagged a little. "Thank you, sir," he muttered, then stared at the fan with such concentration that Akitada handed it back.

"Sorry. You weren't here then. You recall my telling you how a farmer was murdered on the road and his daughter abducted?"

Genba nodded. He still looked doubtful. “You think this was hers?”

“It must be. The farmer and the girl were returning from a market on the other side of the mountain when they were attacked. I bet the father bought this for her.”

“That means she was with the monks.”

“Yes. I don’t know precisely where Saburo found the fan, but the fact that he hid it so carefully means he thought it proved that the monks were in league with the bandits. That was what he set out to prove.”

“What will you do, sir? There’s not much time. Tomorrow we planned to go home.”

“Yes, but that’s now impossible anyway. I shall not leave Saburo like this.”

Genba returned the fan, looking relieved. He even tried a smile. “He’ll mend fast, sir. Saburo’s been through worse.”

“Perhaps. But while he’s recovering, you and I must finish what he’s started.”

22

The Fan

Akitada went first to see Sergeant Shibata. He hated dealing with the man since he had become uncooperative and rude. Worse, there was a chance that Shibata could not be trusted, that he had known or suspected all along what was happening and that he had decided to turn a blind eye. Akitada did not think he would have gone so far as to be part of the plot, but being left here without resources or support from the governor had probably taught him not to get involved.

Well, he was involved and would have to be reminded of his duty.

Shibata was in his office. Akitada reported the attack on Saburo.

Shibata bit his lip. "He probably ran into the bandits. I had a notion they hadn't left. How is he?"

"Unconscious. He lost a lot of blood. When he regains consciousness, I'll know more."

To Akitada's surprise, Shibata looked uneasy. To his even greater surprise, he bowed his head and said, "I'm sorry, sir. I feel responsible. What can I do to help?"

Akitada was instantly suspicious. "Nothing at the moment. Did something happen?"

Shibata flushed. "I beg your pardon?"

"Your manner has changed rather abruptly. I can only assume that something has happened that made you change your mind about me. Has the governor contacted you?"

"No, sir. He never contacts me but to threaten." Shibata was bitter. "As you know, I'm on my own here with a handful of local men as my constables. It's pretty much beyond me."

Akitada was inclined to soften his attitude. "Well, that's why I wrote Lord Minamoto. I'm sorry he decided to take it as a criticism."

Shibata nodded. "I didn't dare do anything to irritate his Excellency further."

"Yes. But unfortunately that made things worse."

Shibata hung his head. "I'm afraid so."

A short silence fell. Then Akitada asked, "Well, will you tell me what happened?"

Shibata heaved a sigh and nodded. "Sadamoto's killer has escaped."

"What? When?"

Shibata actually blushed. "My men have been on double duty lately. The one who was here to watch the jail during the night fell asleep. I couldn't in fairness even have him whipped. And I can't afford to fire him."

Akitada gave Shibata credit for his humanity to the guard, but that did not explain the situation completely. "Aren't your jail cells locked?"

Shibata nodded. "Someone slipped the latch from the outside. I don't know how."

It was possible to unlock a door without a key. Akitada had learned this much from Saburo who had all sorts of tools and tricks from his years as a spy. He said, "I think this proves that there is more involved than a murder by an ignorant servant. Asano's daughter believes Shigeie killed her cousin, and perhaps her father out of loyalty to her brother."

"Do you believe that?"

"No. I didn't believe it when she told me, but she believes it. And I do think her brother is involved in some way."

"He wouldn't murder his own father."

"Perhaps not. I'm just beginning to learn some facts about young Asano. It's too soon to make judgments. What do you know about him?"

Shibata pursed his lips and thought. Finally he said, "He's only nineteen, and not very mature. I think he would be too timid to raise a hand against his father. But people say the boy is lazy and spends too much time on the other side of the mountain." Shibata paused again. When Akitada said nothing, he went on, "In Sunomata there's much that can lead a young man astray and he kept bad company." He clamped his lips together when he got that far.

"You mean Lord Otomo's son?"

Shibata's jaw fell. "How did you know?"

"I told you I talked to his sister. I also talked to Asano's servant Moroe. I got the impression that Toshiyasu has been losing a lot of money. They think he was gambling and spending it on women. Apparently Asano took a long time finding it out, but there was a quarrel between father and son on the day of the murder. And Sadamoto must have discovered the same thing when he started going through the books."

Shibata was astonished. "How did you learn the secrets of the Asano family so quickly? They didn't tell me such things."

Akitada could have pointed out that Shibata had already settled on Saburo as the killer and therefore did not look any further, but he only said, "People tend to guard family problems from their neighbors. I'm an outsider and both Maeko and Moroe think I may be able to help them."

The sergeant looked slightly dazed. "I don't understand any of this. You don't think the son committed both murders?"

"As you said, he seems too immature to take such an action, but he has his father's temper. He blusters, but that may be due to the fact that he's scared. I think there are other secrets. We must wait. But I came for another reason." He related what had happened to Saburo and showed him the remnants of the fan.

"That temple!" cried Shibata, clenching his fists. "I knew it. I knew those bandits are there. We'll go back and look again, and this time, I'll make things very uncomfortable for Abbot Shinsho."

Akitada shook his head. "Not yet. We need to know more. Tonight is the last night of *O-bon.* There will be crowds. You'll have your hands full, and I have promised my children they could go. Then you'll have to find Shigeie. He knows about the murders, but I'm not convinced he is the killer."

"His confession was somewhat garbled." Shibata looked deflated. "How could things go so awry," he muttered. "This is a peaceful valley. We had a few drunks, some thefts, and a couple of husbands beating their wives, but now all hell has broken loose and monsters and goblins walk among us. It all started with the bandits."

They sat in silence for a while, contemplating the changes that had come to the valley. Akitada asked eventually, "Do I assume that the monks behaved peacefully before?"

"Yes. Mind you, they made trouble sometimes, talking people into giving part of their harvest and their hard-earned coppers to the temple, but all monks beg, and they are poor."

"I see. Well, you have your work cut out for you. Let me see what I can learn."

Shibata was coming out of his mood of dejection. He said angrily, "This time, when I find Shigeie, I won't be gentle with him. He knows more than he told me. He was drunk at the time, so I didn't really force the issue."

Akitada nodded. He did not envy Shigeie his interrogation when he was brought back to the jail.

They parted, and Akitada returned to Kojiro's house to check on Saburo.

Yoshiko and one of the maids were with him. Saburo's eyes were closed and he was restless, muttering and tossing his head.

"He's awake?" Akitada asked.

Yoshiko looked up at him, her face worried. "No. He's been like this since you left. It's the fever. He's mumbling and talking, but he doesn't hear us and we don't understand what he says."

Akitada saw now that the maid had a basin of water and was wringing out a cloth, which Yoshiko placed on Saburo's chest. He said, "The wound is infected. We need a doctor. Someone who can drain the poison."

"There's no one but the monk, and you don't want him. But the wound looks clean. I think it's the fact that he's been lying in the forest, bleeding all those hours. It was too much for him, poor man."

Akitada felt a surprising jolt of grief, surprising, because so recently he had felt a furious anger at Saburo's defiance and the fact that he had as much as called him a coward for not pursuing the matter of the bandits. "Saburo's tough," he said.

Yoshiko said nothing.

Feeling useless, Akitada left again. This time he took a horse to Taro's farm. He found that the widow had managed to bring in the harvest with the help of neighbors and Kojiro's people. She was in the house, preparing rice dumplings, and knelt when Akitada walked in, bowing her head low.

"Please get up," he said, looking around. "I see you're busy."

"I've been so busy with the harvest that I had nothing to put in front of the altar for Taro." She paused and added, "My husband and my daughter both loved dumplings with bean paste." She looked at the dumplings and sighed deeply."

"Your daughter isn't dead," Akitada said.

"I hope," she said. "But what must have been done to her! She's so young, much too young to be used so."

"Yes. I'm very sorry. If we find her . . ." He paused, searching her face.

"Oh!" She clasped her hands. "Can you find her, sir? I pray every night and every morning to the Buddha that she will come back to me."

"You're not afraid of what people will say?"

"No! Never! She's my child. She's all I have left. She and I will go away as soon as Lord Otomo pays me for leaving. We'll go live elsewhere where nobody knows us."

Akitada nodded. He did not want Otomo to win, but he saw now that taking her child away from here was more important than holding on to their land. He pulled out the broken fan again. "My servant found this on the mountain. I wondered if it might have been your daughter's."

She took the pieces of wood and paper. "No," she said. "Kuniko didn't have a fan. She always wanted one. Silly girl." She blinked away tears. "She dreamed of being a fine lady. The girls, Tameko and Kuniko, spent a lot of time together, and Tameko had read books and talked about the lives of the good people. I told my daughter it was foolishness because she'd never have use for such things." She paused and looked at him sadly. "I shouldn't have been so hard on her. They say those men sell the girls to the trade along the highways. Maybe now she'll have things like this." With a shudder she pushed the broken fan back at Akitada.

"I'm sorry to cause you grief. There's no harm in pretty things. All girls want them. All young people dream."

She hung her head. "She was such a good girl, so loving. I'm a bad mother."

"No. You're angry at those who took your child. We must try to bring her back."

She brushed away more tears. "You will do that?"

He nodded. "I'll try. But about the fan. They were coming back from the market. Is it possible she might have bought it there?"

She stretched out a hand for the fan, spread the pieces, and studied them. "Cherry blossoms. She loved those. Her father called her *sakura no hana,* Cherry Blossom. It could be. She had no money, but he had some after selling at the market." She suddenly looked hopeful. "Where did you find it?"

"Saburo, my servant, found it on the grounds of the Dragon Temple on the mountain."

"The monks have her?"

"No. I don't think so. But she was probably there."

She sighed. "It's broken."

He knew she was not thinking about the fan. "Will you let me keep it a while longer?"

"Yes. Thank you for your kindness." And she knelt again and bowed to him.

Akitada's spirits had lifted a little during this heart-rending scene. Kuniko would be welcomed home.

If he could find her

23

The Dragon King's Palace

Akitada found Saburo still feverish and muttering. Yoshiko and her maid were taking turns with cold compresses.

Yoshiko looked tired and worried.

"Come outside for a little." Akitada said. "You are doing too much. This is my responsibility. I'll pay some women from Hichiso to come tend to him. And I recall that Shibata mentioned a pharmacist he uses sometimes to examine the dead and treat sick prisoners. Let's send for him."

They went to the main room. Yoshiko pointed to some cushions. "Sit down, Akitada. I'll get us something to drink."

He was glad to rest for a little. He needed to think what was to be done, and in what order. Nothing much could be achieved the rest of the day, for it was the last day of *O-bon,* and everybody would observe the farewell for their ancestors. He thought of Tamako and Yori and hoped they were at peace. His other sister,Akiko, had seen to their memory in his absence.

Yoshiko returned with fruit juice, cool, delicious, and welcome. "I'm worried," she said unnecessarily. "I've never seen such a fever, Akitada. He talks about dragons."

"Dragons?" Akitada was astonished. If Saburo talked in his fever, perhaps he might tell them what had happened to him. "What exactly has he been saying?"

His sister shook her head helplessly. "Oh, things like 'Is it *Watatsumi?* Who is it?' and 'what shall I do, *Watatsumi*? And then he talks to *Mizuchi*."

"The Dragon God of the Sea and the Dragon God of the River," Akitada said with a nod. "Very strange. What put dragons in his mind?"

"Surely it must be because he was at the Dragon Temple."

"Oh, of course. Why do you have a dragon temple on top of a mountain? Don't they live near the water?"

"We have a river. But mainly the entire valley is rice farming land. We need a lot of rain. The rice farmers all pay their respects to the dragon god every spring."

Akitada said dryly, "I'm sure the monks appreciate the donations."

She smiled. "They are poor. And we have had good harvests. Though we could use rain again."

This reminded Akitada of Taro's widow. "Why was Taro in such trouble when all the harvests have been good? His widow says they had to borrow seed rice from you."

Yoshiko's face fell. "Yes. And we could ill afford it. Actually Taro borrowed the money for the seed rice. His storehouse burned last winter and he lost all of his own."

Akitada frowned. "There was another fire recently. Someone lost his harvest, or part of it. Are fires common here?"

"There have been more than usual, but it happens. Lightning, or an oil lamp left unattended."

"Hmm."

"And now the murders of Asano and his nephew. So much trouble in one year."

"Yes. It's peculiar." Akitada frowned. "I don't know. I think there's some connection between all these disasters, but proving it is another matter."

Yoshiko was silent. After a moment, she got up with a sigh. "I wish you hadn't come at such a terrible time. Now you have Saburo at death's door and have to fear for Yasuko."

"Both Saburo and Yasuko took risks. We shall be safe if we're more careful."

Akitada was by no means certain of this. He dreaded this night's *O-bon* celebration. So many things could happen under cover of darkness.

They returned to Saburo's bedside and sent the maid away to get some rest. A moment later, they were startled when their patient opened his eyes and looked at them.

"Saburo!" Akitada leaned over him. "How are you? What happened to you?'

But Saburo closed his eyes again. "The dragon," he whispered hoarsely. "Did you see the dragon?"

"Who attacked you?"

"They use knives. Long knives."

"Who are *they*? Who stabbed you?"

"There was a . . . child. I killed him."

Yoshiko cried out, "A child?"

Akitada took Saburo's hand. "What child, Saburo?"

But Saburo took a long, shuddering breath, and fell silent again.

Yoshiko said, "He doesn't make any sense. It's the fever."

'I don't know. He's rambling, but there may be some sense to this. The dragon business is unlikely, but we know there were knives. He was stabbed. And killing a child doesn't seem to have anything to do with dragons or other supernatural beings."

She was horrified. "Oh, but Akitada, he wouldn't kill a child, surely?"

"It may have been an accident." Akitada scratched his head. "Yes, it's awful. I hope it isn't true."

"There are no children at the temple."

"We cannot be certain what may be at the temple. Besides this could have happened on the road."

After a moment, Yoshiko said, "We will surely hear about it if a child died."

"Yes."

They sat, looking at Saburo, wondering what he had been up to. Something terrible happened on that mountain. Saburo adored children. Suddenly, the feverish mutterings seemed more like the talk of a madman. He thought of the cruel torture Saburo had suffered all those years ago. It could well have taken any man's sanity. And whatever happened on the mountain might have brought the past back. Those monks. What if they were the ones who had tormented and scarred Saburo? It was possible. And now he might well die without ever telling what happened.

The pharmacist arrived after the midday rice. He looked at Saburo—who woke enough to start muttering about knives and dragons again—shook his head, and mixed an herbal draft he gave to Yoshiko to bring the fever down a little. He did not sound hopeful. Akitada paid him generously, and he left.

Genba looked in to ask about the patient. Akitada went into the corridor with him and told him about the fever. Genba shook his head and looked grave. "I think, my men had best go with you tonight, sir," he said. "I have given them instructions. "If you can spare me for a few hours now, I want to go into town. Maybe I can pick up some gossip."

Akitada gave his permission, and returned to Saburo's bedside.

Yoshiko had taken up her sewing. They sat companionably, talking softly about life in general and Saburo's condition in particular.

"It still seems strange, this obsession with dragons," Akitada said. "I wonder what caused it."

"It may be a childhood memory." Yoshiko smiled a little. "Remember the tale, about a man who wandered into the dragon king's palace. He fell in love with the dragon king's daughter and married her. I loved that story."

Akitada chuckled. "Yes, that brings back memories. Your sister used to recite the passage from the lotus sutra where the dragon king's daughter was so pure and brilliant that the Buddha bestowed enlightenment and Buddhahood on her. She said it proved that women could be smarter and better than men. Father told her that her performance in her studies disqualified her."

Yoshiko giggled. "Oh, and then there was the tale of the poor young man who offered his last copper to a man for a small snake the man planned to kill. The young man put the snake into a nearby lake where it swam away. That snake was also one of the dragon king's daughters and the dragon king gave the poor young man a golden rice cake that fed him and his family the rest of his life."

"The kindness of dragons," croaked a voice.

They looked at Saburo, who looked back. Yoshiko felt his forehead. "The fever isn't as bad," she said.

"How are you, Saburo?" Akitada asked, moving closer.

Saburo licked his lips. "Thirsty."

Yoshiko was up in an instant. "I'll get water. And some food, too," she cried and ran from the room.

Saburo looked after her. "Sorry, sir," he mumbled. "I'm a burden."

"Don't be silly. You've been stabbed, lost a lot of blood, and got a fever."

Saburo thought and nodded.

"You didn't really kill a child, did you?"

The wounded man frowned. "A child," he muttered. "Was there a child?"

"I don't know. You talked about killing a child. And about dragons."

Saburo smiled a little. "The dragon saved me."

Akitada felt Saburo's forehead again. It was quite warm. He thought he must still be caught in his dreams. "Don't worry," he advised. "Just rest. It will all come back to you later."

But Saburo used one of his hands to feel around his torso. "The fan," he said. "I had a fan. Where is it?" He was becoming agitated and muttered under his breath.

Akitada caught his hand. "We found the fan. I thought it might belong to Taro's daughter."

Saburo's head fell back. He breathed a sigh of relief. "Yes. I thought so."

"You found it in the Dragon Temple?"

"Near the abbot's house. Caught in a bush."

Yoshiko bustled back in. She carried a pitcher of water and a cup. The maid followed with a tray. On the tray was a bowl that filled the room with an aromatic scent of herbs.

"Water first," Yoshiko said, kneeling and filling her cup from the pitcher. She supported Saburo's head and let him drink his fill. He sank back with a sigh. "You're very kind, Lady Yoshiko," he said, giving her a look of fervent gratitude.

"Now you may have a little of the broth with rice."

"Thank you. Just the water."

Yoshiko was disappointed. "Maybe later?"

Saburo nodded. He looked exhausted.

Akitada wanted to know about the child, but when Saburo's eyes closed, he did not have the heart to wake him again.

24

Speaking of the Dead

Genba made friends easily. The most unlikely people talked to him. The reason was his size, the way he moved, and the fact that he still wore his hair close cut. He looked like a wrestler, though these days his hair was gray.

He found the town quiet after last night's wild excesses. It was the last day of the visit by the dead. Genba had his own dead to mourn, but not here and not today. He must try to take the place of the absent Tora and the wounded Saburo.

After several hours, of roaming about, his efforts of learning the secrets of this place had failed miserably and he was considering giving it up when he became aware again of the pock-marked beggar.

The scrawny fellow in the ragged shirt had followed him for a while. Genba had ignored him. Now he caught up with Genba and stared at his face.

Genba looked back. "What?"

The beggar asked, "You ever wrestle?"

Genba smiled with pleased surprise. "I did! How'd you guess?"

The thin man flushed a little. A strong odor of wine suggested that he had been celebrating. "It's the way you walk. And your size. I love wrestling. Win anything?"

"Yes. The northern circuit championship."

"You didn't!" The little man's eyes widened and his face shone. "You went to the capital?"

"I could've gone, but . . ." Genba's voice trailed off. He had lost his best friend that winter, and after that the joy had gone out of his life, and the wrestling with it. He said, "Some bad things happened and I never wrestled again."

"Aw, man!" The skinny fellow practically had tears in his eyes at such waste. "So you're from up north?"

"Not anymore."

"Where d'you live now?"

"In the capital." It occurred to Genba that investigating crimes was more difficult than he had thought. It appeared people asked him all the questions. But Tora had always said that wine loosened their tongues. He asked, "Care for a cup of wine?"

The skinny man shuffled with pleasure. "Oh, yes. It's an honor to meet a great wrestler. I've always wanted to talk to someone like you. You don't mind drinking with me?"

Genba was surprised, "No, of course not. Why should I?"

The thin man looked down, embarrassed. "I'm nobody."

This was not really the way it was supposed to go. Genba was the one who should be asking the questions. Now he was expected to talk about wrestling. But this little man was surely an outcast and very poor. Genba had a soft heart. Few people wanted to associate with outcasts. He sighed. "Look, I'd just like some company. After I answer some questions about wrestling, let's just talk. And I insist on paying."

The thin man hopped about, grinning broadly. "No, no. I'm flush today. Did a special job. You honor me."

"All right. If you insist. You can call me Genba."

The thin man almost danced with joy. "Come, Genba, I know a good place. Great wine. It'll be quiet today. Everybody's getting ready for tonight."

As they walked to the small wine shop. Genba asked, "You have no family among the dead?"

"None worth mentioning."

Genba recalled that Saburo had paid a visit to the local outcasts. He had not had much luck with them. "I'm sorry."

The thin man looked surprised. "No need. I grew up in the streets and later on the road. It was exciting." He paused, "Well it was when I was young." Then he added a little nervously, "I'm an outcast, you know."

Genba smiled. "I know. Don't let it bother you. We all walk the same road of life whatever we do. Sometimes it's hard, and sometimes it's great."

"Exactly. I could tell you stories. My name's Ikugoro, by the way."

"A pleasure, Ikugoro."

"Genba?" Ikugoro wrinkled his brow.

"What?"

"Your name sounds familiar. Like I heard it somewhere. You staying here?"

"No, just passing through."

They entered the wine shop, a dark place smelling strongly of *sake* and fried food. Genba was fond of greasy food. He sniffed the air hopefully. "Do they make fried buns here?"

The little man clapped his hands happily. "They do indeed." He called out to a sleepy looking man near the wine vat, "Two pitchers of your good stuff, Sakito. And some fried buns."

The man straightened slowly, looked them over, and asked, "Who's paying?"

"Me."

"You? Since when?"

The scrawny fellow gave Genba an embarrassed smile. He pulled a string of coppers from his shirt. Their host turned to fill two wine flasks. Ikugoro told Genba, "I'm flush at the moment, but it's been a hard year."

"You must let me pay for the food since I'm the one who asked for it."

"No, no. It's an honor, Genba. It gives me pleasure."

"Thank you. You're a generous man in addition to being a friend to wrestlers. But allow me to pay. It's a matter of honor."

The scrawny man hesitated, then put his coppers away. "If you insist."

Their host brought the wine. "The fried buns will take longer. But they'll be fresh. I make the best buns in town." He addressed this boast to Genba, whose size promised a good customer.

Genba paid him. They poured and drank. The wine was not bad. "Well," said Genba, "what would you like to know?"

They chatted about wrestling, past champions, the fact that there had been outcast wrestlers of renown, the likelihood of making some money betting on the matches, and Ikugoro's personal experiences along those lines. Genba told him about the preparations for matches, secret holds, special styles, the issue of weight versus agility, and some unusual outcomes. More wine and the fried buns arrived and talk stopped for a while.

Eventually Genba swallowed the last bite, burped, and wiped the grease off his mouth with his sleeve. "Excellent," he pronounced.

Ikugoro asked, "Another order?"

"Another round on me," Genba called out to their host.

The man returned, bearing more wine and another plate of fried buns. Genba paid, eyed the buns and groaned. "I'm getting fat. You eat."

The thin man did. It was astonishing how much food and wine could fit in that skinny belly, Genba thought enviously. His own appetite had effectively shut down his brain. He searched in vain for a way to start his questioning.

"Ah, mmm," he started. "So you've got no family to mourn?"

Ikugoro chewed. "Nobody."

"What sort of work do you do?"

"I take care of the dead," Ikugoro said between bites.

"The dead? You mean like for funerals? You prepare the bodies?" Genba shuddered. For all his tolerance of outcasts, he still retained a horror of death.

Ikugoro stopped eating. "Look, it's work. Some of us can't be choosy," he said resentfully.

"Sorry. No, I see that. I'd just never met anyone like you."

Ikugoro glared. "Bet you wish you hadn't accepted an invitation from someone like me. Or maybe that's why you paid."

"No. Look, I apologize. Tell me about your work."

The other man eyed the remaining buns, sighed, and refilled his cup. "People ought to be grateful we look after their loved ones," he grumbled. "Instead they don't want to be near us. But they pay. They pay well."

"It's useful work."

"You bet it is. And I'm good at it. Respectful. And it's interesting work. Never a dull day." He drained his cup. "You wouldn't believe what we see. And the things we know."

"Really? You mean people tell you secrets when you're in their houses?" Genba breathed a sigh of relief. This conversation could be useful after all.

"I mean we learn from the dead."

"What can you learn from the dead? They don't talk."

"You'd be surprised." Ikugoro seized another dumpling, bit into it, and added, "We've had murders in this town. Three so far this month. My friends and I got the bodies after the police had looked at them. I bet I could tell the police more than that coroner."

"Oh?"

"The first one was a farmer. Stabbed. Professional job."

"Professional?"

"In the back. Between the ribs. There was a gang of bandits working that road."

"Did you tell the police about it?"

Ikugoro snorted. "I don't talk to the police unless I have to. Besides, they figured that one out. Not that they caught the bandits."

"That's terrible. What about the others?"

"Now those were interesting. A rich man and his nephew. The first one was beaten to death and the second was also stabbed. Pretty crude work this time, I can tell you."

"So not the robbers?"

"No. The police caught the killer. Pure stupid luck. He got drunk, was arrested, and talked."

Genba shook his head. "This sounds like a dangerous town."

Ikugoro laughed. "There are dangerous towns everywhere." He hiccoughed and reached for the wine again. It was clear that he was becoming drunk. "Now my last job, that was really something. See, I'd met the dead guy before. And he was a killer himself."

Genba gaped at this. "A killer? How did you meet?"

"I worked in Sunomata last year. Sunomata's a town where you'd expect murder. The place is full of gamblers and whores. They live off the travelers who stop there." He giggled. "Not all those travelers leave again."

"Sunomata? That's just over the mountain, isn't it?"

Sunomata was on the highway at a place where travelers had to cross the Sunomata River by ferry. There was another town on the other side of the river. He had passed through it before turning off into the mountains of Mino Province. That town was called Nogami and was well known for its nightlife.

Ikugoro drank and nodded. His head sagged a little and he yawned.

Genba asked, "And he was a killer?"

"So they say. Unjo worked for the brothels. Mostly doing stunts but he was also the guy who got rid of customers who made trouble."

Genba digested this. "How did he die?"

Ikugoro grinned. "You might say he lost his head." He chuckled. "Lucky for me." He pulled out his string of coppers and some pieces of silver. "S*mall* job, *big* money. Ha, ha, ha!"

Disgusted with the drunken laughter and the guessing games, Genba started to get up. "Very interesting, but I have to be on my way."

Ikugoro waved his hand. "Sit down. I'm not done. Ask me why the job was small."

Genba just stared back.

"Come on! He was small. Small like a child."

Genba said nothing, but he sat down again.

"But he wasn't a child. He was my age. D'you get it?"

"You mean he was one of the little people?"

The outcast nodded and touched his nose. "Unjo was a dwarf. But a mean guy to tackle."

Yes, thought Genba. I should have known. Saburo lay at home with a knife wound in his back. The "child" had been a vicious dwarf. Genba, once a part of the world of entertainment—wrestling bouts attracted large audiences—had become a family man and now disapproved of squandering money on women and drink. But he remembered the life attracted villains of all sorts. Still it was best to make sure.

"What do you mean 'he lost his head'?" he asked.

"In a manner of speaking." Ikugoro mimicked a broken neck.

Saburo had defended himself against a knife-wielding killer. It was a relief that Saburo had not killed a child but a grown man, though a rather small one. "How did it happen?" Genba asked, reaching absentmindedly for the last bun.

Ikugoro cocked his head. "Now there you have me. They didn't say. They just said, 'Dig a hole and cover him up,' and then they said a couple of prayers. And then they paid me."

The monks!

"What do you think happened to him?"

"Well, he could've fallen off the mountain, what with all the gullies and gorges about, but that wasn't it."

"It wasn't?"

Ikugoro grinned. "I'm an undertaker. I strip the dead and wash them. There wasn't a mark on him, except on his neck, and that had finger marks."

Genba widened his eyes. "You don't mean it?"

"I'm sure."

"Did the police get the killer?"

Ikugoro's head had sunk on his chest. He swayed slightly. "Don't be silly. Who would call the police? Not me. We don't get along."

Genba nodded. "That explains your generous fee," he said dryly. "Time for bed, my friend."

Ikugoro chuckled. "I was lucky."

Genba gave their host a nod, and left.

25

Of Dwarves and Dragons

The recent events had subdued the children's enthusiasm. When it got dark, they gathered with their parents and set off quietly, each carrying a little boat containing a short candle. The parents had lanterns to light the way, though the road was still marked by many small lights that had guided the dead back into the world of the living. Now their short family visit was over.

Akitada had explained to his children that their mother's soul would always find them, wherever they were. The life of a government official involved being sent to faraway places when it pleased the emperor. He had already served three times as governor and expected to be doing so again.

It was a beautiful night with a quarter moon. The skies were clear, the stars sparkled, and the heavenly river was bright. On earth, lights also blinked and shimmered. People came from everywhere to gather at the river banks.

Their group walked in twos and threes. Kojiro and his wife were followed by their children, who were followed by Akitada with his two on either side. Behind them came servants, and finally the armed men Genba had brought with him. They had swords as well as bows and arrows, though the latter were not very helpful at night. Nothing had been left to chance this time.

And so they reached the river and set their small boats into the current while murmuring their farewells. The lights bobbed away, at first slowly as if reluctant, then faster and faster, eager to join the many others that floated away into the night.

Akitada had always been fond of the custom. While he held no strong convictions about the visit of the dead, he liked the way the lights departed, becoming smaller and smaller until they were finally extinguished.

He thought of Tamako and of Seimei. And he thought of young Yori. His memories of their deaths were still very painful, but, oh, what joy they had given him when they had been alive. As he saw the children's boats disappear, the old loneliness seized him again. What was there for him besides memories? How many more times would he watch the small lights go out until it would be his own turn?

There was so little time for joy. His own share had been less than what most people could expect. The children would grow up and go away, and then what? He and Tora, and Genba and Saburo would become old men together and sit in the sun while the world passed them by.

The others were beginning to turn away from the river, when someone came up behind Akitada and touched his shoulder. Instant awareness that he had forgotten the danger while wallowing in self-pity caused him to wheel around, his hand at his sword.

Genba stepped back. "Sorry, sir. Didn't mean to startle you."

Akitada caught his breath and felt foolish. "Don't apologize. You are late for the little boats, but I'm very glad to see you. Did you learn anything in town?"

Genba grinned broadly. "I did indeed! Such news, sir. You'll be very glad to hear it."

"Ah, so it isn't only Tora and Saburo who find out all the secrets."

Genba looked sheepish. "It was by accident, sir. Shall I tell you about it?"

"I'll be patient until we get home."

On Akitada's invitation, Kojiro joined him and Genba when they reached the farm Akitada's sister was busy getting the evening meal ready. The three men sat in the main room, supplied with wine, and Genba told them about the outcast Ikugoro. When he was done, Genba said, "And so I thought you'd be glad to know that Saburo hasn't killed any children."

Kojiro shook his head. "It's incredible that such people roam about. I've never seen this dwarf. And you say he was a killer?"

Genba nodded. "I think he meant to kill Saburo."

"Yes, yes. I can see that." Kojiro still shook his head. "So the monks are really behind this?"

Akitada said, "Until now I wasn't sure. But they ordered this outcast to bury the dwarf secretly and paid him for his silence. I wish we knew who gave the order."

Genba looked embarrassed. "Sorry, sir. I didn't ask." He brightened. "But the bastard's name was Unjo."

"Well, that's something. Besides, too many questions, and he would have stopped talking."

"That's true. I think he only kept talking because he was drunk. And I'd told him I was just passing through the area."

"Yes. Let's see if Saburo is well enough to tell us more."

Saburo was still feverish, but he was much more alert. Yoshiko looked in and bustled off to get the patient his nourishing gruel and then to see to their evening rice.

Akitada and Genba settled on either side of the patient while Kojiro hovered near.

Saburo managed a smile. "Sorry to be such a nuisance," he said hoarsely.

"Does it hurt to speak?" Akitada asked.

"Not really."

"We have some news and a lot of questions."

Saburo nodded.

"Genba encountered a fellow in town who is an undertaker. It seems he's handled four bodies lately, all murdered."

Saburo grimaced. "Four?"

"Yes. The fourth murder just happened recently. The undertaker was in town celebrating his good fortune."

"Good fortune?"

"Yes. He was particularly well paid to see this latest one underground."

Saburo's mouth twitched. "Ah! So they found him."

"You thought he was a child?"

"No. I thought a monkey with a knife had dropped on my back."

This made Akitada smile. "A surprise attack?"

"Should've looked up. He was a dwarf."

"Yes. And apparently also a hired killer."

"Really? How do you know?"

"Genba here talked to the fellow who buried your victim. He knew him."

Saburo's eyes went to Genba. "Do tell!

Genba blushed a little. "It was a lucky accident. The guy likes wrestlers."

Saburo's lip twitched again. "Well, you used to be, but there's quite a lot of gray in your hair now."

Genba's blush deepened. "Seems like you can tell from a man's walk. And his size."

"Fair enough. Who was he?"

"An outcast. Name of Ikugoro. Works for the monks when there's a funeral."

"Wait. I think I may know him. Shot dice with him and some others."

Genba nodded. "Badly pock-marked. I think you used my name."

Saburo looked embarrassed. "Yes, brother. Sorry. I was afraid they'd link me to the master."

Akitada cast up his eyes. "Thank the gods for small favors." But he smiled.

Saburo said, "It's all right. But how did you get this character to tell you about this?

"He was drunk. And he wanted to know about wrestling. I bought him some wine and just let him talk."

A brief silence fell. Then Saburo chuckled. "Why didn't I think of getting someone drunk? So I take it the dwarf belonged to the monks, and they didn't want Shibata to know? Remember that monkey Yoshi saw in the rain storm?""

Akitada nodded. "Yes. A look-out, no doubt. You were right all along, though just how deeply the monks are involved we still don't know. I think there's something else going on and the answer to that may be in Sunomata."

Saburo looked puzzled, and Genba explained, "Ikugoro knew the dwarf from Sunomata. They both worked in the brothels there. He had a reputation as a secret killer."

"I think," said Akitada, "we'll have to have a look at that place."

Saburo looked at him. "Because of what happened to me?"

"Because of what's been happening here. When they attacked you, it became my problem."

Saburo cleared his throat. "Thank you, sir."

At this point, Yoshiko came in with gruel for her patient. She took a look at him and cried, "You're wearing him out. Leave him alone now. He must rest."

They got up and left then, even though Saburo protested.

She knelt beside him, propped up his head, and fed him the broth. "All this talking," she scolded. "You eat all your gruel and then you sleep."

"I'm not sleepy."

"Nonsense."

When the bowl was empty, he said, "Please don't leave, Lady Yoshiko."

"No need for 'Lady'."

He looked at her with such adoration that she became uncomfortable. "What can I do for you?"

"You have done too much already. A servant could have done all this. It isn't right that my master's sister should look after me."

"Oh! What nonsense!" She looked and sounded irritated. "Believe me, I know more about nursing the sick than any of our people."

He accepted this. "I thank you. You are the goddess Kannon to me."

She shook her head. "Enough or I'll leave."

Saburo chuckled. "Very well."

A brief silence fell. Then she asked, "In your fever dreams you talked about dragons. Why was that?"

He remembered. Not the dream, but the moment on the steps to the hall. The moment when his strength had left him and it no longer mattered that he was dying. He had looked up and seen the dragon on the ceiling looking down at him. "The kindness of dragons," he said softly.

"Yes, that's what you said. What did you mean?"

"The dragon saved me from certain death."

Yoshiko frowned. "How so?"

"The monks were coming back and there I was, in full sight, when they opened the gate. On the steps of the main hall. They couldn't have missed me. They would have killed me."

"I see. You know, I have a hard time thinking of the monks in the Dragon Temple as killers."

He grimaced. "I have no trouble at all thinking of monks as killers."

She looked at him searchingly. "You were a monk once. Akitada said you were tortured. Did monks do that to you?"

"Yes. Or those who served them."

"But then they were very far from the teachings of the Buddha."

"Yes."

She thought about it and looked unhappy. "I like to believe in goodness," she said.

He smiled. "Yes, I know."

She caught the adoring look again and blushed. "But what about the dragon? What happened?"

"I thought the dragon spoke to me, warned me. I found the will to crawl a few more steps and hid inside the hall."

Yoshiko smiled and clapped her hands. "Oh, I see. I'm very glad. We think dragons are kind when they bring us rain, but I never thought of them saving human lives. It's a very good story."

"A story, yes. Except it saved my life. Who am I to question the goodness of dragons?"

She nodded. "I recall, I read a story about their kindness when I was a girl. It was also about a monk and a dragon."

"Yes." Saburo's face lit up. "I know it. About that old monk who chanted the sutra day in and day out. And a dragon would come to listen, so they became friends." Saburo frowned. "That had something to do with rain, didn't it?"

"Yes. They'd been having a terrible drought and people were starving. The emperor sent for the monk because he was so holy that a dragon was his friend and ordered him to make the dragon bring rain. And if he didn't do it, then the monk would be banished from Japan forever."

"Oh. Yes, but the dragon had to die if he did what he was asked. Do dragons die?"

"We must assume they do. But perhaps they too return for a visit during *O-bon*."

Saburo was dubious, but he nodded. "Anyway, the rain fell, the people were saved, and the monk went to bury the dragon in a nearby lake and built a temple to remember him." He yawned and closed his eyes. "It's a good story. Thank you for reminding me."

She extinguished all but one of the oil lamps, and rose quietly to see to the rest of her family.

26

Toshiyasu

Akitada was up at dawn. He considered his options. The armed men Genba had brought with him had been hired to protect them on their return journey. Now they were an expense and a drain on Kojiro's resources, since they had to be fed and housed. Genba had instructed them to lend a hand on the farm, but they were soldiers and not very useful. Akitada was tempted to dismiss them with their pay and send them home. But the attack on Saburo had changed matters. They could not leave yet. And while Akitada and Genba started asking questions, his family was unprotected. In the end, he decided that they must stay and guard his brother-in-law's farm and the family. He would find a way to make it up to Kojiro.

He next looked in on Saburo and found him still asleep. In the kitchen, he found the maid eating her morning gruel. Suddenly ravenously hungry, he asked for a bowl, ate it, then carried a pail of hot water to the bath, where he washed, shaved and retied his hair. All this time, his thoughts ran in circles among the various pieces of what he had learned recently and the events of the past weeks. Nothing connected. There were still too many facts missing.

He wondered, for example, about Shigeie's confession. It had seemed altogether too simple, and he did not believe that Shigeie had killed his master to protect Toshiyasu. But he knew about the murders, both of them. He thought also about Maeko, another enigma in her role as dutiful daughter and loving sister. He was convinced she had a secret, one that made her desperately unhappy. Whatever it was, was it connected with her father's murder? And what about Sadamoto? Was he truly just a generous man who had rushed to help his young cousins after their father's murder? He knew next to nothing about Sadamoto. And Toshiyasu had quarreled with both.

And then there was the matter of the bandits. Who were they? Did they work for themselves or someone else, some shadowy entity who directed from afar? The monks were certainly the most likely, given that the murder of the farmer and abduction of his daughter had happened on the road to the temple, and that Saburo had found a fan that might have belonged to Taro's daughter on the temple grounds.

There was also a puzzle of the dwarf. What was his role in all of this? The outcast had recognized him and linked him to crimes in Sunomata. Akitada was familiar with life around brothels. Men's need for women drove them to prostitutes, and this led to a very good business for unscrupulous men. It was a pernicious business, but one so filled with rewards as gold changed hands that their low status in society mattered little when wealth promised comforts they could not otherwise expect.

Akitada, who disliked prostitution, had experienced its lure on several occasions and knew its power to make a man weak with longing. He was able to pity the women, who invariably had little to look forward to once they passed their thirtieth year. He abhorred the abuse most of them suffered at the hands of their masters and their clients, but he did not blind himself to the fact that they could be ruthless in the pursuit of wealth and freedom from this life.

On the other hand, he felt no pity whatsoever for the men involved in this business. He thought them all criminal, even if they did not commit outright crimes. The prostitution business attracted gamblers and male entertainers, all of whom hoped to fleece the women's clients. The nightlife in brothel quarters had ruined many a family man who had merely looked for some pleasure in his life of hard work.

Considering all these disparate things, Akitada wandered into the courtyard where he found Genba at the well, splashing water on his face and head from a bucket. Like Tora, Genba had never lost the custom of washing himself outdoors, even though he had lived for years now in a nobleman's house that offered bathing facilities.

"Morning, sir," he shouted cheerfully, using his shirt to dry himself.

"Good morning, Genba. Have you eaten?"

"Not yet, sir. It can wait, if you need me."

"No, no. Go to the kitchen. The maid has some gruel ready. I'll look in on Saburo. After that we'll ride into town and have a word with Sergeant Shibata."

Saburo was awake. His face lit up when he saw Akitada. He struggled to sit up and Akitada quickly pushed him back down.

"Careful. Don't do anything to open that wound. How are you?"

"Much better, sir. Your lady sister is an angel. I am ashamed that she must help me."

"Yoshiko is a very loving person and she has a weakness for men in trouble," Akitada said with a smile. "You know how she came to marry Kojiro, I think?"

Saburo nodded. "Such kindness and generosity isn't of this world. Nobody is that unselfish."

Akitada sat down. "I'll let you in on a secret. Of my two sisters, Yoshiko is the happier. And she always got her way. Yoshiko knows what she wants and she's very strong. I should know. I was totally opposed to her marrying Kojiro."

Saburo chuckled weakly. "I wish her all the happiness in this world. What will you do today, sir?"

"There are many unanswered questions. Even though your trip to the Dragon Temple has cleared up a few things, it has also brought new questions. Genba and I will go into town. Maybe we'll ask the right questions this time."

"I wish I could help."

"You can. Tell me about the outcast village. Did you meet this Ikugoro?"

"I think he may have been one of the two guys who prepare the dead. They bragged about making good money working for the temple. Whatever good money means in an outcast village. They played for small coins. I used Genba's name. If the man was there, he may remember."

"Well, we must hope he doesn't. What about the woman Miyo. I caught her trying to abduct Yasuko."

Saburo jerked up again, grimaced and fell back. "What? I thought she was a victim. She said they mistreated her and she ran away with her child. Are you sure"

"I saw her myself. And Yasuko told me she lied about taking her to the abducted girl. Now Shibata says she's left the village."

Saburo clenched his fists. "I'll kill her."

"They're very poor. And the woman has a child. In desperation people will do terrible things."

"Not what *she* planned to do. I'm sorry, sir. It's my fault. I should have been more careful."

"I also believed her. Anyway, no harm was done."

Except to Akitada's mind.

He left Saburo and joined Genba, who was still chewing.

"Got one of the buns," he said, smacking his lips. "I wish I knew how she makes them. My wife would be pleased to know."

Privately, Akitada doubted that, but he said nothing. They rode into town and stopped at the police station. Shibata was standing outside. He came up to speak to them.

"My lord?"

"Have you caught Shigeie yet?"

"No, sir. I think he must be in the next province by now. I don't have the men to send after him. I've posted warrants for his arrest for murder here and at the border. If he takes the great eastern highway, they'll get him."

Akitada did not think this likely. "How exactly did he get out?"

Shibata grimaced. "Someone let him out. Nobody saw anything."

"What about the woman Miyo."

Shibata just shook his head.

Akitada sighed. "What do you know about Asano's son?"

"Toshiyasu? Why?"

"I like to know as much as possible about the people involved in a murder."

Shibata looked uncomfortable. "Shigeie did it."

"According to the sister, Shigeie killed Asano to help Toshiyasu."

Shibata thought about this for a moment. "Shigeie's not too bright. He might've thought he was helping."

"Ah, but what if Toshiyasu told him to do it?"

The sergeant looked shocked. "You can't think a son would kill his own father. No, Toshiyasu isn't bad. He might drink a bit much sometimes and chase the girls, but they all do that."

"So he has come to your attention in the past?"

"Yes, but his father took care of it. Asano doted on the boy. There was no more trouble after that. Asano told me his son was finally taking an interest in working for Lord Otomo. He spent most of his time at his lordship's estate in Owari Province."

"That isn't very far from Sunomata, is it?"

Shibata frowned. "Not far, no."

"I'm just trying to work out distances. Thank you for your time, Sergeant."

As Akitada and Genba left, Akitada said, "We must have a look at Sunomata. I think the answers we want are there. But let's stop at that shop over there. The women who own it dye fabrics and I want to buy another present for my sister. She's been burdened with all of us for weeks and now she has to nurse Saburo."

They dismounted and went inside. Only two of the women were there, the grandmother and the young one. Akitada introduced Genba and told them that his sister had been so pleased with her present of *shibori* cloth that he had come for more.

"My daughter's gone to the market in Sunomata," the old woman said, "but we can show you what we have."

A lengthy period of displaying fabrics ensued. They admired, discussed how the patterns were achieved, and selected what to buy. Genba decided to get a present for his wife Ohira. Akitada splurged and bought several lengths on this occasion, and eventually turned the discussion to the shocking events of the recent weeks.

"Do you know the Asanos well?" he asked the grandmother.

She made a face. "We've lived in the same place all our lives. Yes, we know them." A glance passed between grandmother and granddaughter."

Akitada noted it hopefully. "The father had a bad temper, I think."

She pursed her lips. "He had cause enough."

"The children?" Akitada guessed.

"Not Maeko," her granddaughter said quickly. "Maeko's very nice. She bought some fabrics from us."

"The son, then?"

They looked at each other again and said nothing.

"I understood from Sergeant Shibata and from the late Sadamoto that Toshiyasu was a little wild. But they all said he'd grown out of it."

"Huh!" the grandmother said and compressed her lips.

"Do you know something that suggests otherwise?"

Akitada became aware that the young girl had turned rather red. Given Toshiyasu's reputation, he took a guess. "Did he treat you disrespectfully?" he asked her?

The granddaughter jumped up and left the room. The grandmother looked after her and sighed.

Akitada said gently, "We can keep a secret. There's something going on in this valley that puts young girls at risk. Several have been abducted and haven't been seen again. People think the robbers sell them to brothels on the great highway. Is Toshiyasu involved?"

The grandmother sighed again. "He and his friends bothered my granddaughter. She'd taken our fabrics to Sunomata to sell them on the market. Toshiyasu was with two others, young men. They convinced her to come with them to look at a temple garden nearby. The foolish girl went."

"I'm sorry. Did she know the other young men?"

The old woman hesitated. "I don't think so. But she was lucky. They were drunk and she didn't like the way they talked. When she started to run, Toshiyasu tripped her. They jumped on her, but she's very strong. In our work, women get strong. She gave one a bloody nose, pushed them off, and ran. Toshiyasu was bad when he was small, and he hasn't changed."

"When was this?"

"A few weeks ago. After the trouble in town, old Asano kept his son busy going to Sunomata on business. But Toshiyasu got even worse there."

"Is that why you won't let your granddaughter go to the market any longer."

"That and the bandits. This world is no place for a young girl if she's pretty."

"Your granddaughter was lucky."

The old woman nodded. "She'll be married soon and we can stop worrying."

Akitada smiled. "Then I wish her much happiness."

They paid, and left with their purchases.

"That confirms my suspicions about Toshiyasu," Akitada said. "And it seems more likely now that he was responsible for his father's murder. No doubt Asano found out what his son had been up to in Sunomata and intended to punish him. But proving it is another matter. We need Shigeie for that."

They returned to the house where they found the coroner inspecting and rebandaging Saburo's wound. Saburo was sitting up, his face pale from the pain, but he looked more alert.

The coroner bowed. Akitada said, "Please don't let us interrupt. How is the patient?"

"Very well, my lord. I'm amazed. He heals fast. The fever's gone."

"I'm glad to hear it. Saburo, we'll probably go to Sunomata tomorrow."

Saburo nodded. "I wish I could come."

The coroner chuckled. "Not quite yet, I'm afraid." He said to Akitada, "Lord Otomo has a magnificent place outside Sunomata. You must see it, my lord. Lord Otomo is very affable. He will make you welcome."

Akitada doubted it. "I take it, he's a powerful man in Owari Province?"

"Yes, indeed. They all kneel to him. He expects it here, too, but people don't care much for him." The coroner chuckled again. "Nothing he can do about it. All he has here is a hunting lodge."

As they walked out of Saburo's room, Genba looked back over his shoulder. "Didn't you say, sir, that Lord Otomo has been trying to buy land here?"

"Yes. A very curious situation. Apparently he wishes to expand his holdings. I've met him, by the way."

"Oh? Did you like him?"

"No."

"Ah." Genba waited for more, but Akitada was not sure how Otomo was involved and did not elaborate. "I think I'll pay another visit to the Asano family after our midday rice."

27

Brother and Sister

When they arrived at the Asano farm, they found Moroe in the courtyard, talking to a tall man in a brilliant green hunting costume who carried a bow and arrows over his shoulder. When they noticed their arrival, the man turned and walked away. Akitada recognized the oddly slanted eyebrows. He had been here before.

Moroe came, bowing as always and bidding them welcome.

"I hope I see you well, Moroe," Akitada said. "I've come to speak to your master or mistress."

"Miss Maeko is inside. Master Toshiyasu, I regret, is with Lord Otomo in Owari."

They dismounted, and on a gesture from Moroe, a servant took their horses. As they walked inside, Akitada asked, "Who was that tall man you were talking to?"

"Jugoro serves Lord Otomo. He arranges his lordship's hunting trips. He brought a message."

Akitada wished to know what that message was but could not pry. He said instead, "Does Toshiyasu's presence at Lord Otomo's mean that he has been confirmed as his new *betto*?"

Moroe hesitated. "I think it may be a trial period. He's very young and has much to learn."

They stopped again at the late Asano's work room.

"I suppose," Akitada said with a smile, Miss Maeko takes care of business here in the meantime."

Moroe returned the smile. "She does indeed, sir. She's very devoted to her brother."

Maeko was bent over a fat ledger, an abacus in one hand, and a brush in the other. Their arrival flustered her. She dropped the abacus and quickly put down the brush. Rising, she bowed.

"My lord. You honor us again?"

Akitada ignored the hint of impatience and said, "Forgive the interruption. There have been some developments and I wondered if I might ask you a few more questions."

"Please be seated."

She looked curiously at Genba, and Akitada introduced him as his *betto*. "Oh," she said to Genba, waving a hand at the ledger, "you will know this business then. So much paperwork, but I enjoy it."

Genba smiled. "I can't say I like paperwork. Saburo does that at home. I look after the property."

She lost interest and turned back to Akitada. "How may I help you? Has something happened?"

"Yes. There have been two separate attacks, one on my secretary and one on my daughter. Fortunately I was in time to rescue my daughter, but my secretary was severely wounded."

She gasped and raised a hand to her mouth. "How terrible! What is happening?"

"I'm not sure. That's why I came to see you."

She paled a little. "I assure you, my lord, we know nothing about any of this. As you know, the murders in my family were committed by one of our own people."

Akitada nodded. "Yes, but Shigeie has escaped."

"Oh. Do you think he attacked your secretary and your daughter?"

"No, but Shigeie must be found. He knows more than has been given out. Your brother is away?"

She said quickly, "Toshiyasu is with Lord Otomo. He couldn't have had anything to do with all of this."

"I assume you know that Toshiyasu has been in trouble before? It seems to be common knowledge in Hichiso, and Sergeant Shibata has confirmed it."

"My brother is young and sometimes foolish, but he's good at heart." Her voice was calm enough, but her hand shook a little as she brushed back a strand of hair. "There was some small incident when he had had too much wine. Father dealt with it and it never happened again."

"You mean when he attacked a young woman in Sunomata?"

She flushed. "If you mean the dyers' girl, he was drunk. Toshiyasu is not a violent person."

Akitada did not believe this for a moment. His own brief encounter with the young man had given him a very poor opinion of him. He said, "I'm glad to hear it. Is he staying long in Sunomata?'

"He's not in Sunomata. He's staying with Lord Otomo."

"Who, I understand, resides just outside Sunomata."

"Yes, but Toshiyasu is working on the estate. He's learning the business. He has no time to go anywhere."

And that answer proved that Maeko thought he might indeed be up to other things."

"What about his friends? Young men his age usually have some male companions."

She hesitated, looking down at her interrupted work, and hid her shaking hands in her sleeves. "I know nothing about his friends," she murmured.

Akitada rose, thanked her, and they left. He was becoming very curious about the young men Toshiyasu had been with.

As they got on their horses outside, Sergeant Shibata arrived on horseback. When he saw them, he halted his horse, considered a moment, and then approached. He had exchanged his policeman's uniform for an attractive robe and a small black hat.

Shibata bowed, then dismounted and tied up his horse by the stairs.

"There you are again, Sergeant," Akitada greeted him with raised eyebrows. "And dressed very handsomely. Are you following me?"

Shibata flushed. "No, sir. I'm here to clear up a small matter concerning Shigeie. And you, sir?"

The question was impertinent. Akitada smiled. "The same. Well, good luck, Sergeant."

As they rode out through the gate, Genba observed, "He wasn't dressed for work."

"No. I wonder what his real business was."

"Do you suspect him?"

"Not really. I don't see him as the mastermind of what's been going on here. But I no longer trust him either."

"What do you make of young Toshiyasu?"

"Him I do suspect. I don't like at all what I've seen and what we've been hearing. But I don't know what he has done; only that he isn't innocent. Shibata suggested some mild offense, like drunkenness and brawling. Moroe seemed to lean more toward gambling and womanizing. The shibori makers thought attempted rape. His sister is protecting him. And so was Sadamoto. And now I think about it, Shibata does also. I wonder why."

"Surely someone in this town knows what he's been up to."

"I doubt it. I think Toshiyasu's activities moved to Sunomata after his father chastised him. But I'm thirsty after all that talking. We'll have some wine in the best wine shop there."

The best wine shop went by the colorful name "Bridge of Magpies." The reference was to the Tanabata legend of the heavenly herdsman crossing a bridge of magpies spanning the Milky Way to meet with his beloved. Perhaps whoever named the place hoped to suggest that *sake* in liberal quantities would also bring happiness.

It was spacious and clean inside, and the wine their elderly host brought was decent. He had few customers at this time. A few old-timers sat near the *sake* vat and played *go.*

Akitada paid and said, "You had an excellent *O-bon* festival here. I imagine business was good."

The old man grinned. "It was, sir. We were busy."

"Will you sit and share a cup of your excellent wine?"

"Thank you, sir. That's very generous." He shuffled back to get another cup and then joined them. As Akitada poured, he said, "You would be the gentleman from the capital, sir? Visiting family?"

"I am. You have a good eye."

"In this business it pays to know one's customers." The old man raised his cup and drank.

Akitada said, "I hear there was some trouble with the young Asano heir at one time."

Their host nodded and held out his cup. "That one! Yes, it was bad. Mind you, that friend of his was worse."

Akitada poured again. Genba said, "I suppose all young men take some time before they learn their limit."

"That's what they say," Their host looked morose. "Mind you, old Asano paid."

Akitada asked, "Who was Toshiyasu's friend?"

"I don't know. That was the only time I saw him. He had plenty of money to spend. And his clothes were silk. A visitor perhaps. Toshiyasu liked him. He laughed at everything the pretty fellow said.

"What exactly did they do that caused so much trouble?"

"Oh, they cut off a fellow's ear. There was blood all over the place and people ran."

Genba muttered something under his breath.

Akitada said, "Dear heaven! You called the constables?"

"Yes. But it was late at night. By the time they came, the two had gone."

"What happened next?"

"Shibata went to talk to Asano. Asano paid the fellow with the missing ear. He paid a lot. And he came to see me and apologized."

"Did anyone find out who Toshiyasu's friend was?"

"No, sir. And I don't think Shibata did either. I asked him."

Akitada wondered. Perhaps Shibata knew and had decided to keep the young man's identity to himself.

He thanked their host, paid, and they left.

28

The Road to Sunomata

The following morning, Akitada set out with Genba. Both wore nondescript clothing of the type that a traveling merchant might wear, but they were armed with swords. The armed men stayed behind to guard the family.

It was dawn, the weather was clear, and already people from Hichiso and the surrounding valley were on their way to the market on the other side of the mountain. They had oxen pulling carts if they could afford them, but many pulled their own heavily laden two-wheeled vehicles or carried their loads on their backs. It was a hard journey for hardworking farmers and their families. And it had become dangerous.

Akitada and Genba, mounted on fresh horses, passed them easily and received friendly greetings and bows. The unarmed poor were glad to see armed men on the same road.

They reached the mountain top before the sun had removed the slight fog rising from the dew on the ferns and mosses by the roadside. Genba rode up to the gate and pounded on it with his fist.

The gate opened and a sleepy-looking young monk blinked up at them, then opened his eyes wide. He had recognized Akitada.

"So much for religious discipline," Akitada muttered.

Genba shook his head in disgust. "My master has come to speak to your abbot," he told the monk. "Run to tell him."

The monk slammed the gate closed in their faces.

Genba, irate, was about to pound and kick it, but Akitada stopped him. "No point! He'll be back."

He did return, with reinforcement. When the gate opened again, a senior monk stood beside him.

Genba, still furious, drove his horse forward, pushing the gate wide open. It knocked the two monks to the ground. Akitada followed Genba inside and looked around. Like Saburo, he had not had time to get a good look on their last visit. There was nobody about but the two monks at the gate.

After scrambling to their feet, the young one closed the gate and the older one said angrily, "You can't do this. The Dragon Temple is a holy place."

Genba growled, "We just did. You need to learn respect for your betters."

The monk snapped, "We serve the Buddha, not ordinary men."

Genba was about to continue the argument, but Akitada interrupted, "Quiet! Take me to your abbot. Now!"

It was enough. Looking highly affronted, the senior monk turned and walked away. Akitada dismounted, telling Genba, "Stay here with the horses. I'll be back shortly."

He followed the monk past the main hall, glancing up at it as he went. Up there, on those steps, Saburo had collapsed, unable to move further. And up there above him was the painting of the dragon he believed had warned him to hide when the monks had returned from their O-bon services. Akitada had little faith in dragon warnings. It seemed to him that this particular dragon should have been watching all along over the people of the valley below.

They walked down the same path as on his first visit and ended up at the abbot's house. Ushered inside, Akitada found the room empty. He seated himself on a cushion and waited.

Abbot Shinsho bustled in, looking irritable and adjusting his stole. Clearly he normally started his day later than this. He stared at Akitada after seating himself with a grunt.

"Abbot." Akitada did not bother to bow.

Neither did the abbot. "What brings you this time?"

"Irregularities at this temple. I'm on my way to Sunomata and decided to stop by to hear your explanation."

"You must be misinformed. There are no irregularities here. I would warn you about spreading false rumors like this. We have friends in the capital, and His Majesty dislikes attacks on the Buddhist clergy."

Akitada smiled. "That will not stop me from reporting to the prime minister if my suspicions prove correct."

The abbot blinked. "What suspicions? We're a poor temple and have done nothing but serve the Buddha and look after the people of the valley."

"Sergeant Shibata suspects you of aiding the bandits who murder people and take their young girls."

"The sergeant is mad. I have so informed his Excellency, the governor. Do you know Lord Minamoto Tamenori?"

"Not personally, no."

"Well, the good sergeant is about to be replaced by a more respectful man."

This was entirely possible. Akitada wondered if the sergeant knew it. Shibata's behavior remained a puzzle. He said, "Hmm. Be that as it may, there is also the matter of an illegal burial."

The abbot's hands twitched. For a moment, his whole body seemed to tense. Then he said angrily, "Pah! Nonsense. What are you talking about?"

"You had the body of the dwarf Unjo buried secretly and without notifying the police."

"A lie. Who says so?"

Akitada smiled. "Let's just say that the dragon of this temple sees and hears all things."

The abbot calmed down. "You speak in riddles. There have been no illegal burials. One of our monks has died. He was quite old and it pleased the Buddha to accept his life of service and reward him with eternal life. As is customary, we bury our own on temple grounds."

Akitada did not believe this tale for a moment, but he had no way of proving the lie. Before he could say anything else, the abbot said, "Since you harbor such suspicions about us, allow me to show you around so that you may satisfy yourself about us and our lives."

This was a surprise. Akitada considered briefly. He had not wanted to spend much time here. His intention had been to find out how far the abbot was implicated in what had been happening. He now knew. On the other hand, he could not well refuse, and the tour might offer some other clues.

He accepted, and the abbot led him first to the monks' quarters. By now, with the sun up, these were mostly empty. The small wooden cubicles contained little beyond a woven mat and a wooden pillow, but in one they found a young boy, still asleep.

"Well, Sochi," said the abbot, chuckling, "how can you be so lazy? Up, up! The others are at their morning gruel."

The child struggled up and blinked at them. He gasped, then knelt and bowed. "Good morning, Reverence," he said. "I'm very sorry." Then he scrambled up and ran past them out the door.

The abbot smiled. "Children need a lot of sleep," he said.

Akitada would have softened his opinion of Shinsho, but he had seen both the child's beautiful face and his fine blue silk robe. Senior monks customarily chose the prettiest of their young charges as disciples for sexual rather than spiritual reasons. All his prejudices against Buddhist clergy returned.

The tour took them next to the dining hall, where some twenty monks were interrupting their meal to bow to the abbot and stare at Akitada. Akitada stared back, searching every face. He did not see the blind giant, and could make little of the blank faces he saw. They next passed to the modest kitchen and service buildings, and then visited the various halls. Nowhere was there any sign of outsiders. They ended at the main hall. Genba was still waiting in the courtyard, surprised to see Akitada with the abbot. They climbed the steps to the veranda, and Akitada looked up at Saburo's dragon. It looked very fierce, and he thought it little wonder that Saburo, lightheaded from blood loss, should have hallucinated about the dragon coming alive. He saw no blood stains, but they had surely been removed.

The hall was empty, more dragons writhing on the columns, and the altar gleaming dully in the light that came from the open doors.

"Well," asked the abbot, "are you satisfied? There is no one here but a handful of poor monks and myself."

Akitada nodded. "It seems that way," he said vaguely. "Thank you for showing me." He inclined his head and walked back to Genba and their horses.

The gatekeeper monk stood ready to throw the gate wide, and they rode out of the Dragon Temple.

As soon as they had passed through and the gate had closed behind them, Genba said, "They sent out a monk while you were busy. It looked urgent from the speed with which he departed. He may be carrying a message."

"Could you see which way he went?"

"No, sir."

"Too bad. Interesting, though." Akitada paused, then said, "You must avoid calling me 'sir'. Remember we are two ordinary merchants from the capital, enjoying a journey that combines business with pleasure."

"Oh. Sorry. But what should I call you then?"

"Let's see. How about Akiyoshi. That combines the first syllable of my name with that of my son's. Do you want a new name?"

Genba laughed. "I've always wanted to be called Kagemitsu. It has a certain ring to it."

"I agree. Akiyoshi and Kagemitsu it is."

They took the road down the other side of the mountain in good spirits. In dry weather it proved a more pleasurable ride. Farther down the mountain, the road became wider, smoother, and less steep. They made better time and soon came out of the foothills. Before them spread another valley dotted with farms. A broad river bisected it and a road crossed the river to disappear in the distance among hazy mountains.

Genba pointed. "Look! Isn't that our monk?"

The small brown figure was still jogging. He had nearly reached the highway junction. As they watched, he made the turn and disappeared among a stand of pines at the roadside.

"He's going to Sunomata," Akitada said.

"Yes. What do you suppose he's doing?"

"I wish I knew. The bandits may have a foothold in Sunomata. The dwarf certainly came from there. But there is also Lord Otomo."

"Do you think he's involved with the bandits."

"I don't know."

Genba thought about it. "Why would a nobleman with many acres of land need bandits, sir?"

"Please remember who we are, Kagemitsu."

"Oh! Sorry, Akiyoshi. Umm, this will be difficult for me. I mean, it's not very respectful."

Akitada chuckled. The sense of adventure was still with him. "Enjoy it while it lasts. Tora would."

29

Travelers

The town of Sunomata was little more than a wide place in the road, but it marked the point where the great highway crossed the Sunomata River to continue on the other side. The inhabitants had seen a business opportunity in the delays that travelers encountered when the ferry did not cross or when the river was not passable. They saw to it that guests spent as much money as possible before moving on. This included not only charging outrageous prices for food and lodging, but also a concerted effort to provide costly entertainment. Dancers and singers were available and willing to spend the night with a stranger who was far from home and in need of affection.

Genba and Akitada quickly attracted the attention of shop keepers, doormen, and maids at various establishments lining the narrow street. Sharp eyes separated travelers with money from messengers, workers, and farmers. The fact that they were on horseback made this easy, as they towered above the rest and clearly could afford to rent horses. Shouts of welcome reached their ears, hands grasped their legs, eager faces looked up at them. The wonders awaiting them inside the establishments seemed endless and irresistible.

They ignored them, looked around instead to get a feel for the town and its people, and hoped for another glimpse of the monk who had preceded them. At the crossing, where boats and horse trains ferried people to the other side, they found a post station.

At the moment, the river was low. It had not rained for a while and the rice fields upstream had drawn its water. It was possible to ride across, and people could rent horses and a guide to negotiate the tricky crossing.

Akitada was abundantly familiar with the challenges of travel in the provinces. He stopped to watch the ferrymen guiding travelers across. The sun was high and the river, though reduced in width, gleamed like a silver ribbon between the golden sand of its shores. Brown houses clustered there, and the deep green hills and mountains rose beyond, gradually fading into blue and losing themselves in the sky.

"It's a beautiful place, this land of ours," he said.

Genba eyed the crossing. "There's much traffic, going and coming."

"We're a nation of travelers. As the poet says, 'I go this way, and you that, but we shall meet again someday.'"

"That's a good poem. It's hopeful. Not like all those sad parting songs."

Akitada thought of Sadako. She would not return. They would never meet again. His heart contracted painfully. "The sun's very bright," he said. "Let's leave the horses at the post station and walk."

They took only their money, their identification papers and tokens, and their swords with them, tucking everything away under their robes or in their sashes. They looked like most traveling merchants or small landowners.

Almost immediately they came to the town's temple and a busy market. The temple was small, perhaps even smaller than the Dragon Temple, but clearly well-endowed. It boasted plenty of lacquer and some gilding. The red lacquer tablet with its gold inscription told them it was the Temple of Boundless Mercy.

Genba grumbled, "From all we've heard about this place, they need it."

Akitada turned to look at the market stalls that lined both sides of the street, offering vegetables, fruit, fresh fish, eggs, utensils, fabrics, or mementos. He said, "There are also the poor farmers and their families. They labor all week in their fields and then come over the mountains to sell what they have grown or made."

Genba's nose twitched. Here as elsewhere, food vendors called out their wares. Tempting smells rose from kettles and baskets holding noodles or fried shrimp. "Time for refreshments, do you think, my dear Akiyoshi?" he said with a grin.

Akitada chuckled. "If you like, but I thought we might postpone our main meal until later."

Genba purchased a handful of greasy shrimp wrapped in a large cabbage leaf and was munching as they walked between the stands. Housewives and cooks shopped for vegetables and fish. Travelers paused before displays of amulets or perhaps bargained for a length of fabric for a wife left behind. They had almost reached the end of the market, when Akitada paused before a woman who sold cheap knick-knacks: neat rows of sandals woven from sea grass, little painted wooden boxes on strings to carry one's medicines attached to one's belt, tiny carved and painted animals for children, and inexpensive paper fans.

The middle-aged woman knelt behind her wares and bowed deeply. In the soft sing-song tone of the country people, she called out, "Very pretty things here for the gentlemen and their little ones."

Akitada picked up a blue fan. It was painted with pink and white cherry blossoms. "Did you paint these?" he asked, gesturing to the fans.

She bowed again. "I did. Poor work only, but the colors are pretty and young women like them." She smiled at Akitada.

He said stiffly, "I have a daughter."

She chuckled. "Ah, young girls like them, too."

"By any chance, did you sell one like this about three weeks ago?"

"I don't remember, sir. I sell so many of them. Three weeks is a long time. And the cherry blossoms are a favorite."

"It would have been bought by a farmer for his young daughter."

Her face lit up. "Oh, how did you know? Taro bought one for his girl. He'd had a good day and she begged him for it. Do you know them?"

Akitada was astonished. "Yes. How do you know his name?"

"Taro's a regular. He sells his vegetables here." She wrinkled her forehead. "Though, come to think of it, I haven't seen him lately. Must be busy with the rice harvest."

"Taro was killed on his way home the day he bought your fan. By bandits."

Her eyes went wide with shock. "Oh, no!"

Akitada was pleased that he had solved the mystery of the fan and had been right about the monks, but here was the woman's dismay and the memory of the grieving wife and mother back in Hichiso. One should never forget the pain a death caused the living.

"And the little girl?" the woman asked anxiously.

"They took her."

"Oh, oh!" she wailed. Her hands covered her face as she rocked back and forth. "May the Merciful Kannon, protect her!"

Akitada glanced over at the temple. "Yes. And may the evil that resides here be driven out."

She lowered her hands and looked at him. "Here? In Sunomata?"

"The bandits bring the young girls to sell into prostitution, I'm told."

She looked from him to Genba and back again. "You think she's here? Will you find her? Oh, I grieve for her mother."

"We shall try. Do you know where we might look?"

But here their luck ran out. Being a poor married woman, she had never set foot in a brothel and knew next to nothing about such businesses. Akitada bought the fan, left a generous gift, and they walked on.

They found a small, clean eating place and sat down on benches outside. The owner came to recite his selection of food and praise his wine. They ordered.

Akitada leaned back against the wall of the house and looked across the roofs on the other side of the street. The land rose beyond, rice field by rice field, and on the crest of the hill were many big trees and large tiled roofs. "Look," he said to Genba, "I wonder who lives there."

Their host had returned, carrying wine and cups. He followed Akitada's eyes and said, "Oh, that's Lord Otomo's mansion. It's magnificent. He lives there like a king, I think."

"Does he indeed?" Akitada was impressed, and the man volunteered a number of anecdotes illustrating Otomo's wealth.

"Does he have a large household?" Genba asked.

"Many, many servants and retainers. And many warriors. You should see him when he travels to the capital. His mounted warriors and runners, his wagons for his wives and their maids, and his personal horses take up the road from his residence all the way through town and halfway to the next post station."

"You don't say," Akitada murmured. "Could you bring the food now?"

They ate quietly. The sun had set when they paid and returned to the main street of Sunomata.

30

More Dragons

Neither Akitada nor Genba had ever used brothels, though Genba had found his wife in one. They passed quickly by the Dew of Paradise, the Jasmine Bower, the Peony Garden. None looked precisely fragrant or tempting. The houses were barely clean, and the women peering out, though mostly young and colorfully dressed, seemed listless or forced in their manner. They heard some music and saw one dancer performing inside the open front room. In the capital, entertainers did not normally sell their bodies but might be persuaded. Here, things were different. At each of the establishments, Akitada looked for very young girls. He saw none. Either they were kept out of sight, or the heavy make-up these women wore disguised their ages.

"Look!" Genba stopped and pointed. Up ahead was a house whose name in large black characters read "Rain Dragon." A violently colored picture of a writhing dragon accompanied the inscription.

"Yes. That *is* interesting. It may not mean anything, but . . ."

A young boy in rags had been following them for a while. He was skinny as a rail and looked half-starved. Akitada felt for his money and found it safe in his sash. After a moment's relief, he detached a couple of coppers from the string and tossed them to the youngster. He scrabbled eagerly for them in the dirt, then stood and grinned at them. "Need help finding pretty girls?" he asked.

Akitada said disapprovingly, "Thanks, we'll find our own. But do you know anything about the Rain Dragon?"

The boy grinned more widely and sidled up to Akitada. "Yeah. What do you want to know?"

"Well. Anything. Who owns it? What goes on inside?"

The youngster's eyebrows shot up. "That'll cost."

"How much?"

"Ten coppers?"

Akitada felt his sash for his string of coins. The boy watched him. "For each question," he amended.

"Don't be greedy." Akitada passed him some coppers.

The boy clutched the coins. "My mother's sick and we got five hungry kids at home," he whined.

"Does your father work?"

"He ran away."

"Well, talk first. If I like your information, there may be a bit more."

The youngster nodded and said, "Let's walk a little."

Akitada glanced across and saw that they had attracted the attention of the man at the door. They walked on and turned a corner. The boy was gone. Genba said, "He stole your money."

But he had not. He materialized suddenly beside them and asked Akitada, "What were those questions?"

"Who owns the place?"

"The man who runs it is called Kaemon."

"Ah, but who owns it?"

The boy glanced up at the hill above Sunomata. "His lordship owns most of the town."

"Lord Otomo?"

"He's the only lordship around."

"Don't be snotty! What goes on inside?"

"A little of this. A little of that." Seeing Akitada's expression, the boy said. "They gamble. They have the best wine in town. They put on shows to entertain their guests. You know, acrobats, actors, singers, dancers. It's the best place in town and people come from far away to spend their money there."

"I see. It didn't look large enough for all of that."

"There's places in back. A big garden, small garden houses. Private, you know."

"Very well, I take your word for it." Akitada fully intended to verify all of this himself. "What about the women? Any very young girls?"

The boy eyed them both. "Girls? You want girls? How young? I have a sister. She's eleven. Very pretty."

Genba cried, "You should be ashamed! Your own sister!"

The boy was unfazed. "She's as hungry as the rest of us."

Akitada said firmly. "No, thank you. I want to know about any other young girls. I mean girls who work here."

"There might be some. They get girls sometimes."

"Really?" Akitada considered the Rain Dragon. It had looked well taken care of. "You say people go there to gamble? They must make a lot of money."

"The gods smile on them. And his lordship as well. His oldest son likes the place."

Akitada thought of Toshiyasu's gambling debts. On an impulse, he asked, "Do you happen to know anything about a dwarf who used to work in Sunomata?"

"Unjo?" The boy made a face. "Stay away from him. He's little but he's bad. He works at the Rain Dragon."

"You don't say." Akitada paid him another handful of coppers and told Genba, "Let's pay them a visit."

The man at the door was pock-marked. He watched their approach with narrowed eyes. For a moment, Akitada thought he would bar their way but he bowed and said in an incongruously high voice, "I'm Kaemon. How may we serve you?"

"Let's see what you have first."

Kaemon shook his head. "No. Our guests don't come to look. We make sure they stay."

"Can you afford to turn them away at the door?"

The man grinned, revealing missing teeth. He folded his arms across a barrel like chest. "You have money?"

Offended, Genba stepped forward. "Do we look like beggars? We're successful merchants from the capital."

The man sneered. "You'd be surprised how little some respectable people have. Gambling and women are expensive. So show me your money."

Genba wanted to argue further, but Akitada said, "Never mind, Kagemitsu." He reached into his sash and brought out a handful of gold and silver. "Is this enough?"

The man nodded, stepped aside, and they walked in.

The anteroom was surprisingly luxurious with straw matting, scroll paintings, and a large planter filled with bamboo. A handsome youngster in a pale green silk robe approached and asked for their boots and weapons.

Akitada readily relinquished his short sword and, after a brief hesitation, Genba did the same but he was clearly unhappy. Their property was placed on a shelf near the entrance, and they received tokens.

A second boy appeared. His head was shaved, making him look like a novice monk, but he, too, was wearing silk, rose-colored in his case, and had melting eyes and rouged lips. He bowed them into the next room.

There they found groups of men seated on cushions placed on the wood floor. They were engrossed in games of dice or *go* and had small piles of coins before them. More boys in colorful robes passed between them, serving wine and refreshments. From the back of the building came the sounds of zither, flute, and drum.

"What is your game, sirs?" asked their guide, smiling up at Akitada.

The boy could not be more than fourteen, and it suddenly occurred to Akitada that the Rain Dragon catered to a different type of customer than the other places, and that there was probably more going on than gambling. He said, "Later. I understand you have entertainment."

The next room was larger. Its doors stood open to a garden where colored paper lanterns hung among the shrubs and trees. Inside, men sat on the floor with seductive companions, watching as a young woman danced on a raised dais to the music of three musicians. She was nearly naked. Both the music and the dancing were surprisingly skillful. They seated themselves, and the young boy served them wine and food. The price, collected immediately, was exorbitant, but the food was good and the wine strong.

Genba cheered up. He dipped into a bowl of fried octopus, tasted, and sighed blissfully. "This is excellent," he said. "And the dancer is amazing."

Akitada was not as happy. The Rain Dragon seemed much better, even luxurious, compared to the other places, but nothing suggested they catered to a taste in very young girls. In fact . . . that dancer was a man. He decided to be patient a little longer and looked around the room.

He had intended to ask one of the handsome boy waiters if they knew Toshiyasu, but this turned out unnecessary. On the other side of the room sat two young men. They were kissing. And one of them was Toshiyasu.

The other was a little taller and older. As Akitada watched, he turned away from his companion and shouted, "Kaemon! Come here this instant!" Akitada saw that he had a haughty but handsome face with a small mustache and chin beard.

The music stopped. The dancer froze in an elegant pose. The guests stirred and looked around. And Akitada lowered his head and said to Genba, "I think we should leave."

The young man, who wore red silk, cursed and got to his feet, but the boy had already run for the manager, and Kaemon came quickly. A brief conversation ensued. Kaemon bowed, and the young man in red sat back down. After a moment, the musicians started again and the dancer danced.

Genba sat, a last bite in his hand. "What the devil was that about?"

Keeping his head down, Akitada said, "I'm not sure, but we'd better leave."

"Why?"

Akitada pulled Genba by the arm. They walked out quickly, past the gamblers, and to the entrance where they collected their boots and swords, and left. There was no sign of Kaemon.

Genba looked over his shoulder. "What happened?"

"Toshiyasu, the son of the murdered *betto,* was there with the young man in the red robe. I hope he didn't see me."

"Oh." Genba was philosophical. "I doubt it. They were kissing. No wonder his father was upset. Was the other one a *chigo*?"

"He looked too old for that. But I could be wrong. I know little about them."

The young man had been expensively dressed and he painted his lips. Toshiyasu had also worn paint like a woman. It was unlikely that Asano's son worked as a male prostitute. More likely, the pair were lovers who used the Rain Dragon for their meetings. Akitada guessed the young man in red was Otomo's son. If so, the relationship between Toshiyasu and his friend was closer than he had assumed.

"Come," he said. "We still have to look for Taro's daughter. Let's check out the brothels.

31

The Fragrance of the Plum Tree

Unlike Tora, Genba was basically awkward about buying sexual favors. The seductive ways of professional women frightened him. Sometimes it seemed a miracle that he had found a wife at all, let alone in a brothel. But Ohira had not worked there long and came from a farm deep in the countryside. Genba had chosen well. Or perhaps *she* had. Ohira had made him a good wife and given him a daughter he doted on.

Thus, when Akitada suggested visiting a brothel, Genba blushed. "Do you mean . . . you know . . . um . . . do anything?"

Akitada chuckled. "No, it would waste time, and already half the night is gone. I'm trying to find Taro's daughter. And maybe one or two of the men who killed her father."

"But you don't know what they look like."

"True enough. But if I don't look, I will certainly learn nothing."

The Sunomata brothels lacked the luxuriousness of the Rain Dragon and offered only sexual pleasures. When they enquired in the Peony Garden about very young girls, an interest that raised no eyebrows, they were told to see Aunty Orchid at the Fragrant Plum Tree.

The Fragrant Plum Tree was, if anything, shabbier than the rest and a particularly repulsive man served as its doorman. He was bald, had a scarred face, and his bulging arms and legs were decorated with tattoos. They hesitated, but a young boy of about nine ran out to them. He wore a stained red silk jacket and small red shoes. Bowing deeply, he announced in a piercing voice, "Very beautiful flowers inside. Please, you must see the beautiful flowers. Come!" He straightened, smiled, and waved them forward.

"I don't know," said Genba, looking nervous. "Don't you think we'll raise suspicions by just browsing?"

Akitada said firmly, "Not at all. We are hard to please," and started for the door.

The boy bounced ahead, shouting, "Auntie Orchid, customers. Fine customers!"

Genba muttered, "Have you forgotten that monk? He's probably announced us everywhere."

Akitada stopped and turned. "You're right. But didn't he take off before I had finished with the abbot?"

Genba thought. "Maybe."

"Then he cannot have known what we have in mind."

The little boy was back, pulling Akitada's sleeve. "Come, sir. Come. Only see the lovely flowers. Come, please!"

They followed and were received by Auntie Orchid, a bony, sharp-featured woman dressed in brown silk, with her dyed hair gathered on top of her head. She bowed several times, saying, "Welcome!" each time.

A maid came in, placed two cushions, and they sat. Auntie Orchid poured wine and offered the cups.

Akitada did not like her. Usually aunties were former prostitutes who had saved up to buy their own business. They retained some of their training in polite manners. This woman had none. She was all business. But he reminded himself that he was not in the capital, and that the women here had grown up on poor farms or lived with vagrant troupes of entertainers. He also recalled his experiences in the Yodo River pleasure towns. There were many people in this country who merely exploited the women working for them without caring about them in the least.

"May we see your youngest girls?" he asked, as he had previously.

Auntie Orchid narrowed her eyes. "How young? All of my girls are exceptional. Allow me to make the choice for you. Perhaps if you would tell me what your interest is?" She looked from Akitada to Genba, who gulped.

Akitada laid a gold coin on the floor. "I would like to speak to them first."

The woman eyed the gold coin and called the maid. "Bring refreshments and call in Amber, Lotus, Gold, Jasmine, and Pearl," she instructed.

The maid bobbed a bow and disappeared. A moment later, a second maid brought a platter of pickled plums and nuts. Auntie Orchid refilled their cups, and said, "I trust you'll find what you desire." She smirked. "All five are lovely and fresh. Two are quite adept for their age. I trained them myself. They know the ten positions and the fifteen methods of encouraging desire even if a gentleman is in his seventies or eighties. But both of you, being still young and strong, will not need such help I'm sure."

Genba cleared his throat. Akitada said nothing. They watched the young girls file into the room. They wore silk in bright colors, and their hair was loose. Their faces were heavily made up with white paint, the eyes outlined in black, and their lips were tinted red. They were all quite young, but two were still mere children.

Auntie Orchid called on Lotus first. She was the tallest and performed a brief dance, waving her long green sleeves about. Amber, a thin, fragile-looking girl, sang a song about lost love. Gold recited a poem, rather badly, but she made up for it with suggestive gestures and melting looks. The last two were both smaller and younger than these. They looked terrified.

Auntie Orchid introduced them, saying, "I'm afraid these two have no talent, but they are very fresh. Some gentlemen like to teach a young girl about the joys to be found in the privacy of the bedroom. I need not point out that such innocence is more expensive."

She did not offer them as virgins, however. Akitada bit his lip. Someone else had already paid for that. Taking the cheap fan from his sleeve, Akitada fanned himself as he pretended to study all five thoughtfully. He was almost sure that one of the two youngest girls was Taro's daughter. Her eyes had fixed on the fan with a look of recognition. He exchanged a glance and a nod with Genba, who turned red and started sweating, then said to the auntie, "Charming, those two little ones. Yes, you may have something there. If my friend agrees, we'll enjoy the company of these two. Together."

Genba gasped audibly, but Auntie Orchid giggled and put a hand on his arm. "Oh, you will not be disappointed. Just be patient. They're very willing." Then she took the gold piece and said to Akitada, "Two girls, for two gentlemen?"

Akitada bit his lip and pulled out another gold piece. She nodded.

They were shown into a backroom, small, poorly furnished, and with thin walls. The sounds from next door left little to the imagination.

The two young girls stood, white-faced and trembling.

A coarse-faced maid, unperturbed by their fate, spread two grass mats and laid some fairly dirty quilts on top. After placing four wooden head rests, she grinned, bowed and departed.

Akitada shook his head and sighed. Looking at the girls, he said, "Please don't be frightened."

It was useless. They drew closer together.

Genba said, "Sir, I don't like this a bit. It isn't right. We are frightening them. This is despicable. Let's go."

Akitada gave him a sharp look. "Hush! How soon we forget, Kagemitsu. We were agreed."

"Oh. Sorry, Akiyoshi. But they're so little."

Akitada ignored this. He sat down and said to the girls, "Please, sit. We're not going to hurt you." After a moment, Genba sat also.

The girls glanced at the bedding, then knelt on the floor.

"What are your names?"

The taller one said, "I'm called Jasmine. She is Pearl."

"How long have you been here?"

"I came thirty-five days ago."

Akitada looked at Pearl. "And you?"

"Twenty-one days," she said softly.

They had been counting days since they had been taken.

"And where are you from?"

They were silent.

"Come, where did you live before this?"

Jasmine murmured, "We mustn't tell."

Akitada nodded and turned to Pearl again. "Your real name is Kuniko, isn't it? And you are from Hichiso?"

She stared at him. Her lower lip started to tremble.

"Your father's name was Taro. Am I right?"

Now the tears came. She sobbed, "They killed him."

"Yes. I'm very sorry. Your mother grieves for you. We came to take you home."

Sudden joy sprang up in her face. She wiped her eyes and pressed both hands together. "Oh, please! Oh, sir!" she cried. She crawled forward and flung herself down before him, sobbing, clutching his knees, begging, "Can we leave now? Please?"

Akitada glanced at the walls. "Hush! Not so loud."

Jasmine found her speech again. "You mustn't," she cried in a panic. "They'll kill us. They've said so. Oh, Pearl, don't you remember how they beat you when you tried to run away?"

Kuniko-Pearl sat up. She looked suddenly doubtful. All the joy left her face. "Can you really take us from here?" she asked in a small voice.

Before Akitada could answer, the door slid open, and Auntie Orchid ducked into the room. Behind her loomed the doorman, looking huge in the small room as he peered over her shoulder. He was grinning.

Or maybe he was baring his teeth.

"What is the meaning of this interruption?" Akitada snapped.

Auntie Orchid hesitated, then bowed. "Your pardon. It sounded as if the girls were being troublesome. As I said, they're very new." She turned to the girls. "Now, what is this? Get ready for bed! Untie those sashes and loosen your trouser cords. The quicker you are, the faster it will be over." She paused, perhaps considering how this must have sounded to her customers, and explained, "They are still a bit frightened. But some gentlemen find this reluctance very much to their taste. It increases desire. They'll find pleasure soon enough in the lovemaking when an experienced older gentleman shows them how it's done."

Akitada felt nauseated. He sought for something to say and failed.

She looked concerned. "Would you like me to have a talk with them?"

Genba shouted, "No!"

She chuckled. "Very well. Then we'll leave you."

Akitada found his tongue. "No! There is clearly no privacy to be had here. I believe we'll try elsewhere. Return our money!"

She gasped. The girls burst into tears and threw themselves down before him. Akitada was afraid they would give away his plan. He hesitated.

The woman said quickly, "Sorry, very sorry. I know it's very noisy." She gestured to the walls. Another room perhaps?"

Akitada frowned. "The walls are too thin. And the slightest noise apparently brings your strongman."

She wrung her hands. "He won't bother you again. He'll stay outside the entrance. How about the garden house? It's a little dusty, but you will be away from other guests there."

"Hmm." Akitada turned to Genba and winked. "Perhaps? What do you think, Kagemitsu?"

Genba nodded enthusiastically and bent to help the girls to their feet."

Auntie Orchid clapped her hands. "Excellent!" she cried, and sent the maid who appeared to dust the garden house and spread bedding. "And have them take some refreshments out so the gentleman won't be disturbed," she instructed. The doorman scowled and slouched away.

32

The Escape

After a short wait, during which they sat mostly silent, Auntie Orchid returned.

"It's ready," she announced. She herded the girls before them, whispering urgent instructions as they walked through an overgrown garden. Akitada tried to look around, but the trees and shrubs had grown wild and it was pitch dark under the branches. He hoped any fences might be in as much disrepair as the vegetation.

The "summer house" turned out to be a mere store house with a single door and no windows, but it was solidly built and dry. Someone had removed its contents, swept it, and brushed down most of the cobwebs. Paper lanterns hung from the beams, and two maids spread bedding. Another maid brought trays with food and a large flask of wine. Apparently, Auntie was making an effort to hold on to the generous payment this time.

At last they were alone. Akitada opened the door and looked after the departing staff. He saw only the one path in the surrounding thicket of vegetation, and when the flickering light of the last maid's lantern disappeared, there was nothing but night. Their problems were far from solved.

He closed the door again and turned to the others. "I'll try to find a way out. Meanwhile it will be best if you make the sort of noise associated with entertainment. Can either of you girls sing?"

They were frightened again, though perhaps no longer of Akitada and Genba. They looked at each other and nodded reluctantly.

Kuniko said, "We know the songs we used to sing at home. We haven't learned anything yet."

Genba laughed. "Good. Those are probably the very songs we used to sing. Let's sing." He glanced over at the food. "And let's eat and drink, too. We are going to have a good time." He made faces signaling his delight and patted his belly.

The girls giggled.

Akitada slipped outside into the blackness. It took a moment to adjust his eyes. A thin glow of lights came from the main house, but the house itself could not be seen behind the black mass of trees. Another faint glow hovered over the trees to his right, probably the lights of the next house. He tried to orientate himself. If he recalled, there was a narrow alley between the houses. He turned that way.

Getting through the shrubbery in the dark without making noise was problematic. Branches grabbed at his clothes and snagged. Thorns ripped at his hands and forearms. He stumbled over unseen objects on the ground. But eventually he fought his way through, found the brightness increasing, and stood before a tall, well-built wooden fence.

He could not see over it and saw no way of climbing it. It was well-maintained. The only advantage in that was that the vegetation had been hacked away, leaving a narrow path along the fence. Auntie Orchid had made sure that none of her girls could escape by climbing a tree and jumping down on the other side.

Discouraged, he walked along the fence hoping for a gate. He did not find a gate, but at the far corner, a large branch had broken from a tall pine. It had fallen on the fence, breaking its top, with one end resting on the ground.

Akitada stepped on it and found that he could walk on it and peer over the broken section of the fence. The break was fresh, and the branch must have fallen only recently. On the other side was a narrow alley filled mostly with knee-high nettles, and then another high fence of the neighbor's back garden. Music came from the house. There, too, guests were being entertained. Akitada gauged the distance down into the nettles of the alley, and his heart lifted. Luck was with them. Now if only the rest was this easy.

He returned, with some difficulty, to the garden house. They were still singing inside. He opened the door and slipped inside. If someone had seen him, they would assume he had relieved himself.

Inside, the others fell silent and looked at him anxiously. He nodded.

"Extinguish all but one of the lights," he told Genba. To the girls, he said, "We have to climb a fence. You must be very quiet. I'll go first to show you the way. Then you follow, holding on to each other, and Genba will come last. Can you do that?"

They nodded solemnly.

Genba darkened the room. It would make any watchers think they had gone to bed. Akitada opened the door, peered out cautiously, then stepped out. The girls followed. Genba closed the door behind them.

They crept through the shrubbery, not as noiselessly as he had hoped. The girls gasped once or twice. Genba muttered a curse. Then they reached the fence, and the going was easier. At the broken section, Akitada explained his plan in a whisper.

Genba climbed over, and Akitada helped the two girls up. They jumped down and Genba caught them. Then Akitada himself negotiated the broken limb, the gap in the fence, and the jump down. He tore his clothes, but the thicket had already ripped them. More serious was the fact that he turned his ankle when he landed.

The initial pain was sharp and he sank to his knee with a groan.

Genba hissed, "Sssh!" When Akitada did not immediately get up, he asked in a whisper, "What's wrong?"

Akitada bit his lip and stood, putting most of his weight on the good foot. He saw why Genba had hushed him. They were near the end of the alley, and people were passing on the main street. They had to get away. He tried to hobble a few steps, gritting his teeth. It was bad, but it could not be helped.

"Go ahead to the post station stable and get our horses," he told Genba in a low voice. We'll wait under the trees of that grove just past the temple."

Genba hesitated. "You hurt your leg?"

"Go!" Akitada gave him a push.

Genba departed.

Akitada looked at the girls. They looked back at him. Their faces expressed concern, but also trust. Taro's daughter came and took his hand. "Lean on me, sir," she said softly. "I'm very strong."

This touched and amused Akitada. He chuckled. "Thank you, my dear." He put his hand on her shoulder. Jasmine came to his other side. In this manner, they hobbled to the main street and paused to see if it was clear.

It was very late even for a night in Sunomata. A drunk staggered from a wine shop, propelled by the doorman. He walked a few steps, then sat down in front of the next house and went to sleep. Nothing else moved.

"Come," said Akitada, and they made their way slowly and unsteadily toward the temple. Akitada hoped that if anyone saw them, he would assume he was a drunk who was taking two women back to his room with him. His foot grew more painful and started to swell inside his boot. Somehow they made it past the temple and into the grove. There they sat down on the ground and waited.

A night watchman passed, sounding his wooden clapper and calling the hour. It would soon be dawn. Akitada hoped Genba would have no problems getting their horses.

It was a chilly night. The girls sat close together and shivered in their thin silk gowns. Akitada tried to ignore the pain in his foot. The boot would have to be cut off, but that was for later. Now they must concentrate on getting the girls away. His plan had worked. But he had not thought much beyond it. Now he had a second girl on his hands. He also had not learned anything about the bandits. Their connection to Sunomata was clear, since they had brought the girls here, but nothing else was known. They would return to Hichiso to take Kuniko to her mother. He wished he could turn to Shibata for help but it had become apparent that the sergeant was covering for Toshiyasu. And Toshiyasu was involved with the bandits and most likely had killed his own father and cousin.

At this point in his glum thoughts, Kuniko whispered, "Look! I hope he doesn't see us."

Akitada looked and saw a tall figure in red striding down the main street. It was the young man from the Rain Dragon. He looked preoccupied as he passed with quick steps and turned the next corner.

"Do you know him?" Akitada asked Kuniko.

"Oh, yes. That was Master Tabito."

Toshiyasu's lover was Otomo's son. And that was very interesting indeed. It explained Toshiyasu's behavior. Most likely it meant Otomo's son had had a hand in the troubles in Hichiso.

Akitada asked, "How did you come to know Master Tabito?"

"Oh, he comes to Hichiso. *Betto* Asano works for his father, the great lord, and Master Tabito and Toshiyasu are best friends."

Before Akitada could ask more questions, Genba appeared with the horses. The girls tucked their long skirts in their sashes and climbed up to ride behind Genba and Akitada. And so they left Sunomata and took the road back across the mountain.

33

Trouble

As long as they were within sight of Sunomata, they did not speak.

The connection between the two young men suggested all sorts of possibilities. From what he had witnessed in the Rain Dragon, the nature of their relationship was now clear. Akitada wanted to know more but did not want to ask Kuniko. In spite of her shocking experience, she seemed too young.

Still, there was the other matter, the one they had failed to solve.

After they were well into the forest, he asked, "The men who killed your father and took you with them, do you know anything about them?"

She did not answer, but he felt her hands tremble and he felt bad. "I'm sorry," he said. "We need to arrest them so they cannot do such things again."

"Yes," she said in a soft voice. "There were four of them. One was a dwarf. He was horrible. He laughed when they killed Father and later when they . . . raped me."

"He is dead."

She gave a small choking sob. "I'm glad."

"You may not know that *Betto* Asano is also dead. He was murdered."

"Oh! Was it Toshiyasu?"

Startled, Akitada asked, "What makes you think so?"

"Toshiyasu was very angry because his father said he couldn't have his money."

"When was that?"

"It was before Father and I went to market. Master Tabito and Toshiyasu came to speak to Father. Master Tabito told Father he'd better sell the farm to the great lord or bad things would happen. Father said he wouldn't sell. When Master Tabito turned to leave, Toshiyasu said, 'Bad things need to happen to my father, and quickly. I need money.' Do you think he killed him?"

Akitada did not answer. She was silent for a moment, then asked, "Why doesn't he work if he needs money?"

Why indeed? "What did Tabito say?"

"He just laughed."

Akitada returned to her own story. "Have you seen any of the men who attacked you and your father before or since?"

He could feel her tensing again before she answered. "They had cloths wrapped around their faces. I could only see their eyes." And after a moment, "It was the same for Jasmine."

Probably the same gang. "A pity you cannot identify them."

"I hope I never see them again."

They were both quiet after that. Akitada did not know how to proceed without help from the capital. The governor of Mino Province had ignored his requests for help and instead threatened Shibata. Akitada was not well acquainted with any of the Minamoto, though there were many of them, and all of them seemed to be seeking power at court. They were a provincial clan and kept standing armies, and the court was increasingly reliant on using their troops to put down rebellions in distant provinces. No, he must work through the bureaucratic channels that were open to him. As soon as he reached his sister and brother-in-law's home, he would write the necessary letters. If he was lucky, the prime minister's office would direct the governor to investigate the crimes and arrest the killers. And then he and his children could return home.

When the road became steeper, they rode single file. The sun had come up, but in the dense forest, it was still shady and cool. The girls seemed to have gone to sleep, and Akitada felt drowsy also. His foot had stopped hurting. They would soon reach the Dragon Temple, and then it was all downhill, slow at first as the horses found their way on loose stones, then faster when they left the woods and reached the open fields and paddies. And then they would be home. How happy Kuniko's mother would be!

It happened near the summit where the road made a sharp turn. Akitada was dimly aware that his horse had pricked up its ears. He scanned his surroundings, but it was too late. They were already on them and then all around them a moment later: Men with covered faces, armed with knives. Akitada's horse shied. Both girls screamed and kept screaming.

Akitada drew his sword and shouted, "Get down, girls! Run and hide!" Behind him, Genba cursed. Akitada slashed down at one bandit who tried to cut his horse. He missed as the man jumped clear, and the horse reared. Akitada managed to get his feet out of the stirrups and jumped as the horse, with Kuniko still hanging on, took off.

On foot, they had a better chance of dealing with the bandits–there were five of them–who only had long knives and had not dealt with well-armed travelers before. Both Akitada and Genba had fought against soldiers in their younger years and, while both were no longer as agile as then, there are things you never forget. Besides, fury took over and a bitter hatred for these men who had killed and raped children.

Akitada elbowed his closest attacker viciously across his face and, swung his whole body around, striking the raised arm of another with his sword. A good sword will cut through bone. The bandit screamed. He lost his knife hand and part of his forearm. Akitada heard Genba grunting behind and another scream. Akitada's opponent fell, but the rest of the bandits were running away, uphill toward the Dragon Temple.

There was no sign of the girls or the horses.

Genba checked his bloody arm.

"You got cut?"

"It's nothing. Just a scratch." Genba grinned suddenly. "That felt good. I haven't felt this good in many years. Are you all right, sir?"

Akitada tested his foot. Jumping off his horse had not improved matters, but it did not feel worse. "Yes, but we've lost the horses and the girls. And those bandits got away. Let's hope they don't bring a horde of armed monks down upon us."

Genba looked around. "We'll have to walk."

Akitada shook his head. "Let's rest a bit. I'm not sure I can walk."

Genba glared at the wounded bandit, who was trying to get to his knees, and gave him a vicious kick, raising his sword again."

"Don't bother. He lost his arm. He'll bleed out before he can get help."

"Ah! Serves him right."

The wounded bandit whimpered for help. Akitada bent to tear the cloth from his face and recognized the pock-marked features of the manager of the Rain Dragon. "Who do you work for?" he asked. The man did not answer and fainted a moment later.

But Akitada knew the answer. It was unlikely that these bandits could have followed them from Sunomata, passing them somehow in the forest. Therefore they had been dispatched earlier to set up an ambush while Akitada and Genba were still in the Fragrant Plum Tree. And that meant they had been recognized in the Rain Dragon. Toshiyasu had seen them and told Otomo's son. It always came back to the Rain Dragon and to Otomo.

There was another connection between the bandits and Lord Otomo. They appeared to do their mischief to those whose land Otomo was trying to buy. Otomo was playing a dangerous game that would have failed if the governor of Mino had protected his people. But that governor had refused to deal with the bandits in the southernmost corner of his province. Out of lazy negligence? Or because he was complicit with Otomo?

It was high time Akitada alerted the central government. They frowned on local gentry seizing power in a province.

Meanwhile, they had lost the girls and their horses. Akitada cast another look around and got to his feet, "Come on! Let's hope the girls didn't get hurt."

His progress was slow, but the top of the mountain was not far and his foot seemed to improve gradually. He debated pounding on the gate of the Dragon Temple to ask about the escaped bandits but discarded the idea. They passed the temple and started down.

Just around the first bend, they found their two horses, each with a girl on its back, awaiting them. The girls, who had been looking anxious, burst into cries of joy.

Akitada smiled and Genba applauded.

"How did you manage this?" Akitada asked Kuniko. "I thought the horse would throw you. I was afraid we'd lost the horses and would find you two with broken bones."

Kuniko grinned, as she made room for him to get in the saddle. "We both ride. We like horses. Oxen, too, if we cannot get a horse."

Genba laughed. "There you have it, sir. They grow up as strong and able as boys on the land."

Akitada thought of the life the girls had just escaped and felt a sense of contentment. He hoped Jasmine, or whatever her real name was, would find a welcome in her own family.

34

Shíbata

They returned to Hichiso among stares from the people in the street. Sergeant Shibata was standing outside the police office when they drew up and Akitada dismounted.

He stared at their bloodied clothes and at the two girls. "What's this?" he asked, looking irritable.

Akitada tied up his horse. To Shibata, he said, "Inside, Sergeant."

Shibata made a face but obeyed. Akitada did not bother to sit down. He faced Shibata and said bluntly, "I've been doing your work. I've brought back Kuniko from Sunomata. The other girl is her friend and was also abducted by the bandits. On the return we were ambushed by them. One is dead. The rest escaped, probably to the Dragon Temple. The dead man worked for Otomo and his son. You will go and get the body and try to arrest the other men. There are other matters to discuss, but I don't have time now."

With this he turned and went back outside, ignoring Shibata's questions, and got back on his horse.

To his relief, he found all well at Kojiro's place. The household surrounded the girls, offering welcome, rest, food, and joy on seeing them free.

Yoshiko wanted to take the girls inside, and Kojiro asked anxious questions about the blood on Akitada's and Genba's clothing, but Akitada said, "First Kuniko will want to see her mother. Everything else can happen later. He turned to Jasmine. "Do you want to stay here or go with Kuniko? What is your name, by the way, and where are your parents?"

The girls drew together. Jasmine looked scared. "How can I go home now?" she whispered.

Kuniko said, "She'll come with me. Mother will make her welcome. And her name is Akiyo."

There it was again: the fear of having a daughter who had been a prostitute and was no longer useful for marriage. Even in the poorest families, marriages affected the well-being of the whole family. There was a fear that poor Akiyo's fate might somehow contaminate the whole family. But Akitada said nothing. He nodded, had new horses brought out, and took both girls to Taro's farm. He needed to see for himself that Kuniko, that brave young girl, was safe. He needed to see her mother's joy. He needed to feel good about something again.

They saw the farm from a distance, lying peacefully under the wide blue sky. A small female figure was filling a bucket at the well.

Kuniko cried, "Mother!" and spurred on her horse.

They were still too far for the woman to have heard the cry, but she paused what she was doing, and turned. Then the full bucket fell from her hand, spilling water, and she was running toward the girl on the horse.

Akitada and Akiyo followed more slowly. Kuniko slid from the horse and threw herself into her mother's arms, and both were laughing and crying.

Akiyo smiled, then looked very sad. Not for her such a homecoming.

But Kuniko recalled herself and turned to introduce them. Kuniko's mother looked up at Akitada with a shining face and said, "Oh, thank you, sir!" then went past him to the other girl and opened her arms.

By then, Akitada had tears in his eyes. Kuniko came and touched his knee. "I shall never forget you, sir. Akiyo will stay with us unless her family wants her home. Mother and I hope she'll stay."

Akitada looked at Akiyo, saw her brushing tears from her face and smiling shyly as Kuniko's mother tucked her hair back and put an arm around her shoulders. Then he gathered the other two horses and rode home, his heart filled with gratitude that the gods or the dragons had allowed him to accomplish part of what he had set out to do.

He spent the next few hours composing some very important letters. The first one was addressed to the prime minister himself and included detailed reports of what had happened in Hichiso and Sunomata.. It was fortunate that this man, who ruled the nation on behalf of the emperor, had reason to be grateful to Akitada.

Nevertheless Akitada was careful to formulate his letter in the official language of a bureaucrat reporting on conditions in the province of Mino. He described the activities of the bandits, stressing the fact that they targeted small farmers and took their daughters to sell them into prostitution in the neighboring province in towns like Sunomata. He described conditions in Sunomata with minimal reference to Otomo Muroya and counted on the fact that the prime minister or someone close to him would make the connection.

He would have liked to confront Otomo with his suspicions but knew that would be futile and only increase the danger to himself and his family.

His next letter was to his own superior, the minister of justice. He explained his delay in returning to his post. They got on well together, and he could count on his support and, perhaps, information. In this case, Akitada mentioned the bandits and their connection with the Dragon Temple, asking for suggestions on how to proceed against Abbot Shinsho and his monks. It was just as well to alert the government to rogue religious institutions. They tended to keep a wary eye on them in any case since the disturbances caused by the monks in Omi Province.

His third letter was to his friend Nakatoshi, senior secretary in the Bureau of Ceremonial. Nakatoshi was a fount of court gossip since he worked daily with ranks and promotions and knew who was striving for what position or rank and what his chances were. He wanted to know more about Otomo and also about Minamoto Tamenori.

When all three letters had been written out neatly, he stamped them with his personal seal and addressed them. One of the hired men Genba had brought with him would carry them back to the capital and return the next day with answers, if any.

Finally, Akitada went to see Shibata.

He found the sergeant in conference with two constables. All three looked perplexed.

Shibata saw Akitada and made a face, as if to say "What next?" He dismissed the constables with the words, "Keep asking questions!"

Akitada seated himself, uninvited, and commented, "Appropriate words. I have come to ask some questions of my own."

Shibata said resentfully, "You always ask questions."

"And rarely get the right answers."

"What do you want now, sir?"

"How close is your relationship with Asano's daughter?"

Shibata paled, then flushed. "We're friends. She's a very capable lady whom I admire."

"Indeed. Does your admiration for Maeko extend to protecting her brother?"

Shibata blinked. "What do you mean?"

"It should have been obvious to you, a man who investigates crimes, a man who knows the people of this town, and a man who is close to the Asano family, that of all the people only Toshiyasu had the perfect motive for killing his father. He's a spoiled youngster with a reputation for gambling, drinking, and chasing after sexual pleasures. Furthermore, his father was known to have disciplined him shortly before his death. He had refused his son his greatest wish, to send him to the capital, and he is known to have threatened to disinherit him. Did you at all investigate Toshiyasu's involvement?"

Shibata looked extremely uncomfortable. "Toshiyasu wasn't home at the time. He was in Sunomata."

"And who told you that?"

Shibata hesitated, then said reluctantly, "His sister. But we know now that it was Toshiyasu's servant Shigeie who killed Sadamoto. He must also have killed Asano earlier."

"Ah, the elusive Shigeie. First he confesses. Then he mysteriously escapes from prison . . ."

Shibata cried, "I had nothing to do with that."

Akitada smiled. "Really? It was your jail and he was your responsibility."

Shibata looked around the room helplessly. "It was *O-bon*. It was a madhouse. I wasn't near the jail all day and night."

"On purpose?"

Shibata threw up his hands. "What difference does it make? Shigeie's dead. The case is closed."

Akitada stared at him. "He's dead? How do you know?"

Shibata snapped, "Because someone found him in the woods, that's how."

"Where's the body?"

Shibata gave a sigh of defeat. "Out back. With an arrow through his body. A hunting accident."

Akitada remembered that Otomo regularly hunted in the area. He stood up. "Let's go. I want to see the body."

The sergeant shook his head. "It isn't fresh. Must've happened two or three days ago. And it's been hot."

"I've seen decomposing bodies before."

Shibata got up reluctantly and led the way out the back of the building and to the jail. Shigeie's corpse lay in a small side room. He smelled bad and had started to look puffy. Flies rose and buzzed around him.

"What does your coroner say?" Akitada walked around the body. Shigeie had been young and must have been handsome once. Now his mouth hung open as if in surprise. Blood had trickles from his nose and lips and several flies crawled in and out. In death, he looked repulsive.

"He hasn't come yet. They just brought the body in."

"Turn him over!"

Shibata bent down and rolled the body on its side and then on its back. The back of his shirt was blood-soaked. Akitada sucked in a breath, then bent and touched the center of the stain. "Who removed the arrow?"

"The constables. They shouldn't have, but they wanted to see who he was. The arrow was in the way."

Akitada straightened. "So," he said heavily, "Shigeie was shot in the back. Conveniently, it seems."

35

The Murder of Shigeie

Suddenly nothing was simple any longer. Akitada had never believed the story that a servant had murdered his master and later another member of the family to protect an eighteen-year-old heir. No, he had always thought that Toshiyasu was responsible, perhaps with the assistance of his sister. He had hoped to clear the sister somehow, but when he realized that she had used Shibata's love for her to cover up what happened, he no longer trusted her.

He had intended to have Toshiyasu arrested and questioned, but the murder of Shigeie had happened while Toshiyasu was in Sunomata.

And Toshiyasu's activities there with Otomo's son opened up all sorts of new possibilities.

Now he looked down at Shigeie's body and said, "This was no hunting accident. He was shot to keep him from talking."

Shibata said, "We don't know that."

Akitada gave him a pitying look. "And you claim to be a police officer! Where is the arrow now?"

"In my office." Shibata fidgeted. "I'm duly assigned to this post. It is my case."

"Not much longer!"

"You can't do that. You have no jurisdiction."

"You think not?" Akitada turned his back on him and walked out.

Shibata followed Akitada back to his office where Akitada looked at the arrow.

It was longer than his arm, made of bamboo and lacquered. The tip was metal; the type called a willow leaf. At the moment it was caked with black blood. The blood extended up the shaft, showing that the arrow had penetrated Shigeie's back deeply. The arrow was fletched with black and white eagle's feathers, the long slightly curved feathers from the wing.

Many years ago, when Akitada was a boy and a young man, he had been trained in the use of the great bow. It had been a sport for him and his friends, a way of showing off one's skill at hitting targets, perhaps even from the back of a galloping horse. He had never used the bow and arrow to kill men, but it was the weapon of choice in warfare. In the few close action battles he had fought, he had used a sword. But he remembered enough to know that this was no ordinary arrow. It had been made by a master craftsman.

He touched it with a finger. "Who uses arrows like this?"

Shibata looked blank. "I don't know. It looks expensive. The local people use plain bamboo sharpened at the end. The feathers look special, too."

"Yes. This was made by a master. Maybe in the capital. So you know of no one around here who makes such arrows?"

"No."

"Then it stands to reason that its owner gets his hunting equipment elsewhere."

Shibata frowned. "I know of only Lord Otomo who's likely to do that. He keeps his hunting bows and arrows at his lodge."

"I think tomorrow you'd better check if he's missing an arrow," Akitada said.

"I don't think he's been hunting lately."

"Is anyone staying there in his absence?"

"Only Jugoro."

"Lock up the arrow, then go and ask Jugoro to show you Lord Otomo's arrows."

Shibata nodded. "I still think it was an accident," he muttered.

"Tell this Jugoro that it was an accident, but that you need to make sure."

Shibata looked uncertain. "But you don't think it was?"

Akitada sighed. "No. Of course not. I want to know if the arrow came from Otomo's lodge."

Shibata shuffled his feet. "Lord Otomo is highly respected in Hichiso."

Akitada said impatiently, "Do your duty, Sergeant. Just this once, do your duty," and walked out.

The next day Akitada went to the Asano farmstead. The elderly Moroe came to greet him. He looked drawn and worried. "I'm sorry, sir, but my mistress is indisposed," he said before Akitada could speak.

Akitada dismounted. "What's wrong with her?" he asked.

Moroe wrung his hands. "It's all been too much for her, sir. She's tried to do it all. She's just a young girl."

Akitada thought of the even younger girls and what they had suffered. "Where is she?" he asked coldly.

Moroe barred his way. "You can't see her, sir. Please, leave her be."

Akitada took his arm and moved him aside, then strode into the house. He checked the office first. It was empty. Glancing into rooms along the corridor, he found them in the rear of the house.

Brother and sister sat together. She held his hand in hers and was speaking softly to him. He was doubled over, weeping. When she saw Akitada, an expression of distaste crossed her face. But she was composed again in a moment. Releasing her brother's hand, she said severely, "My lord, this is a surprise. Where is Moroe?"

"Moroe tried to stop me, but I'm afraid the time has come to face the truth. Your brother is deeply implicated in two murders and probably in other crimes."

"No!" she cried, getting to her feet. "Toshiyasu has done nothing."

Toshiyasu wiped his face. "Don't bother. It doesn't matter anymore. It's all over." He looked blearily at Akitada. "If you've come to arrest me, I don't care. My life's over anyway."

Akitada eyed him without pity. "I've come to get some straight answers. I take it you recognized me in Sunomata and set up the ambush?"

Maeko cried, "What? What is this, Toshiyasu? What happened in Sunomata?"

So he had not told her? Akitada was puzzled for a moment. What, indeed, had happened in Sunomata? He said, "Did you quarrel with Tabito?"

Toshiyasu clenched his fists. "I told him about you. Now he blames me. You had to come snooping into our business."

Maeko shook his arm. "What business? What have you been doing with Tabito?"

Toshiyasu jerked his arm away. "Nothing! Stop nagging. You're always nagging. You and Father. Now see what you have caused."

Akitada said, "You and Tabito were lovers and you organized the bandit attacks together, didn't you?"

Maeko gasped. "No! Not the bandits!"

"We were just having some fun. Life's pretty boring here. We frightened a few peasants, that's all. Father wouldn't let me go to the capital. Or give me money."

"Fun?" Maeko cried. "Fun? Taro died and his daughter was abducted. Did you do that?"

"That one got out of hand. Taro fought our men. They had no choice."

Maeko moaned and put her face in her hands.

Akitada asked, "Were you there?"

"No, but they always reported to us."

"They reported to you and Tabito? Where? In Sunomata?"

Toshiyasu gave a sullen nod. "There never was much money and we split that with the men, and we got little enough for the girls."

His sister sank down and started weeping. Akitada ignored her. "How did you fall in with bandits?"

"I told you, there was nothing to do. This was just some excitement."

"In other words, you took part in what they did?"

"Sometimes." He grinned suddenly. "We covered our faces and pretended we were highwaymen. You should have seen the peasants' faces! Some fell on their knees and knocked their heads in the dirt begging for mercy."

Maeko moaned.

"But how did you find the bandits?"

"They weren't always bandits. Mostly they just worked for Tabito's father."

Maeko sat up "Oh, Toshiyasu, if your father had known, it would have killed him."

Toshiyasu gave a harsh laugh. "That's a pretty stupid thing to say. He's dead, isn't he?"

She shot up, took a step to her brother, and slapped him.

Akitada said quickly, "That brings us to your father's convenient death. Did you murder him?"

Toshiyasu snapped, "No. I wasn't there. And I wasn't there when Sadamoto was killed. You can't pin that on me. I didn't kill anyone."

Maeko, white-faced, asked, "Who killed them?"

Toshiyasu glanced at her. "You figure it out. I've said enough." He suddenly sounded defeated.. Perhaps the memory of the quarrel with Tabito had returned.

Akitada bit his lip. He had no power to arrest Toshiyasu, even though he had confessed to enough to put him in jail. But there was more. Much more. There was Tabito. And there was Lord Otomo.

Before he could decide what to do, Sergeant Shibata walked in.

36

The Lovers

The sergeant looked belligerent. Going to Maeko, he put a hand on her shoulder. "What is this, sir?" he demanded. "Moroe says you were not admitted. Is it customary among noblemen in the capital to force their way into private people's homes?"

Alas, morals among the nobility were such that this was indeed a common occurrence, but Akitada did not say so. It had taken courage for Shibata to speak in this manner. He looked from the sergeant's angry face to his hand on Maeko's shoulder and said calmly, "I take it you and Maeko are lovers."

Neither Shibata nor the young woman answered. It was Toshiyasu who drew himself up and cried, "How dare you insult my sister? I demand satisfaction."

It was both funny and embarrassing, and Akitada regretted that he had been blunt in order to get Maeko to admit to the game they had been playing all along. He sighed and shook his head at Toshiyasu. "Let your sister speak."

Maeko looked up at Shibata, then raised her hand to lay it on his. "Yes," she said. "We are lovers. You're not the only one, Toshiyasu, who rebelled against Father."

Her brother gaped at her. Then he exploded in fury. "You and that penniless policeman? You slut! You shamed our family! Get out of my house and take your bastard of a lover with you!"

Maeko turned white and rose. "You are my brother! How can you speak this way to me? I have protected you. I have kept quiet when I knew you were gambling away our money. I have lied to Father about what you were doing. I have lied for you when they started asking questions about the bandits."

Toshiyasu's fists were balled. "Get out!" he snarled again.

Shibata, looking pale but determined, said, "We shall be husband and wife as soon as Maeko agrees."

"Not as long as I live!" Toshiyasu fired back, apparently having forgotten that he had just thrown his sister out.

A difficult situation.

Toshiyasu, as the surviving male in her family, had the right to forbid Maeko's marriage. Akitada guessed she had kept her secret affair from Toshiyasu because she knew what his reaction would be. It also complicated the case. Shibata would surely refuse to arrest Toshiyasu.

But there he was wrong.

Shibata drew Maeko to his side. He said gently, "My dear, it has gone far enough."

She touched his hand again and bowed her head.

The sergeant stepped forward and told Toshiyasu, "In the name of the emperor, I arrest you, Asano Toshiyasu, on charges of aiding bandits and other criminals who invaded our peaceful valley. You will remain in jail until those charges are investigated and until you can be cleared of the accusation that you plotted the murder of your own father and cousin."

Toshiyasu stood stunned for a moment, then he flew at Shibata with a shout. Shibata, being older and stronger, threw him down quickly and, with Akitada's help, secured him with the thin chain normally carried by constables.

Toshiyasu kicked and cursed him. His sister ran from the room, sobbing.

The chain surprised Akitada. "You came prepared?"

Shibata, looking bleak, nodded. "I waited too long. If you'll keep an eye on him, sir, I have some constables waiting outside."

Toshiyasu, trussed up on the floor, glared up at Akitada. "He'll be sorry," he shouted. You'll be sorry, too. You think just because you're some official from the capital, you can come here and accuse decent people."

Akitada sat down beside him. "Are you hoping that Lord Otomo will protect you?"

"Yes. My father was his *betto* and I shall succeed him."

"You don't think that the falling-out between you and Otomo's son might make that unlikely?"

Toshiyasu gulped. "Tabito and I are lovers. He won't abandon me."

"Most likely he'll be afraid that you'll talk too much about what you and he have been doing."

Toshiyasu looked frightened for a moment. "I would never do that and he knows it," he said stoutly.

"You know very little about the ways in which police get suspects to talk."

"They wouldn't dare!"

Shibata and the constables made a timely entrance. The two constables jerked Toshiyasu to his feet and dragged him away. He was shouting threats the whole way.

When the door had closed behind them, Akitada said to Shibata, "Unpleasant for you, I'm afraid."

Shibata bit his lip. "I don't care about him. He was always a troublemaker and his father knew it well enough. But Maeko is innocent. She had nothing to do with any of this. You mustn't blame her. If I held back what I knew, it is my fault. I wanted to protect her."

"I need to speak to her."

Shibata looked for a moment as if he would protest, but then he nodded and led the way to her own room, proving that he knew the way well. She sat near a door open to a small courtyard and turned a tear-stained face to them. But her spirit was back, and her eyes flashed with anger when she saw Akitada.

"Am I to have no peace?"

"Forgive the intrusion, Maeko, but you must realize that circumstances are such that they overrule matters of propriety."

"I thought the good people prided themselves on never allowing improprieties."

Akitada grimaced. "Don't forget that I'm old enough to be your father and that I serve in the ministry of justice. This allows me certain liberties." He paused, then added a little maliciously, "And Sergeant Shibata has been made welcome here in the past."

She flushed. "That's none of your business."

"I disagree. He has done his best to obstruct the investigation into your brother's activities to protect you. People have died as a result."

Her eyes flew to Shibata, who shuffled his feet and said nothing.

"You won't report him?" she asked Akitada. "Please, you must not. I'll do my best to answer your questions."

Akitada, who had already reported on the inadequate nature of the policing in Hichiso, said, "Sergeant Shibata has had to work without the support he needed. I expect allowances will be made."

She looked unhappy, but nodded.

"Were you aware of the relationship between your brother and Lord Otomo's son?"

She flushed a little and glanced at Shibata who looked impassive. "Toshiyasu admired Tabito. Tabito is older and he's dashing and experienced. He attended the university."

"I assume that was why Toshiyasu was eager to go also."

She nodded. "Father thought it unsuitable. We are farmers; he was only a *betto* on a nobleman's estate. In any case, Tabito failed the examinations and came back. After that the two became inseparable. Father and I thought nothing of it until people came to collect on Toshiyasu's gambling debts. I think this must have led them to rob farmers travelling to market." She sighed.

"Then you didn't know that they had become lovers?"

"I knew. Or I suspected. They are young. The young experiment, but Father was terribly upset when he found out. He heard about it just before he died. He worried about the future of the family."

"And he talked about leaving the farm to his nephew Sadamoto?"

She nodded. "There was a terrible row. Shigeie was there." She glanced pleadingly at Shibata.

Akitada asked, "Was Toshiyasu good with weapons?"

"No. He hated that sort of thing. Why?"

"Shigeie was shot with an arrow."

She gasped. "Oh no! How badly is he hurt?"

"He's dead."

"Murdered?" When Akitada nodded, she said quickly, "It wasn't Toshiyasu. He didn't know how to use bow and arrow."

"Do you have any idea who might have done such a thing?"

She shook her head.

"Does Tabito hunt with bow and arrow?"

This startled her. "He may have done so. With his father."

"Thank you. I think that's all for now."

Akitada left and after a moment Shibata followed him. When he caught up, he said, "You see, she had nothing to do with what Toshiyasu was up to. She only loved him and tried to help him."

"Yes." Akitada sighed. "From what I've seen of her, I wouldn't argue with you. But will she forgive you?"

A quick smile touched Shibata's face. "I hope so. She's strong and she's fair." He paused. "And I think she loves me."

"Congratulations,"

The smile returned. "Thank you, sir. I hope she won't be disappointed. I'm determined to do my best whatever happens."

Shibata's courtship had caused a lot of trouble, but Akitada's anger softened. The sergeant had, belatedly, found the courage to test his love for Maeko and arrest her brother. And she had responded well.

He said, "Meanwhile we may have a problem. Someone released Shigeie from your jail and later someone killed him, possibly the same man. I doubt that Toshiyasu will escape the same fate. He is too deeply implicated and knows who the killers are. I'll send you some of my hired men to make sure you don't find your prisoner with his throat cut."

Shibata paled. "If there's danger, it will come from Lord Otomo or someone close to him."

"I see you understand the situation. Make sure you get a confession quickly and have it witnessed. Send for a judge from the provincial capital."

"The governor will refuse."

"I doubt that. Not this time. He will have heard from court."

Shibata looked at him shyly. "I'm very sorry, sir, that I doubted you. We've never had anyone come here with your rank and authority."

"Authority?" Akitada chortled. "I have no authority, but I know some people who do."

They parted on friendly terms and Akitada rode home thinking about the lovers. Not for him, such happiness. He had found it once and never again. Tamako had died in childbirth with his small son, and Sadako, the only woman who could have taken her place had left forever this past spring. He had been too slow, too unaware, too shy to ask her to stay. Most likely she would have turned him down after witnessing his affair with Aoi. That too had been due to his foolishness. In his loneliness he had made mistakes. First Yukiko, his best friend's daughter–as unsuitable a match as could be imagined between an eighteen-year-old beauty and a middle-aged official–and then he had been about to throw in his lot with Lady Aoi, a practicing medium so unconventional that her high-ranking relatives kept trying to hide her. She, at least, had had the good sense to turn him down.

Never mind. Shibata and Maeko deserved a chance. He'd try to do his best for them unless the prime minister ordered otherwise. He should have an answer soon.

37

Lord Otomo

The next day messengers arrived on lathered horses. They came accompanied by uniformed soldiers and flags. Akitada was amazed at the speed with which the prime minister had acted. To be sure, Akitada's earlier report had set matters in motion. No doubt meetings had been held and precedents consulted, but he felt flattered that his report had been responded to so rapidly and in such a gratifying manner.

The first messenger carried a short letter from the prime minister, thanking him for his report and assuring him that responses would reach him and the Mino governor shortly. It further instructed him to continue supervising the investigation and directing the local officers. This messenger also presented the duly signed and sealed papers that gave him temporary authority in the area and in the neighboring province. Such confidence was a high honor indeed.

A short time later two more messengers arrived. One of them carried a brief note from his superior, the minister of justice. He assured him that the prime minister had authorized his absence personally and added that nothing was known about Abbot Shinsho, but that he had passed Akitada's information on to the authorities.

The other messenger was of the ordinary kind. He came alone and wore ordinary clothes. He brought a letter from Akitada's friend Nakatoshi.

Nakatoshi wrote, "I see you've managed to dig up another mystery even in the remote mountain valleys of Mino Province. How do you do it?" There followed some conventional remarks about family and friends, then Nakatoshi got to the information Akitada had requested.

"As to Minamoto Tamenori: he received the appointment to Mino two years ago. It was in recognition of having provided soldiers to put down an uprising in Shimosa Province. Rumor has it that he was bitterly disappointed, having expected a position at court. The Otomo family of Owari Province are minor in importance. This has not stopped Otomo Muroya, the current family head, to raise eyebrows among the court nobles. Numerous complaints have been received that he was driving peasants off their lands and of negotiating tax-free status by allying himself with local temples who then claim his properties under temple authority, making them tax free. It's a popular trick to get out of remitting taxes. It is said he pays the temples a small fee and passes it off as donations. The court is frustrated but cannot proceed against him and the others."

Akitada folded the letter. He had guessed correctly, and that explained the very gratifying communications by the prime minister. They hoped he would be instrumental in removing two thorns from their side. But he knew well enough, if he did not succeed, both Minamoto and Otomo would make trouble, and the prime minister would be forced to settle complaints by blaming Akitada.

This was not the first time Akitada had had to take this sort of risk. It had become easier after his many years of service, partially because he had forged friendships, and partially because his reputation and authority had both grown. He had no doubts about what he must do next.

He would confront Otomo.

Before taking the road to Sunomata again, Akitada and Genba stopped at the police station. They found a Shibata who was white-faced and shaking. He said, "He has confessed."

Akitada said, "To what?"

Shibata heaved a breath, "He and Tabito organized the bandits. They started out burning storehouses. Then they robbed peasants on the road. Then they had the idea of abducting girls. It seems a brothel owner suggested that to them. They picked young girls because they were easier to subdue."

So Toshiyasu and Tabito had not enjoyed tangling with the young cloth dyer. Akitada asked, "Anything else?"

Shibata looked away. "Toshiyasu had his father and his cousin killed. Tabito sent a message that his father was unhappy with some repairs in the highest paddies. Asano went immediately to check and was beaten to death by the bandits. Tabito also arranged the murder of Sadamoto on Toshiyasu's urging. Shigeie happened to get in the killer's way and got wounded. I expect Toshiyasu paid him to keep quiet."

"I see. Did Toshiyasu say who killed Sadamoto?"

"He doesn't know."

"Doesn't know?"

Shibata got up. "The interrogation was terrible. I've never had to do anything like it before and hope I never shall again. Come see him. Otherwise you'll never trust me."

They walked back to the jail. They could hear weeping as soon as they entered. Shibata had one of the cells opened. Inside lay a wreck of a human being. Toshiyasu's back was soaked in blood. He was moaning and sobbing loudly. Akitada said nothing. He nodded and they left. Outside he said, "I'm going to see Otomo. We need to arrest Tabito. And I suspect that the man Jugoro killed Shigeie."

Shibata said, "It could as easily have been Tabito or his father. Both use those arrows."

"Yes. I'm keeping it in mind.

"I have no jurisdiction in Sunomata."

"I know."

The visit to Otomo was a formal one. In Sunomata they changed into their best clothes. Akitada wore his green silk robe and trousers, as well as his court hat. Genba put on half armor over a red hunting coat and trousers. He wore boots and had his long sword at his side. They had brought an attendant, the brightest and strongest of the hired men. He too was armed. Akitada traveled with his own long sword, but he did not wear it when they set out for Otomo's residence. He carried his special powers inside his robe.

The Otomo estate, previously seen only from the town below and at a distance, proved to be not much different from the palaces of the great nobles in the capital, but Otomo enjoyed the privacy of a great deal of land around the buildings. It was mostly forest except for the approach, which had been opened up to allow the world to see the great gate and the brilliantly white walls with the green tile tops. Beyond lay large roofs, also green-tiled.

"It's a palace, sir," Genba said. "There lives a man who rules his own country."

Akitada frowned. "The court disapproves on such display, and rightly so. You cannot trust a man who strives to be an emperor."

"How did he gain his wealth? Is it an old family?"

"Not at all. Otomo's great grandfather was a farmer like Kojiro. He was the first of a line of greedy men. They made their money by cheating on their rice tax and then used their rice stores to sell seed rice to impoverished peasants at huge rates. When the peasants defaulted, they took their land."

"Why didn't the provincial government stop them?"

"The Otomo family bribed the local authorities."

Genba shook his head.

As they approached the two-story gatehouse, the double gates opened wide. Liveried servants and guards lined up inside to receive them.

Akitada said, "Apparently Otomo has his spies in the town below. We have been announced."

"Maybe someone in Hichiso warned him."

"That, too, is possible. An unpleasant notion."

They passed through the gate and into an expansive graveled courtyard where they dismounted. A senior retainer approached them, bowed deeply, and bade them welcome.

"We are here to see Lord Otomo," Akitada said. "Tell him Sugawara Akitada wants to speak to him."

The man bowed again and hurried off. The hired soldier stayed with their horses.

The old retainer returned quickly and ushered Akitada and Genba inside. After walking through a number of elegant rooms, they arrived in the large, luxurious main hall of the house. Its owner entered through another door. His eyes took in Akitada's formal robe and went to Genba in his half armor.

"My lord," he said with a smile, "this is a surprise. But may my servants relieve your companion of that uncomfortable weapon?"

Akitada said coldly, "No. We won't be staying long."

"Ah. You're on your homeward journey and anxious to be on the road. Very wise precaution. Travel isn't safe these days."

Akitada did not comment on this. "I wished to get some answers about certain activities that have been happening in Hichiso."

"What activities? I hunt sometimes on the other sides of the mountain."

"You have been buying up the land of small farmers. I myself was present when you discussed buying Taro's farm with my brother-in-law."

Otomo chuckled and spread his hands. "I plead guilty. Naturally I try to keep land in production. Terrible things happen when peasants leave the land. You want people to starve? The emperor himself encourages our sacred rice culture."

"Perhaps I should have been clearer. Peasants have been forced to sell you their land. They have been threatened. If they don't sell, certain things begin to happen. Fires burn down rice storehouses, for example. In the case of Taro, he ended up dead and his young daughter was abducted and forced into prostitution in Sunomata's brothels."

Otomo's brows shot up. "Shocking, but it has nothing to do with me. I heard about the bandits. The Hichiso police are too inept to stop them. You really shouldn't blame someone of your own station for such low crimes."

Akitada's chin went up. "I remind you that you're not of my station. You're a provincial landowner and have no rank I'm aware of."

Otomo bristled, but he said nothing.

"Sergeant Shibata has witnesses who implicate your son Tabito in the crimes in Hichiso."

"I don't know what you're talking about, but whatever it is, he must be mistaken. Tabito has just returned from his studies at the imperial university."

"He's been back long enough. And the troubles started soon after his return. This won't do any good, Otomo. Shibata has arrested Asano's son. He has confessed and implicated your son. I think you'll find not only that Tabito hired the bandits who set the fires, raped, and killed, but that he's also mixed up in the murders of Toshiyasu's father and nephew."

"What?" Otomo stared at Akitada with bulging eyes, then he swung round and called for servants.

Akitada tensed. It had been a gamble. They had walked into the tiger's lair, thinking to intimidate him and now the moment had come when they would pay for their audacity. Genba had his sword and would fight for their freedom if Otomo chose to call up his guards, but it would be a hopeless battle.

A servant shot into the room. Otomo stood irresolute for a moment, then said, "Send for my son."

The servant shot back out. They waited in silence. The time stretched. Akitada's skin crawled. Otomo started pacing, muttering under his breath. Suddenly he stopped. "Where is he?" he growled. He turned to them, said, "I'll have his head if what you say is true," and ran from the room.

Akitada stood for a moment, then threw open doors. One led to a covered gallery. He called, "Come, Genba! I'll not be trapped in a cage like an animal."

They walked quickly along the gallery and from there into a large garden. Akitada made for the trees.

Genba, following, was puzzled. "What are we doing, sir? He only went to get his son."

"I don't trust him. What I told him shocked him profoundly. I saw his face; he wanted us dead. We'll have to try to get out."

Genba followed him into the trees. "But he wouldn't dare attack an imperial official. Especially not now when you have the authority to arrest him."

"He doesn't know that yet, and he's a desperate man. The news about his son is shocking."

They ended up in front of a smooth plaster wall twice their height.

Akitada said, "Back to the house. Let's try the galleries again. If we can get to the horses, we have a chance to get out alive."

But when they got back, they could hear that a search was under way. They stopped among the trees.

Men appeared here and there along the covered galleries, looked around, and disappeared again into various parts of the main house or its pavilions.

Genba muttered, "They're armed."

"Yes."

After a while, Otomo himself appeared in the gallery. He leaned on the railing and scanned the garden. "Lord Sugawara," he called. "Are you out here?"

They did not answer.

Otomo called his servants and the armed men back. He spoke to them, gesturing toward the garden, and they ran down the steps and spread out to search. He remained on the gallery to wait.

"We need to get out," said Genba.

"Too late. They'd be on us before we found a way out."

Genba grimaced. "Well then!" He drew his sword.

In spite of the dire situation, Akitada smiled. This was like Genba. He had courage and determination and did not hesitate in the face of what must be inevitable death. "No," he said. "We'll try to talk our way out. Put your sword back. We'll walk out. Act casual!"

It took them only a few steps before they were seen. A servant set up a cry and men came from everywhere to surround them.

Akitada stopped. "What is this?" he demanded. "We were merely looking at the garden." Glancing up at the house, he called out to Otomo, "Call back your men."

Genba drew his sword, ready to meet an attack. The armed men retreated a little.

Otomo laughed. "Why, Lord Sugawara! You thought I'd set my people on you? How very funny!" Another laugh. "No, no! We were just concerned for your safety. My son keeps a wild bear in this garden. Please come back inside. Let's talk."

Akitada was tempted to ask to see the bear, but he let it go. They were not in the clear yet. He exchanged a look with Genba, nodded, and they climbed the steps to the gallery, allowing Otomo to lead them back into his reception room.

This time servants brought cushions, platters of refreshments, and wine. They sat.

Akitada asked, "Where is your son?"

"I'm told he's gone to Hichiso to do some hunting. You have wasted your journey. As for what they told you about him, some of it may be true, but most of it is lies."

Akitada considered this. The partial admission suggested that Tabito's activities had not always met with his father's approval. He asked, "Which part is true?"

Otomo grimaced. "He got in trouble at the university and came home. Since then, he has spent too much time with unsavory characters. This association may be what led to your accusations. I cannot believe that he actually involved himself in anything violent, however. But his . . . er . . . friendship with Toshiyasu has only recently come to my knowledge. I suspected nothing, since Toshiyasu was here quite often on business and they met frequently. I should have taken steps to stop the relationship."

Again Akitada paused to consider. Was the trouble between the two young men explained by Tabito's father realizing the nature of their relationship and putting his foot down? Perhaps, but there remained the fact that Otomo himself had been the one to benefit from the crimes committed in Hichiso, since they all tended toward driving farmers from their land. He did not, however, make that point. Instead he asked, "What do you know about Tabito's role in the murders of Toshiyasu's father and his cousin Sadamoto?"

"Tabito had nothing to do with that. It was a terrible thing. I admit I suspected Toshiyasu. He was in trouble with old Asano who finally caught on that his son had been gambling deeply here in Sunomata. But then I heard the murderer was Toshiyasu's slave. And he confessed."

"He made a garbled confession while drunk. But someone let him out of jail and later killed him."

"Well, good riddance. Can't have slaves killing their masters. Saves the authorities time and money."

"Actually, we are also dealing with other murders. Such a sudden increase in violence in a previously peaceful valley is suspicious. As it is, the authorities in the capital are looking into it. That is, I am looking into it on behalf of the prime minister."

Otomo's chin sagged. "You reported to the prime minister?"

"I did."

"When?"

"Oh, I have been sending in reports on conditions for weeks now."

Otomo got up in some agitation. "Why did you do this? None of it was your business. Now they'll send all sorts of investigators to Hichiso." He started pacing again.

Akitada watched him. "And to Sunomata, I expect."

Otomo stopped. "Well, let's hope they get to the bottom of things quickly and depart. Was there anything else you wished to discuss?"

This trying to get rid of them was sudden. Akitada wondered why, but for the time being, it was a chance to walk away from what could have been a bloody and hopeless confrontation. He said, "No. As your son is in Hichiso, I must ask my questions there."

38

The Hunting Lodge

They were allowed to leave.

As soon as they were back on the road, Genba said, "Whew! For a moment there I thought it was all over. I guess he didn't know what his son was up to."

Akitada, looked glum. "So he says."

"Well whatever, we were lucky."

"Perhaps. But as you said, Otomo realized that having us murdered in his own home could not be explained away very easily."

"You thought he might kill us, sir."

"Yes. I could see the rage in his eyes. And the desperation. Men don't think well in that state of mind."

Genba chuckled. "Well, we escaped."

"For a while."

"What do you mean?"

Akitada said, "The embarrassment of having to explain our bodies in his house does not apply to having them found elsewhere. Especially when bandits are known to roam the region."

Genba turned to look over his shoulder. "You think he will try again?"

"Most likely."

Genba said stoutly, "We'll fight them."

"Of course. But at the moment I'd like to postpone the encounter until we get back. I suspect his son is a greater threat to Otomo than I am."

They drove their horses hard up the steep road to the Dragon Temple, expecting pursuit and another attack, but nothing happened. It was past midday and very hot. The descent was almost as precipitous. The horses slipped and balked and nearly unseated both of them. Finally the valley opened before them and Hichiso lay just ahead.

Clouds were building in the east and the heat rested heavy on the land. The ditches in the rice fields were dry, and clouds of gnats hovered in the air.

"A storm is coming," said Genba. He was red-faced and dripping with sweat. "It will clean the air. And we need the rain."

Akitada grunted. He was exhausted and had feared for a while now that any attack, even by the most unskilled of bandits, would find him barely functioning. And he was afraid what he would find.

But the police station looked peaceful enough. A constable and one of Akitada's hired men lounged outside the door, looking bored. They came to attention when they recognized Akitada.

Shibata came out to greet them. He looked tense. "Very glad to see you, sir. Did you learn anything?"

Akitada dismounted, handing the reins to the hired man. "Otomo is deeply involved, though he denies it. He says his son is here in Hichiso. Has all been quiet?"

Shibata nodded. "Jugoro stopped by. He asked to speak to Toshiyasu. I sent him away."

Akitada frowned. "I don't like it. Take good care of that confession. I expect Otomo's son is at the hunting lodge."

Shibata pursed his lips. "Maybe that's what Jugoro wanted to tell Toshiyasu. Jugoro works for Otomo and lives at the lodge."

"I met him at Asano's farm, I think. He'd delivered a message. I'm glad you didn't let him see Toshiyasu. Remember that arrow?"

Shibata nodded. "You think Jugoro killed Shigeie? But why? It must have been a hunting accident."

"No accident. Shigeie was a danger to the real killer or killers. He was drunk and confused when he confessed. It's time to wrap up these murders. You and your constables had better come with me. Once we arrest Jugoro and Otomo's son, we'll know what happened."

*

The black cloud bank had moved quickly across the valley. A reluctant Shibata led the way. They took a narrow path into the thick forest. It was nearly dark under the trees. The air was heavy with moisture and the smell of pines, and the trees stirred in the first gusts of wind. Akitada hoped they would reach the lodge before the storm broke.

The forest was full of noise and movement as the wind increased and the first drops fell. The trees protected them from the rain, but birds and small animals sought shelter. When they finally saw the lodge, a cluster of wooden buildings with thatched roofs, they heard the first thunder. Inside a wooden palisade was a main house with a veranda and an open stable next to it.

Akitada stopped in the shelter of the trees and scanned the area carefully. There was no sign of life apart from two horses that were tied up in the stable.

Genba said, "Two visitors? Or does this hunter have a horse?"

Shibata came up, looked, and said, "One is Jugoro's. But someone else is here."

"He rides a fine horse," Genba commented.

"Tabito." Akitada liked gray horses. He had once had a very fine one himself. "Come on. We might as well get inside."

They took their horses to the stable and tied them up. Shibata told his constables to wait on the veranda until they were needed and knocked on the door.

The door opened immediately and the man called Jugoro looked out. Akitada recognized him by his slanted brows.

Jugoro nodded to Shibata. "What brings you, Sergeant? And your friends?"

Akitada said, "I take it that Tabito is here?"

Jugoro opened the door wider and stepped aside.

It was dim inside, but candles and oil lamps had been lit. They flickered wildly until they closed the door. The handsome young man they had last seen in Sunomata was seated, sipping wine. He regarded them with raised brows. "I don't believe we've met," he drawled.

Akitada suppressed his irritation at the rudeness. "I'm Sugawara. We've just returned from Sunomata. Your father said you'd come here. There are some matters you need to clear up."

Tabito looked mildly interested. "What matters?"

The fact that the young man had not risen to bow or bothered to ask them to be seated was insulting. It hardened Akitada in his determination to bring him to justice.

"You and Toshiyasu have employed men to terrorize, murder, and rape in this valley. Toshiyasu has been arrested and has confessed."

"He lied if he said I was with him. Toshiyasu and I just broke up. He's angry and is trying to take revenge."

"There are witnesses, so don't waste my time."

Tabito smiled. "Then they are lying, too. I must remind all of you that you have no business here. This is my father's property."

"It's over, Tabito. For you and for Toshiyasu. The sergeant is here to arrest you and Jugoro."

Tabito laughed.

They were both too calm. They should at least have protested. An uneasy feeling took hold of Akitada. Outside, thunder rumbled. Best get on with what they came for. They would get drenched on the way back, but Akitada had a bad feeling about this place.

He said, "You've been involved with the bandits. Those activities include arson, murder, and the abduction of young girls to sell to the brothels in Sunomata; Toshiyasu is also charged with the murders of his father and cousin. And we will prove that Jugoro killed Shigeie to keep him from talking." He looked at Shibata. "Do your duty, Sergeant!"

Shibata called for his constables to come in with their chains.

Nothing happened. Tabito and Jugoro grinned.

Shibata cursed and went to the door. Before he got there, it opened and Lord Otomo walked in.

He was not smiling.

Three armed soldiers followed him. In the flickering light, their helmets gleamed and the lacquered breastplates shimmered as they moved. Their hands were on their swords.

Akitada's heart fell. They were trapped. The moment he had dreaded since Sunomata had come. Otomo and his men must have been waiting in the forest. The storm outside had covered Otomo's arrival. Though there were only three armed men with Otomo, it was likely that there were others outside. Even these three seemed to fill the room.

Akitada considered their chances of fighting their way outside. Otomo wore a sword but did not look agile enough to be much of an opponent. Jugoro and Tabito were another matter, but they had not made a move to reach for weapons. They still sat there, grinning.

They had expected this.

"I see you found my son," Otomo said heavily.

The situation was unnerving. Akitada swallowed and said, "Yes. We were about to arrest him."

"I heard the charges." Otomo shook his head. "Tabito, you have finally bought yourself more trouble than I can get you out of."

The utter astonishment Akitada felt at those words was mirrored on Tabito's face. His grin faltered. He glanced at Jugoro, who stumbled up to kneel before Otomo and knock his head against the floorboards.

Lightning flashed briefly. It was a while before thunder sounded again. The storm was coming, but it was still a distance away.

Tabito slowly got to his feet. He looked confused. "Father? What do you mean? Jugoro and I did what you told us to do."

"Fool!" thundered Otomo and, stepping forward, he slapped his son. Hard.

Tabito stumbled from the force of the blow. He cried out and put a hand to his face.

His father roared, "How dare you get me involved in your dirty games? Don't think I don't know how you and that son of Asano's have been carrying on in the brothels. You're a disgusting coward and no son of mine."

Tabito lowered his hand. He was quite pale and the handprint stood out sharply on his face. "You cannot do this, Father," he wailed. "I'm your son. I'm your heir. None of this is true. Toshiyasu's been lying to cover his crimes. It was him all the time."

"Get out of my sight!" Otomo turned his back on him and faced Akitada. "You may arrest him. I don't care. And Jugoro as well. I will not be used to cover the sort of crimes you described."

Akitada found it hard to adjust to Otomo's surprising behavior, but he told Shibata to go and find his constables.

Shibata was equally stunned, but he passed by the three armed men, who stepped aside.

Tabito was kneeling and wailing. Jugoro looked desperate enough to run, but Otomo's men moved to block him.

When Shibata returned with the constables, they chained their prisoners and took them away.

Akitada and Genba were left with Otomo. Otomo had ignored Genba before and ignored him now. Looking at Akitada, he said, "I trust you'll tell them in the capital that I'd rather sacrifice my son than break the laws of this land."

Akitada said stiffly, "I shall inform the prime minister of what happened here."

Otomo nodded. "I wish you a safe journey home then. I shall stay for a day or so for some hunting and then return to Sunomata."

Dazed by the events, Akitada and Genba walked out of the lodge. It was almost dark, the wind came in gusts, and large drops fell. They were alone. Sergeant Shibata had left with his constables and the prisoners, no doubt eager to make it back before the storm broke.

The case of the bandits of Hichiso was over. They would be identified by Toshiyasu and Tabito, and Sergeant Shibata would round them up for trial. Akitada wondered about Otomo and what his decision to sacrifice his son had done to the case against him. Akitada believed him guilty. Tabito had been about to give it all away when Otomo had slapped him into silence. Perhaps nothing else would happen to him, but losing your son and heir was a heavy punishment.

They had almost reached the place where the path to the lodge joined the road to Hichiso, when his plans came to nothing. There was a shout and men burst from the shrubbery and threw themselves at their horses.

Genba cursed and reached for his sword. Too late. The bandit had already slashed the animal's hindquarter. The horse screamed, reared, and threw Genba off.

Akitada was sliding out of the saddle, sword in hand. The surprise was devastating and he blamed himself. He hit the ground upright, saved perhaps by the dancing and kicking of his own horse. The attackers, their faces covered,–there were several of them, he could not be sure how many–had jumped out of the way. Genba was still cursing, but Akitada had no time to look for him. He met his first bandit, who was armed with a short sword, with a fury that was partially due to having walked into the trap and partially to satisfaction for the chance to avenge Taro and his daughter and all the other victims of these villains. He killed the man efficiently enough, and quickly turned to meet another. There were more than four, he thought, as he fended off a blow aimed at his legs by slashing the man's thigh. "Genba?" he shouted, going for two other men, one of whom was swinging a chain.

"Get the bastards!" shouted Genba from somewhere behind him, and then "Ow!"

No time to look. Akitada killed one of the men, but the other's chain came whistling his way. It was a clever way of disarming a man with a sword. He realized that these were not all untrained bandits.

They were Otomo's men.

Akitada ducked and went for the man's legs. The chain caught the side of his head, and searing pain coursed down his face and neck. He managed to slash the man's knee and pushed him back until he fell. Seeing another attacker through a veil of blood, Akitada aimed at the fallen man's belly with the desperation of knowing he was outnumbered and about to be overpowered and killed.

Because Otomo had lied. This had been the plan all along.

He gripped his sword, tried to see, tried to ignore the pain in his head, the searing, hot pain. He wiped at his eyes with his free hand and glimpsed a giant coming at him, sword raised, his face a snarling mask. The elusive Togo? Akitada could see with only one eye, and his enemy kept shifting. Crouching, he held his sword steady and expected to die.

There was a blinding flash of lightning, followed by a crack of thunder that was deafening.

The giant faltered in mid stroke. It was enough. Raising his sword high and jumping forward at the same time, Akitada brought his blade down at the giant's shoulder with all his remaining strength.

It would have struck the giant's armor harmlessly, but the heavens opened up and the rain gushed down in buckets. It caused Akitada to twist the blade a little, and made his opponent move. The sword sliced deep into his unprotected neck.

The giant's blood gushed forth as the rain fell in sheets. The big man stood for a moment, then he swayed and crumpled to the ground.

Akitada staggered back, raised his face to the rain and wiped it with his left hand. The rain felt clean and cool on his skin, though the pain still hammered inside his head, dizzying and remorseless. In the flash of the next lightning, he saw that he was the only one left standing.

The rain dragon, he thought. The rain dragon has saved me.

And Genba?

Thunder rumbled again. Akitada searched the area, checking bodies. He found him sitting with his back against a tree.

"Genba?" he croaked, afraid.

"Yes, sir?"

"Thank heaven! Are you hurt?"

"Just my leg." A pause, then, "Sir! Your head! You're bleeding. Sit down."

Akitada felt laughter bubbling up. "It's nothing," he said and walked stiffly to Genba. There were bodies. Five, maybe six. None moved. All dead.

But he and Genba were alive. A strange kind of joy filled him.

"Your leg? Is it bad?"

"Flesh wound."

Akitada knelt and looked. Genba had a long and deep slash in his right thigh. He peeled away the cloth and saw it was bleeding badly. Getting up again, he passed among the dead, making sure they were indeed dead, and collected belts, sashes, scarves and a shirt. These he used to fashion bandages. His head was still bleeding, though the rain was washing the blood away.

"You shouldn't do this, sir," Genba protested, when Akitada started wrapping his leg.. "You look ill. Let me see to that head wound. My leg barely hurts."

Akitada's head hurt viciously. He let Genba tie a piece of cloth around it. It seemed to dull the pain a little. Then he made sure that Genba's wound was covered, the bleeding stopped, and the bandage was good and tight.

"It's a little tight," Genba complained.

"It has to be. I don't want it to slip. We have to walk."

"Walk?"

"The horses are gone and I'm afraid to take the time to look for them. And there are no girls this time."

Genba stared at him. Then he looked around. "How many were there?"

"Six are dead. There may have been more."

"You think there are more?"

"It's likely."

Genba struggled to his feet and stood swaying for a moment. Let's go!" he said stoutly.

39

The Dragon's Gift

They supported each other as they staggered through the rain to the main road. Every moment, Akitada expected more of Otomo's men to catch up with them.

The storm had abated slightly. The rain was cool and refreshing. This long hot summer had finally broken. The farmers would be glad. Akitada thought again of the rain dragon. And then he thought of being alive, and the splitting pain in his head did not matter.

They heard the first sounds vaguely, masked by the final rumblings of the receding storm. Akitada stopped.

"Listen!"

Genba said, "Horses. And men. A lot of them."

"Quick! Into the trees."

They scrambled as best they could into the forest, hiding behind some small pines and a rock outcropping. The soldiers appeared, riding by twos as quickly as was manageable on the wet rocky ground.

They carried sodden banners on their backs. Ten of them preceded a sedan chair carried by four sturdy bearers. More warriors followed after.

Akitada stood up. "They've come for us," he said happily.

Genba, grabbed his arm, hissed, "Get down!"

Akitada laughed out loud. "Oh, Genba! Look at the flags. It's the imperial guard. The prime minister has sent them." And he staggered out of the trees, shouting "Halt!"

The cavalcade faltered. Someone shouted, then the guardsmen stopped to gaze at the bloody pair limping from the woods. The sedan chair was put down, and from it emerged an elegantly gowned elderly courtier. He stood for a moment glaring at the rain, then walked gingerly up to them.

Akitada recognized the senior investigator from the *Danjodai*, the Bureau of Censors. He was a man who used to instill fear into him in years past. Now he greeted him with half-crazed delight, crying, "Your Excellency! Well met! We thought we were dead and here you come, our deliverance!"

The elderly courtier narrowed his eyes. "Who the devil are you? And what do you mean, stopping an imperial emissary?"

Akitada still smiling broadly, said, "I'm Sugawara, my Lord."

The bushy gray eyebrows rose. "Sugawara? You look terrible. How did you get into such a disgraceful shape?"

"We were attacked by Otomo's men, sir."

"You were? Hmmph." He paused, thought, and said, "We'll see about that. You'd better take two of our horses and go to have those wounds seen to. I shall be in touch."

And with that, he turned and got back into his sedan chair.

Akitada looked after him and laughed again. "A man of few words and much action, I think."

Their return created considerable excitement. Kojiro and Saburo asked questions. Akitada's sister exclaimed and bustled about for water, bandages, and ointments. The children stood about wide-eyed and frightened. Akitada answered their questions briefly and retreated to the bath, whence he emerged cleaner and feeling better.

They had sent for the coroner to see to Genba's leg and Akitada's head wound. He arrived full of news about events in Hichiso.

"There's some high-ranking nobleman from the capital at the police station. He brought mounted soldiers. And Sergeant Shibata brought in Lord Otomo's son and the hunter Jugoro and put them in jail. Such developments! Can you imagine?" he asked Akitada.

Akitada was relieved that Shibata had not been waylaid and Otomo's son and Jugoro were now securely in the hands of the imperial investigator.

While tending to Genba's leg wound, the coroner added, "You know, sir, that arrow in Shigeie's back? That looked uncommonly like the ones Jugoro uses."

"Yes. I wouldn't be surprised," Akitada said.

The coroner paused in his bandaging. "But why would Jugoro shoot Shigeie in the back? Jugoro is too good a marksman and hunter to make such a mistake."

Akitada nodded gravely. "I agree completely. You must make that point when the judge asks you about Shigeie's manner of death."

The coroner looked thoughtful. "Lord Otomo won't like any of this."

"Do *you* like Lord Otomo?"

The other man was startled by the question. "No," he said after a moment and smiled. Being satisfied that Genba's wound was taken care of, he had a look at Akitada's head. "Hmm," he muttered with some painful poking, "you lost some skin there, sir. I'd best stick this flab back down securely. The hair should grow back. But your ear is missing a bit. And you'll have a scar."

"No matter. Patch it up. I expect a visit from the high-ranking official later and don't want to look a fright. No unsightly bandages, please!"

His sister, who had watched anxiously, said, "Now there's a surprise! My brother is as vain as a woman."

They all laughed. It stung worse than the coroner's ministrations, and Akitada grimaced at her.

His Excellency, Lord Fujiwara Otsugu, senior secretary of the Board of Censors, arrived at Kojiro's farm after sunset. He looked drawn and tired, and Akitada marveled again that a man of his rank had been dispatched to look into banditry in an obscure valley in Mino Province.

He said, "Did you speak to Sergeant Shibata and his prisoners?"

His Excellency looked Akitada over and nodded. "I did. And I see you cleaned up well. When I saw you last, you looked more like a mauled rat that had been drowned."

Akitada chuckled. "I was never so glad to see anyone, Excellency. Your journey cannot have been very pleasant either."

The other man did not bother to answer that. He sighed and said, "It's a fine mess, but you have a talent for drawing us into them."

"I'm very sorry. Please sit down. What about your accommodations? Where are you staying?"

"Hmmph." His Excellency sat, looked around, and said dismally, "They'll spread a blanket for me at the police station."

"Well, that mustn't be. May I offer sharing my room here? The farm is bursting at the seams with guests at the moment, but my room is quite spacious and my sister serves the most delicious meals. And there is a bath. I think you'd be much more comfortable."

His Excellency brightened. "That is very good of you. Yes. It will make our work easier, too, because we can talk this situation through. What about your brother-in-law, though?"

Kojiro was in his fields to check for damage from the storm, but Akitada went to look for Yoshiko, who came, shyly when informed of the rank of her guest, and confirmed the invitation, then bustled off to see about special delicacies for His Excellency's evening rice.

And so Akitada and Lord Otsugu set to work to untangle the mysterious events in Hichiso.

His Excellency said, "There was one problem when we arrived in Hichiso. A prisoner had committed suicide."

Akitada looked up. "Not Toshiyasu?"

"I believe that was his name. The Sergeant was quite angry that nobody noticed. Is it important?"

"To his sister, I think." For a moment, Akitada wondered if Toshiyasu had been killed like Shigeie, to keep him from talking. But given his condition after his confession, it seemed likely that he had committed suicide in despair.

"Well, there are now two new prisoners in the jail. The sergeant seems capable. And he wasn't there when that other fellow hanged himself."

Akitada did not inform the great man of Shibata's courtship of Toshiyasu's sister and his earlier lack of cooperation. There was enough misery for Maeko already.

Lord Otsugu continued, "I have, of course, read the reports you sent the prime minister. Do you have anything to add?"

Akitada told him about events in Sunomata and about the strange confrontations with Otomo. When Akitada described the attack on himself and Genba by Otomo's people, the elderly courtier's eyes widened.

"Is that what happened just before we found you?"

"Yes. I'm afraid we left some bodies behind. I should have mentioned it, but I could see you were in a hurry and I was afraid Otomo would send more men. His willingness to let his son take the punishment seemed too good to be true."

"Shocking! He was probably sure he had plenty of time after he had eliminated you. Hmm." The secretary pursed his lips. "Awkward."

"What will you do?"

"It depends on what his son and the other man have to say. They haven't talked yet." He added grimly, "But they will."

"They need to identify those involved in the attacks on the peasants. They have also set fires to burn some farmers' harvest or seed rice. All of this was meant to make the peasants sell their land to Otomo."

"Ah, yes. The emperor does not tolerate the abuse of our rice farmers. And the administration frowns on anything that removes land from the tax rolls."

The secretary was as efficient as he had been from the start. Within a week, Hichiso was a peaceful town again. A judge appeared on the scene, dispatched from the provincial capital, and Tabito and Jugoro were tried for the crimes they had committed in Mino Province.

When they realized there was no help coming from Tabito's father, they both confessed, implicating others. The bandit raids had been organized by Tabito and Toshiyasu. Toshiyasu had considered it good fun and Tabito was being helpful to his father by terrorizing the farmers into selling their land. Jugoro had taken part in the raids and arranged the murders of Asano and Sadamoto, both of which were carried out by their gang. He had killed Shigeie himself. Both Tabito and Jugoro were found guilty and received the maximum penalty. They were sent into exile: Jugoro to hard labor and Tabito to fight border wars in the far north. The latter sentence was a privilege accorded to men of noble blood. Both sentences usually meant death.

The bandits were from Sunomata and were either in Otomo's employ or worked in the brothels there. Tabito and Jugoro identified them all, and the police in Owari Province arrested them. Those who took part in the murders, also received the most severe penalty. They had used the Dragon Temple as their refuge and the place where they planned their raids. This information was passed on to the Buddhist authorities and the Bureau of Buddhism in the Central Administration. Abbot Shinsho was removed soon after.

Akitada was no longer in Hichiso when Tabito and Jugoro went to trial, but Shibata wrote to him about it.

Nothing happened to Otomo senior, but he would never again drive peasants from their land. Threats from above, both by the central government and the provincial administration of Owari, made sure of that.

But by then, Akitada had returned home with his children and his wounded. Both Saburo and Genba were mending, and Akitada had only a scar on the side of his head where his hair would hide it.

He parted sadly from Yoshiko and Kojiro. Too much of their time together had been spoiled by the events in Hichiso, but he treasured the peaceful and loving moments he had shared with his sister. He had also made his peace with Kojiro and found a new respect for him, while Kojiro had responded with friendship and gratitude. And the children invited their cousins, hoping to show them the wonders of the capital.

Akitada's homecoming was memorable for another, very personal reason. They had sent a messenger ahead and found the double gates of the Sugawara residence wide open in welcome. Tora waited in the courtyard, a broad smile on his face, his teeth brilliant in the sunshine.

Akitada's heart lifted: Tora was back! He swung down from his horse and went to embrace him He had missed Tora's good humor more than he had realized.

Tora gave a shout of laughter as he returned the embrace. "Welcome back, sir! Wait till you see! Such a surprise! You'll never guess!"

"Thanks, Tora. You look well. You had a good journey?"

"Yes, yes. Lady Sadako's brother treated me very well, and we've seen such sights. But wait till you see the surprise."

Lady Sadako? Yes, the poor widow who had been Yasuko's companion had found her family and with it her former rank. The grief of losing Sadako was back again and took away Akitada's pleasure of seeing Tora. "Well, I'm glad all is well," he said. "But now I think we'll just go inside and rest. We've had a hard time of it on this journey. We'll trade stories later."

Tora ignored this. "Yes, come inside and see who's here!"

Akitada sighed. His sister Akiko no doubt, anxious to hear about their other sister and her family. Or, heaven forbid, some official sent by the prime minister. "We're all tired, Tora," he said plaintively, "and Genba and Saburo are recovering from serious wounds. They need to rest and be seen by the doctor later."

"Of course." Tora was momentarily distracted and went to greet both Genba and Saburo. Having been reassured by them, he returned, still irrepressibly cheerful. "Well? Come on!"

Akitada saw that his wounded were surrounded by wives and children and that the hired men and the stable boy were lending a hand. Mrs. Kuruda, Saburo's mother, directed them. The children had already rushed into the house, and now Saburo and Genba went off with their own families.

Tired and feeling a little envious, Akitada finally turned to enter his own house, wondering what awaited him inside.

Tora was still standing at the foot of the stairs, still smiling.

"Who is here?" Akitada asked irritably.

"You'll see."

"Tora!"

But then a soft voice called from the veranda, "Welcome home, my lord."

He looked up, not believing his ears, and gasped. "Sadako?"

She smiled and nodded.

He ran up the stairs two steps at a time, arriving out of breath, and stumbling on the last step. He would have fallen if Sadako had not caught him.

He steadied himself with his hands on her shoulders, happy that she felt real and was not a figment of his overheated imagination.

Sadako, for whom he had longed all those weeks!

Sadako, whom he had thought lost.

Sadako whom he would never let go again.

On that thought, he drew her close and held her. "You came back," he said, quite inadequately. "You really came? And you won't leave again?"

She nodded and shook her head, and laughed a little with tears in her eyes.

And Akitada was filled with gratitude for the kindness of dragons.

Historical Note

At the time of this novel (1034), Japan was ruled by an emperor and a government of nobles. The capital was Heian-Kyo, the modern Kyoto. The form of government was based on that of T'ang China, as was much of Japanese culture of the time, but by the Heian era (794-1185) certain changes were beginning to take place. The power gradually shifted to one noble family, the Fujiwara, who filled most upper government positions and married their daughters to emperors. This court aristocracy left military matters to provincial families and, while the central government continued, greedy appointees to provincial governorships enriched themselves while turning a blind eyes to local corruption. Eventually, the provincial aristocracy would seize power and bring about the end of imperial rule. The Samurai age began.

Heian Japan was divided into provinces, each with its own provincial government. Court-appointed governors served for four years. Such appointments were considered hardships by court nobles who preferred to serve in the capital. Nevertheless, they were sought after because they offered opportunities to gain family wealth. The governors were responsible for the people and the economy of each province and collected taxes they annually dispatched to the capital. In this, they were aided by local officials who gradually gained influence and wealth.

In order to control the country more efficiently, the government established early on a road system that was maintained through corvée labor. Its purpose was to connect even the most distant provinces to the capital. The most famous of these roads is the Tokaido. The provinces of Mino and Owari in this novel are on the Tosando, the Eastern Mountain Road. The roads had frequent post stations that kept horses for government messengers and controlled the movement of people throughout the country. While government tax convoys traveled under the protection of armed guards, ordinary travelers were not so lucky. Highwaymen worked all the major roads.

Sunomata was one of the stops on the Tosando. It is mentioned in the diary of an eleventh century noblewoman who traveled from Kazusa Province to the capital. She mentions a group of entertainers who were hired to sing for them (*As I Crossed a Bridge of Dreams: Recollections of a Woman in Eleventh-Century Japan,* transl. by Ivan Morris). Such entertainers are mentioned elsewhere as roaming the highways and making a living selling their talents and bodies to travelers and local landowners. Nothing is known of brothels along the Tosando, though these existed in other places, for example on the Yodo River.

The origin of outcasts in Japanese society is obscure. They may have originated as prisoners taken in the many wars of the past. Eventually they became involved in performing services other people found repulsive or that were taboo for religious reasons. They were the street cleaners, undertakers, butchers, and tanners. They lived either in separate villages or were vagrants. The traveling entertainers and prostitutes of the time belonged to the outcasts, as did ex-convicts.

The Festival of the Dead *(O-bon, Urabon)* takes place in late summer and celebrates the return of the spirits of the dead for a brief visit to their homes and families. It originated in Chinese ancestor worship and is one of the Buddhist observances. The Japanese practiced both Buddhism and Shintoism, often side by side in the same temple. Shinto is the native faith, is animistic, and is closely tied to the rice culture. The emperor traditionally observes all the Shinto rites. Shinto is also responsible for the various taboos that existed, most significantly the abhorrence of death and contamination from dead bodies. Hence funerals were handled by Buddhist temples and the dead were prepared (usually for cremation) by outcasts.

The Japanese economy depended on rice. It not only fed the nation, but it often substituted for money in business transactions. Certainly, taxes were primarily paid in rice, though other goods could be substituted, and corvée was also involved. The rice culture requires water and intensive labor. In the Heian age, the court encouraged cultivation of wasteland by making the reclaimed acreage tax free property. Noblemen or temples, as well as peasants, could benefit from this. A prosperous peasant could evade provincial taxation by becoming a land manager for a nobleman's estate, as in the case of Asano who served as *betto* for Lord Otomo.

Dragons play a major role both in Chinese and Japanese mythology and religion. They are generally associated with water. There are, for example, the four dragons of the four seas. Dragons can dwell in the ocean, or in a lake or river. As rain deities they are of great importance in agricultural areas, hence there are dragon temples. The tales about dragons used in this novel come from *Uji shui monogatari* and *Konjaku monogatari shu* , translated in *Japanese Tales* by Royall Tyler. These collections date to the twelfth century, but the tales themselves are much older.

About the Author

I. J. Parker was born and educated in Europe and turned to mystery writing after an academic career in the U.S. She has published her Akitada stories in *Alfred Hitchcock's Mystery Magazine,* winning the Shamus award in 2000. Several stories have also appeared in collections, such as *Fifty Years of Crime and Suspense* and *Shaken.* The award-winning "Akitada's First Case" is available as a podcast.

Many of the stories have been collected in *Akitada and the Way of Justice.*

The Akitada series of crime novels features the same protagonist, an eleventh century Japanese nobleman/detective. *The Kindness of Dragons* is number eighteen. The books are available as e-books, in print, and in audio format, and have been translated into twelve languages. The early novels are published by Penguin.

Books by I. J. Parker

The Akitada series in chronological order

The Dragon Scroll
Rashomon Gate
Black Arrow
Island of Exiles
The Hell Screen
The Convict's Sword
The Masuda Affair
The Fires of the Gods
Death on an Autumn River
The Emperor's Woman
Death of a Doll Maker
The Crane Pavilion
The Old Men of Omi
The Shrine Virgin
The Assassin's Daughter
The Island of the Gods
Ikiryo: Revenge and Justice
The Kindness of Dragons

The collection of stories
Akitada and the Way of Justice

Other Historical Novels

The HOLLOW REED saga:

Dream of a Spring Night

Dust before the Wind

The Sword Master

The Left-Handed God

Contact Information

Please visit I.J.Parker's web site at www.ijparker.com. You may contact her via e-mail from there. (This way you will be informed when new books come out.)

The novels may be ordered from Amazon or Barnes&Noble as trade paperbacks. There are electronic versions of all the works. Please do post reviews. They help sell books and keep Akitada novels coming.

Thank you for your support.

Made in the USA
San Bernardino, CA
13 August 2019